V.C. ANDREWS®

SHADOWS OF FOXWORTH

Gallery Books

New York   London   Toronto   Sydney   New Delhi

Gallery Books
An Imprint of Simon & Schuster, Inc.
1230 Avenue of the Americas
New York, NY 10020

Following the death of Virginia Andrews, the Andrews family worked with a carefully selected writer to organize and complete Virginia Andrews's stories and to create additional novels, of which this is one, inspired by her storytelling genius.

This book is a work of fiction. Any references to historical events, real people, or real places are used fictitiously. Other names, characters, places, and events are products of the author's imagination, and any resemblance to actual events or places or persons, living or dead, is entirely coincidental.

First Gallery Books hardcover edition June 2020

V.C. ANDREWS® and VIRGINIA ANDREWS® are registered trademarks of Vanda Productions, LLC

GALLERY BOOKS and colophon are registered trademarks of Simon & Schuster, Inc.

For information about special discounts for bulk purchases, please contact Simon & Schuster Special Sales at 1-866-506-1949 or business@simonandschuster.com.

Interior design by Erika Genova

Manufactured in the United States of America

10   9   8   7   6   5   4   3   2   1

The Library of Congress has cataloged the trade edition as follows:

Names: Andrews, V. C. (Virginia C.), author.
Title: Shadows of Foxworth / V.C. Andrews.
Description: First edition. | New York : Gallery Books, 2020.
Identifiers: LCCN 2019056134 (print) | LCCN 2019056135 (ebook)
    | ISBN 9781982114459 (hardcover) | ISBN 9781982114442
    (paperback) | ISBN 9781982114466 (ebook)
Subjects: LCSH: Domestic fiction.
Classification: LCC PS3551.N454 S52 2020 (print) | LCC PS3551.N454
    (ebook) | DDC 813/.54--dc23
LC record available at https://lccn.loc.gov/2019056134
LC ebook record available at https://lccn.loc.gov/2019056135

ISBN 978-1-9821-1445-9
ISBN 978-1-9821-1446-6 (ebook)

SHADOWS
OF
FOXWORTH

V.C. Andrews® Books

SHADOWS
OF
FOXWORTH

PROLOGUE

When I was a little girl, I believed my mother was really an angel. Not my brother, not even my father knew she had told me so through her eyes, through her smile, and through the graceful softness of her touch. In dreams she hovered over me while I slept, her feathered white wings fanning the air gently, washing my face with warmth and raining down kisses tenderly, each one popping like a soap bubble against my cheek. Nestled in her loving embrace, I was unafraid of darkness and fell asleep easily.

During my earliest years, we lived in a small beige stone house with white shutters so close to the beach that the Mediterranean Sea sang my lullaby every night. Its waves combed the shore for me to run barefoot in the morning, the sand caressing me between my toes with that evening coolness still clinging to the damp grains. My brother, Yvon, would be sitting behind me, "digging his way to China," as my father would say. He dug with an intensity that made most people laugh because it looked like my father wasn't exaggerating.

Wearing a long white shirt, black pants, and his handmade tan leather sandals, Papa might already be at his easel capturing some vision he had of a sailboat smoothly riding the waves, a seagull born out of a cloud on the horizon, or something he could see but no one else could because he had the artist's eye. His raven-black hair cut just below the nape of his neck fluttered around him as if his every creative thought made the strands hop with joy.

Or he might just be sipping his coffee from a black ceramic mug and standing beside my mother, who was looking out at the water, her face a cameo with her perfect profile, her ankle-length indigo peasant skirt dancing around her legs, and her beauty feeling quite at home in a world that seemed untouched by anything ugly or dark. The soft fingers of the breeze brushed through her golden hair as lovingly as I would. Even the rain was apologetic here.

"If you listen to the wind just before it showers," my mother said, "you will hear the clouds say, 'Excusez-moi,' the rain sometimes remaining nothing more than mist. Good for your complexion, ma chérie."

I believed her. An angel would know. I listened for it, and when I was sure I had heard it, I'd run to my mother to tell her, and she would embrace me and laugh, with her laugh always followed by her kisses.

"I did! I did hear it, Mama!"

"Of course you did," she would say, and tickle my ears with her nose. "Didn't I tell you that you would?"

She would press me to her soft, perfumed breasts and hold me so tightly that I used to feel she wanted me back inside her, safe in her womb.

If Papa overheard us while he was working, he would pause like someone stepping back into this world, smile, and then quickly return to his own. We were never to interrupt him while he worked or make too much noise nearby. His artistic creations were gaining more and more in popularity. From farther and farther away, people were coming to consider and buy one of his paintings. A couple even came from Paris to purchase one of his landscapes. He placed them in the small gallery that Monsieur and Madame Passard owned in the village. They had been operating it for decades and ten years ago had met the world-famous Edgar Degas, who let them sell one of his smaller sculptures.

Mama's favorite of Papa's paintings was the one he created of a swan in our village fountain. Everyone who saw it thought it was mystical, because although there were swans in France, there was none on the seaside of Villefranche. Papa would tease Mama sometimes by threatening to give it to the gallery, "just so we can see what it would bring in."

"Don't you dare," she would tell him, and he would laugh.

He hung it over their bed, and there was never a time when I wasn't fascinated by the look on its face and the beauty of its wings and neck. In my heart of hearts I knew that Papa would never, ever really even think of selling it.

However, Papa was still often the gallery's artist of the month. Jean-Paul Vitton, my father's mentor and our godfather, had been their featured artist almost from the day they had opened the gallery. He was still Villefranche-sur-Mer's most well known, but he didn't work as much anymore. He was eighty-two and joked that Papa would soon catch up to him before he was half his age.

"Your papa is driven by his work, perhaps even chased. Do not be angry at him if he ignores you for days," Jean-Paul warned both Yvon and me often. "Artists hear other voices, but neither you nor your mama is ever far from his loving eyes. I promise. You are a special family."

Why shouldn't we believe him? When Yvon and I were much younger, people in the village of Villefranche-sur-Mer told my father that his family was a beautiful living painting in and of itself. Just seeing the four of us walking over a pebblestone street toward the open market to get our fruit and vegetables or fresh fish, I holding my brother Yvon's hand and my mother's, she holding my father's, would bring a smile to their faces. Papa brought fame to our little village, and Mama brought beauty and love.

Older people saw their own childhood in Yvon and me. They would stop us when we walked together without my parents; Yvon, even at only six, would hold tightly to my hand, his back straight, his shoulders firm, and his face so serious that it looked like it was sculptured from granite. Nevertheless, he was always polite and attentive. They would tell us their personal childhood stories, tales that always ended with the same lesson or warning stated one way or another. "Love your parents. Listen to them. What they want for you, they wanted for themselves. Their dream is that whatever they couldn't have for themselves, you will have."

We nodded, but Yvon and I were too young to understand or appreciate it fully. We spoke French fluently, of course, and our parents spoke and taught us English. They were both Americans. Language was never our problem, whether it was English or French or even a little Spanish and Italian. I think we were simply puzzled by how intensely people spoke to us when they spoke about our parents and us. Maybe we would never fully understand their admonitions or fully envision the images of dangers and disasters they projected with their terrifying expressions.

Perhaps we felt too high above all that, too protected and too perfect. The difference between Yvon and me was that I didn't want to think about it, ever, whereas he never stopped.

Monsieur Appert certainly agreed there were all sorts of dangers swirling about everyone, and he was confident he knew why. "It's Eve's fault," the village tailor would say, even if the disaster was merely his poking his thumb while he was sewing. He would look at the tiny pinprick of blood and shake his head, mumbling about the first female. He said the same thing after any mistake, any tragedy anywhere in the world: "It's Eve's fault."

"How could it be Eve's fault that you stuck your finger, Monsieur Appert?" I would ask. "She isn't here." He'd look at me and smile. Then he'd suddenly stop smiling and nod.

"It's her fault. Everything would be perfect if she hadn't disobeyed the Commandment. There would be no pain, no sickness. We wouldn't even age!"

He'd shake his poked finger with its spot of blood, holding the needle and thread in his other hand, and then he would laugh at me because I would look like I could cry at any moment.

"It's all right, it's all right," he would say. "I don't feel a thing. Nothing. *Rien.* I'm too old to feel anything. Now, here's the stitch you want to learn," he would continue, and then demonstrate. I often wondered if everyone in the world but me believed I was destined to become a seamstress. But the list of opportunities for women wasn't very long in France in 1912, or anywhere else for that matter.

The truth was, I'd often stop at his shop to watch him work, mainly because he had a candy for me or a fresh apple. Then I would skip off to tell my mother what he had said and had done to himself. She would nod, which wasn't anywhere near enough of a reaction to satisfy me. I'd have to get her to understand and react to how serious this was. I'd be bouncing on my feet and nearly crying.

"There was blood!"

She'd stop whatever she was doing and look at me as if my words had just caught up with her thoughts.

"I'm surprised there's any blood left in that man," she would say. "He has so many holes in his fingers. And the next time he blames Eve, you tell him Adam didn't have to follow her. Why didn't he have a mind of his own? Men are always blaming women for what they do themselves."

My father would laugh, but Yvon would scowl. It was as if he distrusted his own laughter. He was afraid of not being tough. He often had a suspicious, angry look in his eyes as he panned our surroundings, wherever we were, especially at home. It frightened me a little more than I revealed.

It was as if he was expecting something terrible, someone horrible to come to our front door. My heart might even skip a beat imagining the sound of a stranger pounding his fist on the gray wood built from the ribs of an old fisherman's boat. He had come to tell us something so bad it would shake the foundations of our home. When I got older, I would ask Yvon, "What's wrong? What are you worrying about now?"

"*Rien,*" he would quickly say, and look away, his neck stiff and his shoulders raised and turned in as if he had just been whipped.

Everything about him told me it wasn't "nothing," and his refusal to speak about it only reinforced my fears. Trepidation overflowed through his steely blue eyes, which were often firmly fixed on the incoming tide or the highway that led into our village.

I, too, looked hard and looked often in those directions, even when he wasn't there. Although I didn't feel it as intensely as Yvon, I knew in my heart that there was something out there, something beyond the horizon, something riding the waves or bouncing in a horse-drawn carriage and coming toward us. In dark dreams, it was a hearse drawn by two black horses or a masked rider rushing toward us to bring the dreadful message he carried. Sometimes it was on fire in his hand.

As I grew older, I was confident that Yvon knew exactly what it was, but he was always protecting me, even from bad news or thoughts. However, the more he kept it to himself, the more convinced I became that there was something, something that could rattle our family like an earthquake. Eventually, we would stop holding hands, and my mother would lose her angel wings. In nightmares, faces were torn and stretched in agony, and everyone's kisses were blown away like dead leaves to float in the sea and disappear in the waves.

Someday I would learn that Yvon had known about all this for years but harbored it in his heart and suffered with it alone. I would come to understand that his not sharing the pain it brought to him was even worse than what it was.

No one was lonelier than someone lonely in fear.

1

"Louis is close friends with your brother only because of you, Marlena," Regine Besnier said, or rather whined, while we were walking back to my new, larger home after going to the farmers' market for potatoes and onions for my mother's bouillabaisse. She had learned the recipe from Jean-Paul's woman friend, Anne Bise. They had never married. Jean-Paul claimed it would ruin their forty-year relationship. But Papa told him he was as good as married and more henpecked than any other married man in the village.

Regine's voice was so nasal that you would think someone had his hands tightening around her long, narrow neck. I don't know why I wanted her as a best friend. She often would utter nasty and mean things disguised as facts or supposedly helpful suggestions. Actually, I knew why but was afraid to admit it, especially to myself. Her envy of me stroked my ego, which was something for which my mother had a particular distaste: conceit and vanity.

"Vanity, even in small bites, will poison your soul," she told me more than a dozen times if she told me once. It was something she was particularly sensitive to herself. She made it sound like a trap set by the devil just outside the door, waiting to ensnare you as soon as you left your house.

"You do me a disservice by encouraging me to think too much of myself," my mother would tell those who gave her lavish compliments, especially about her beauty. She was so adamant about it, especially in front of me, that whoever had praised or admired her would stutter and apologize.

Her anger and her intensity puzzled me. She wasn't usually so unfairly sharp toward or critical of others in our village, but I assumed that this reaction to praise was her way of teaching me a lesson. I'd see she was looking to be sure I or Yvon had heard her. That was always the first reason our parents would do something unexpected or even unpleasant: they were showing us an example of what not to do. Our parents were perfect. How could they ever deliberately have done or do anything wrong? Refusing to believe that was true was the same as refusing to believe in angels.

"Louis and Yvon have been friends for ages, Regine. I had barely grown out of diapers when they began to do everything together. Seeing them playing together in the yard is one of my earliest memories. Please, don't be ridiculous."

"I'm not!" she protested, her round, deeply set, coffee-bean-brown eyes practically exploding. "Maybe that was true once, but now he can't stop looking at you every chance he has. I see it," she insisted. "Besides, why be upset about it? Louis Pinault is one of the best-looking boys in Villefranche. He's not as good-looking as your brother, of course, but few boys are."

She folded her arms and brought them down forcefully against her stomach. It was one of her *And that's that* statements. Sometimes she could be so stubborn and determined that she would cause my stomach to be tied in knots. Few could stand it. It was another reason I was practically her only friend.

But I wasn't going to disagree with her about Louis's looks. He was handsome, and if I was being truthful, I would admit that I had the feeling he was looking at me differently lately. I just didn't want to give Regine the satisfaction of being right, being so astute, although I didn't want to appear oblivious like some child. Truthfully, lately I had been wondering about myself, not about him. What was it about me that had suddenly opened Louis's eyes?

Perhaps it was how Mama was fixing my much longer hair or the clothes she permitted me to wear, which clearly revealed that my bosom was rapidly developing. I was afraid to ask her if I could use her lipstick. Once I had snuck it on, and Yvon got so upset that I ran to the spring to wash every trace of it away. He didn't tell our mother. He never wanted to get me in trouble and often took blame for something stupid I had done, something I had misplaced or broken.

For some reason I couldn't quite understand myself, I thought if I ever responded to Louis's smiles and looks, Yvon would be angry, not only with me but with Louis, and I'd feel terrible about breaking up their long friendship. Despite what she was saying, I thought Regine wouldn't be happy if I welcomed Louis's affections, either.

"I'm not upset about it, Regine, but I think perhaps it is you who can't stop looking at him," I said.

Showing her I could read her romantic feelings was like stripping her naked in the street. A flush came quickly to her face. I can't say I didn't enjoy my effect on her. Mama would shake her head at me if she heard me doing it. I did tease Regine often.

"That's not true," Regine said, but not with confidence.

"Of course it's true. Don't be so coy. Give him a strong hint how you feel about him, and maybe he'll start looking at you. Some boys need a little push or donkey tug. They're not shy; they're just . . . oblivious."

She looked at me askance, clearly wondering. "How do you know so much about boys? You've never had a boyfriend."

I shrugged. "Some things are just obvious."

"Or your mother told you," Regine said sadly, her eyes filled with jealousy. Her mother had her late in life. She had two older brothers who were already married, with one's wife expecting. "My mama won't even say the word 'sex' to me and pretends I still haven't gotten monthlies. Everything I know about it and sex, I know because of what your mother told you and you told me," she whined. "You two are more like sisters."

I smiled to myself. *Yes*, I thought, *we are*.

Regine was silent for a few moments. Then she just stopped, so I stopped.

"What now?"

"You really think Louis could like me?"

"How will you know if you don't give him some reason to

hope?" I asked, as if it was as clear a fact as daytime. I smiled to myself. Only someone looking into my eyes could see that what I really believed about her and Louis was the complete opposite of what I had just said.

Nevertheless, how sophisticated I sounded for someone just a little less than fifteen, I thought. The truth was that if Mama overheard me, she would hate it and give me one of her critical looks so sharp that Papa would say it would cut through the walls of the old fortress built by the Duke of the Savoy in 1557 to guard the port. He claimed to have the scars to prove it after she had given him similar looks.

"Do you really think so?" Regine asked. Her face looked like a balloon blown up with hope. I had turned lights on in her eyes, lights that she didn't dare turn on herself for fear she would reveal her true feelings and be the object of ridicule.

"You have to think so yourself, Regine. You can't go by what others think when it comes to romance."

"But you really think I can get him to like me? You're not just saying it to shut me up?"

Honestly, I was hoping to shut her up about the way Louis was looking at me these days, and as far as Louis liking her, definitely not, I thought, but didn't say it. Regine's nose was too thin and a bit too long. Her lips were a little crooked, especially when she was thinking hard. She was lean, still more boyish, and she was a good two inches or so taller than any other girl our age. Her legs were so long that it looked like she had to stop them from growing or she would become a circus freak. The rest of her body needed years to catch up, especially her bosom, which was still asleep in her childlike body, despite her introduction to what many of the older women told me was a woman's curse.

But she did have thick, butter-smooth black hair and a perennial tan, which gave her a dark-peach complexion, highlighting her eyes. Her biggest fault was that she talked too much, talked as if she was afraid of any silence. Any boy she fancied would have difficulty thinking, much less getting a word in before she had started another sentence, and I knew that boys hated that. They had to be the ones to control the conversations. If we were clever, we would let them believe they were controlling everything, even though they weren't.

I grunted rather than say *Oui*.

Maybe I was simply too critical of Regine, too critical especially when it came to other girls. I was always envying someone for something, even though I was told I had the best features of my parents and would surely grow to be as beautiful as if not more beautiful than my mother. There was no reason for me to lack any self-confidence, and I didn't like pretending to be shy, even though my mother favored girls who were.

Yvon agreed with me, however. He said very shy girls were probably turtles in an earlier life. He told our mother that he didn't trust girls who were too shy. "They're laying traps with their blushing," he said. "Marlena has more intelligent things to say than most of my friends. Why force her to keep quiet just because she is a girl?"

If Papa heard him, he would start to smile and then quickly look away before Mama saw him. She didn't disagree with Yvon. She often told me I was bright and beautiful. However, she always pointed out that it was all right for her to say it because she was my mother, and mothers had almost an obligation to praise and brag about their children.

Mama wouldn't let Papa paint me, however. There was nothing I dreamed of more, but I wouldn't say or ask for it.

"Don't stroke her ego that much yet, Beau," she would tell him, with her eyes fixed on me, if he as much as suggested he might. "Humility will save her from making all-too-familiar mistakes."

Papa looked at her and nodded in agreement. Whatever she implied kept him from putting up any argument. But what did that mean? What familiar mistakes was she referring to? I wondered. Was she talking about my future ones or mistakes she and Papa had made? Neither Yvon nor I ever heard our parents confess to any serious errors. We overheard other adults, parents of other children, declare they had made this wrong decision or that, most of the time admitting they had not listened to their mothers or fathers and nearly ruined their own lives, but our parents avoided talking about their youth. It was as if they were never children.

They did have deep secrets, I thought, secrets perhaps Yvon didn't know, either, but, like me, he felt them hovering around us. Too often, we would see them whispering, and often when something someone in the village said seemed quite insignificant to us, they would look at each other quickly and sharply, as if they could anticipate the questions that would attack us like angry bees. Sometimes they would move us along, as if we could be infected by the memories other people had of them when they first had come to France with little more than hope. They certainly weren't rich then and weren't truly rich now, but we were comfortable and never lacked for anything like so many other families. We could have been very poor. Maybe they were ashamed of that. Maybe that gave them their nightmares.

A number of times, I overheard my mother say that if it weren't for Jean-Paul and Papa's inheriting his cousin Beverly Morris's money, we'd probably never have lasted here. Jean-Paul Vitton had arranged for our parents to come to France. He had found Papa his first art-teacher job tutoring rich children who had "no ounce of talent." However, it was only that way and other ways that Jean-Paul introduced him to people who would buy his work in France that made our life here possible. He was the closest Yvon and I had to a relative because he was our godfather.

If anything, Mama frightened me with her vague references to early memories that suggested their struggles and fears. Maybe that was why she didn't like to talk about them. When she did, she made it sound as though they were washed ashore with nothing but themselves. It made me wonder. What if Jean-Paul had not been able to help them? What if Papa would have failed to become the artist he was and they were here with no friends or relatives? Just thinking about us wandering Europe like gypsies would make me tremble. I had seen enough of them coming along and begging for bread or a little work to earn some bread.

Yvon had too much self-pride. I was sure that he would have withered away. Mama wouldn't be as beautiful, and Papa would have become so much older quickly, like most of those men we saw pass through, men with faces so empty of expectations for themselves that they looked more like ghosts to me with their gaunt eyes.

Why did our parents come here, anyway? America was where everyone wanted to go to get rich. There was something dark, something hidden between sentences or long silences. I can't remember exactly how young I was when I first felt this sense of mystery about my parents, these clouds of secrets around them, but I did ask Yvon about it more and more as we grew up.

"Mama and Papa whisper a lot, don't they? They're probably thinking about when they were so poor in America. Do you think they were ever as desperate as some of the gypsies? Do they wake up from nightmares about it?"

I didn't really believe that was a possible answer, but I wanted to be sure I wasn't imagining that fearful look on their faces whenever even the slightest reference to their past emerged. Maybe, hopefully, I was making it all seem bigger than it was.

"We don't know if they were ever that poor, Marlena. Stop thinking so much about it. What difference does it make to you now? Besides, everyone has nightmares or memories they'd rather keep to themselves or certainly out of the ears of their children," Yvon said, sounding years older, as he always did. Hearing him, someone would think he was the one who didn't have a real childhood and not our parents.

"But we're older now. They can tell us the truth. We're no longer children."

"Maybe that's more reason for them to keep whatever it is to themselves."

"I don't understand. How could that be more reason?"

Yvon often said things that flew above me. I called them *bird words.*

"Shadows are best left in the shadows."

"What? What shadows?"

Bird words again, I thought.

He said nothing more. I was going to pursue it and force him to reveal what he meant, but the look in his eyes told me not to talk about it, to stop asking questions. How did he know that? How did he know it would be better for us not to talk about Mama and Papa's past, especially in front of them? Did he have so much more wisdom at sixteen than I had at fourteen?

"Parents have an unfair advantage over us," he said just last week as a sort of response to my questions about our parents' whispering and private looks, maybe because I was so much more persistent.

"What do you mean?" Again, I had no idea what he was saying, but this time I was determined to force him to explain. He took one look at me and knew I'd ask him until his ears were stuffed and had turned red.

"They know us from the day we are born, know who we are, how we think, what makes us laugh and cry, and when we do something they might not know or understand, they question us like the gendarmerie. Maybe it's because they worry; maybe it's because they love us so much; maybe it's both. We don't know the same about them. It takes years to, or maybe we never do. That's why it's unfair, especially when they interrogate us like the police might."

I wasn't really surprised he thought our parents could be like the police. Most parents were like that. However, to me it seemed that they were questioning him more than they were me all the time. But then again, he was older, with more opportunities to get into trouble. He was on his own more and wandered off with his friends as far as Nice. When he returned, Mama especially might pounce, demanding to know every detail about what he and his friends had done. I thought she was unfair, always assuming something terrible. What made her think so darkly when it came to my brother? He never did anything that would embarrass or trouble her so.

"Your mother is right to be concerned," Madame Cosse, the butcher's wife, told me when I mentioned how intense my mother could be when she questioned my brother. "Boys, because of their nature, have more access to trouble. Never let a boy dare you to do anything, Marlena. It's built into them to be more distress for their parents and for themselves."

"But it wasn't Adam. It was Eve who brought the world trouble," I parroted from Monsieur Appert's lessons. "Monsieur Appert says so."

"Of course he does. He's a man. Just listen to me. Always listen to the wiser, older people around you, especially older women. Women are born with more wisdom," she insisted, and then muttered, "It's just wasted because men are deaf. But it's not wasted on you."

It seemed to me that everyone in this village, from the baker to the cabinet maker to the street cleaner, was always looking out for me, looking to protect me, and Yvon as well. They wanted to be sure we shared any worldly knowledge that they had acquired. We were like one extended family. Everyone behaved like he or she was an uncle or aunt, maybe more so because they knew Yvon and I had no grandparents. Papa's mother died of cholera when he was no older than I was. He was always a little unclear about how old he was when his father had heart failure. Papa would only say he was in his teens. Mama had told us that her mother died from consumption and then her father died from heart failure the following year.

If we, especially I, asked any more questions about our grandparents, they both advised us to leave what was buried, buried. It was all too sad, and why dwell on sadness? Yvon didn't have to be told twice, but I couldn't stop being curious.

Our family was different from other families in the village in that way. Neither of our parents liked to talk about their families very much. Neither mentioned a favorite aunt or uncle. Sometimes I felt we were the first family on earth with no relatives ever.

Our history seemed to have begun with our parents' arrival in France, where they were married in St. Michael's Church in the heart of Villefranche. They said they had gone through a civil service but wanted a religious one. Every time we walked past the church, I imagined them emerging, Mama in a beautiful lily-white wedding dress, holding a bouquet of a variety of flowers, and Papa in his suit and tie looking even more handsome. How silly of me to wish it, but I wished I had been there and stood beside them when they took their vows.

Despite Regine's babbling about Louis, I was still thinking about all that as we headed back to my new home on the hill looking over the harbor of La Darse. The sun had broken free from a patch of clouds and dropped its late-June rays in waves of thunderous heat over us. Thankfully, our new home was only two streets up. Regine lived four streets up, and the way rose so steeply it was painful to go quickly. However, my legs were quite strong, as were the legs of most who lived above the village and had to navigate long and steep stone stairways.

On summer days, especially like this one, I hated doing errands, but as soon as I was old enough to go myself, there was no refusing. Yvon was an apprentice to Monsieur Dufloit, the village cobbler, and had fewer household duties. He did enjoy the work, and thanks to him, I had a fancy pair of Edwardian high-top black leather boots. It was one of his first accomplishments.

My parents, especially my mother, were proud of him for thinking first of me and not making something for himself. He didn't actually give them to me, however. He left them outside my bedroom door, and when I thanked him, giving him a quick peck on the cheek, he blushed and said he didn't know what I was talking about. From what I could see, Yvon was shy only with me. He certainly didn't hesitate to flirt with other girls, especially Marion Veil, whose father was the village doctor. She was the oldest of three daughters and was certainly one of the prettiest girls in Villefranche, with her strawberry-red hair and blue-green eyes.

But Yvon was uncomfortable being called her boyfriend, even though he basically was. I think he just didn't want to commit emotionally to anyone other than his family. It was part of the distrust that ran along with the blood in his veins. When I asked him what if she had told him that she loved him, he grimaced and said he wouldn't believe her if she had.

"Why not?" I asked.

"People lie to each other too much, even married people. Maybe especially married people," he added, with those cerulean-blue eyes of his narrowing over a memory he had stored right behind them.

My heart skipped beats.

"Not Mama and Papa."

"They're not people. They're our parents, and they are really in love with and true to each other."

That made me feel better, but whatever it was, whatever unseemly thing he had witnessed, he kept to himself or at least kept it from me. Sometimes he treated me as if I was made of thin china, so fragile that a nasty thought would shatter me. But he truly cherished me, and I was proud to wear the boots he had made, even though he wanted to pretend it was just as much of a surprise to him.

"The boots just walked up here themselves?" I asked him.

He shrugged.

"Stranger things have happened."

"Oh, sure. It's Eve's fault," I said, and he pressed his lips together and twisted his nose. Then he remembered Monsieur Appert and laughed. It was always so good to hear Yvon laugh. He did it so rarely.

As we approached my house, I could see something unusual was happening. Yvon was home, and there was a crowd of our neighbors circled around something that held their attention on the east side of the house. Their excited voices carried down the hill and were bringing more people out and up.

Jean-Paul, who was too old and arthritic now to walk up the hill from his seaside cottage, was sitting on the far right. Usually, Papa and Yvon carried him up in what my father had built, a litter they amusingly called the "King's Chair." Papa had dressed up the sides by embossing crowns and scepters.

"What's going on?" Regine asked.

I shook my head, and we both started to run up the hill. The wide smile on Yvon's face put even more strength and speed into my legs. Regine, who had a longer stride, still fell behind. As I drew closer, I saw what everyone was looking at and talking about: some sort of red vehicle.

"What is it?" I gasped, first reaching Yvon. "Why is everyone here?"

"Someone very rich wanted Papa's painting with Mama standing on the wall of the fort and looking out at the harbor, and they traded a brand-new red Alfonso XIII Roadster for it. It's one of the first made in a French factory in Paris. This model won the Coupe de L'Auto race. It's named after the Spanish king."

I never heard Yvon sound so excited.

"What exactly is it?" I asked. Regine caught up.

Yvon laughed at me. "What exactly is it? It's an automobile, Marlena, one of the fastest made. It was delivered only a little while ago."

"So it goes by itself?"

"Without horses, yes. It has an engine. I have shown you pictures of such vehicles. This one has one of the first electric starters, too."

I shrugged. Such machines were never as interesting to me as they were to him.

I drew closer. Papa was sitting behind the steering wheel, with a man beside him explaining things. I never saw Papa look so happy and proud.

"Hey," he called when the man got out of the vehicle. "Come sit beside me." He patted the seat.

"Go on," Yvon urged, but with a sadness in his voice. "Go on," he repeated, and pushed me forward.

I walked around the rear of the vehicle slowly. Jean-Paul nodded and smiled. Cautiously, I got in. Mama was standing on the other side with her good friend Madame Blondeau, whose husband was *capitaine* of the local police. Mama looked so excited, too. Papa turned a key, did something in front, and there was a roar from the vehicle. Everyone cheered. Then he moved something else, and we started forward. I screamed and took hold of the door handle as we began to go faster. Was I the first one to take a ride with him? Why didn't he ask Yvon? I looked back. He was watching us, but he wasn't smiling.

Papa turned the car, and we started down the hill.

I screamed again, as I would on a circus ride, and he laughed. Dust flew up around us. He made another turn and followed one of the roads that led out of the village. The vehicle bounced over bumps and through shallow ditches, but Papa didn't slow down. People walking and farmers with horse-drawn carts stopped and moved to the side, watching us go by with amazement.

"It's one of the fastest new motor vehicles," Papa said, as thrilled as a little boy. We bounced so hard once that I rose and fell in the seat, but he went faster and faster, until he slowed down for a sharp turn. Then he brought the vehicle to a stop and sat back. "Wow," he said. "That was a ride, huh, Marlena?"

"It's scary, Papa."

"Only until you get used to it," he said, and started slowly ahead, before turning around and going back almost as fast as we had come. It didn't go quickly up the hill, but I sat back amazed at how much quicker we returned than we would if we were in a horse and wagon.

Everyone was waiting where we had started. As soon as we stopped, Papa beckoned to Mama to get in. She approached and leaned over the door.

"Take Yvon, Beau."

"Of course," Papa said. He beckoned to Yvon. Yvon walked slowly to the car. I could see he wasn't happy. He looked sullen. *He should have been first*, I thought. *He's older, and he's a boy.* I got out quickly.

"It's scary," I told him.

He didn't reply. He got in, and Papa waved to everyone and turned around.

"Your father is like a little boy again," Mama said.

"His painting was worth far more," Jean-Paul muttered. "He sold it too quickly."

I glanced at him with surprise, and he shrugged. "But what do I know? The world is moving too fast for me now, Marlena. What was important is no longer as important."

"Don't complain about it, Jean-Paul. You'll be driven from your house to ours for dinner faster," Mama said. "That's for sure."

"The food couldn't be any better than it is because of that," Jean-Paul told her, and they laughed.

I looked at the cloud of dust and thought about the sad expression on Yvon's face. Why didn't Papa take him first? He surely knew Yvon would be more interested in motorcars. Perhaps he was planning to do something special after he had given me and Mama quick rides, I thought.

As it turned out, I was right. It took them much longer to return, and when they did, Yvon was driving, with his face so washed in a smile that I thought it would never change. To my surprise, when they stopped and got out, Yvon answered more questions about the vehicle than Papa did. Even the man who had brought the vehicle looked impressed with him.

"Where did you learn all that about the automobile?" I

asked him later, after he and Papa washed it so it would remain looking brand-new.

"Newspapers. Papa doesn't care as much about the real world."

"What does that mean? You can be so frustrating sometimes, Yvon, with your bird words."

He laughed. "Papa's an artist. He isn't interested in facts. He's interested in beauty and mystery," he replied. He turned from the vehicle and looked out at the sea, as if he heard voices coming from it, as if all his wisdom was brought in with the tide.

The sun was slipping like a gold plate into the water. Traces of clouds were thinning out and turning into phantoms. When we were younger, Papa would sit with us on the beach sometimes after dinner and ask us to describe clouds at twilight. He said that was when they changed into their true selves. Yvon always saw animals or insects. I saw flowers sometimes and birds most of the time. When I asked Papa what he saw, he thought and said, "They're still becoming what they are. They're people's dreams."

What was Yvon dreaming about now?

"Got to get back to work," he said. "There is a pair of shoes I promised to finish today. See you at dinner." He started away, never having walked with more pride, his shoulders high and straight. He turned once to smile and wave to me.

The crowd of villagers began to break up, everyone shaking Papa's hand and wishing him luck with his new vehicle. For a while afterward, it practically took over our lives. Every night after dinner for the next few weeks, Papa and Yvon would wash the red automobile to keep it looking new. They wouldn't permit a spot of mud on it. Mama and I would stand by and laugh at them, Mama telling Papa he might have to get permission to marry the thing.

"Thing? Thing? You can't call this a thing!" Papa cried. "It's the beginning of the future."

"I can't see how getting somewhere faster makes that much difference unless it's an emergency," she told him.

He threw up his hands and cried, "Women!"

What I did like about the new vehicle was how it seemed to bring Yvon and Papa closer together. They took it for more rides, fidgeted over parts, and planned out trips. It sat only two, so I didn't go along, but I wasn't as excited about it as Yvon was. A little more than a week later, when Papa suggested Yvon take me for a ride, Mama objected.

"He needs more practice with you," she told him. I saw how hurt Yvon was. He always showed his displeasure by looking down and quickly doing something else, especially if Mama said anything remotely negative about him.

"There's not that much to it," Papa told her. "He knows more about it than I do, and he's certainly not going to confront too many of these vehicles out there."

"It goes too fast, Beau. Please," she begged.

Papa softened the blow by deciding to give more time to Yvon's practicing and less time to his painting.

"You'll take your mother for a ride first, then," he told Yvon. "That way, she'll see how good you are."

That seemed to mend his hurt feelings. As it turned out, she told him that he drove better than Papa.

"Your father is too distracted. No matter how fast we go, he sees something he thinks he might paint," she told him.

I was standing beside Papa at the time. He nodded and laughed.

"Who knows me better than your mother?" he said.

After that, she gave Yvon permission to take me for a ride. But she refused to let him take Louis or any other boy.

"I know you'd like to show off," she said, "but I'm afraid of how they might dare you to go too fast."

"No one makes me do what I don't want to do," Yvon snapped back at her, with an unusual abruptness and rage in his eyes.

She just stared at him, but with an expression on her face I couldn't ever recall seeing. It was as if she was looking at someone else and not her son. She glanced at me and realized it, quickly returning to herself.

"We all have our weak moments, Yvon. When you think too much of yourself, you either hurt yourself or someone you love," she said softly.

It made him blink, and he suddenly looked more ashamed than angry. However, he didn't apologize. He looked down, and then he turned and walked away.

"He didn't mean to be disrespectful, Mama," I said. "Yvon doesn't think too much of himself."

She looked after him and then at me, barely changing her expression. "He doesn't know himself completely," she said. "He doesn't know who he is."

"What?" I smiled. Did Yvon inherit bird words from her?

"There are things inside you, inside us all, that we have not yet realized, Marlena. That is why it's best to be more humble and move a little slower at times. We spend most of our lives learning about ourselves and not, as everyone thinks, learning about others."

She looked at Yvon walking away. "Someday he'll understand."

"What about me, Mama?"

"You'll both understand."

She folded her arms, pulled up the collar of her blouse, and walked around the house to go up the hill a little farther to where Papa was working on a new painting. If she didn't fetch him sometimes, he'd forget we were having dinner or that he hadn't eaten.

With Yvon going off in one direction and she in another, I felt a little lost. What was Mama saying? It was as if suddenly we were all strangers, as if the family everyone thought was picture-perfect had become shadows afraid of the coming sunlight.

It was more like I had just stepped out of our comfortable, beautiful world and did what Yvon always advised me to avoid doing, step into one of those clouds of secrets.

In my heart I knew there would be more.

And it would make everything that had come before it an easily forgotten dream.

2

Winter was losing its grip on us. I could feel spring touching us with the tips of its fingers. I looked forward to the first of June because it was my birthday, and the older I became, the closer I felt to Yvon. I knew it was silly to think of this because he wasn't standing still. He was getting older, too, and the year and two months between us would never shorten. It was just a feeling I had, a belief that the more mature Yvon considered me, the more he would love me, because it was an adult loving an adult and not an adult loving a child, which was expected. To me, adult love had more meaning, especially when it was earned. There were so many kinds of love. Both Mama and Papa had taught me that.

Love that was expected because you were related was taken for granted, even though we heard stories about brothers fighting over land, even killing each other over it. Sons grew up hating fathers. Mothers disowned daughters. Grandparents disowned entire families. It was obvious that love in any form was a fragile thing.

I wanted that to never be true about the love I had for Yvon and the love he had for me. I sensed that the more he respected me, the more he would love me, and although he acted as though any show of affection on my part toward him was embarrassing, I also sensed a deep pleasure in him because of how much I adored him. Perhaps he felt he had to keep such happiness his secret so he would look more manly. I never made fun of him or teased him about the way he avoided a touch or a kiss. There was no need for either of us to reassure the other, however. Everything really meaningful that we said to each other we seemed to say with our eyes, which were the same color.

Truthfully, there were never any deep or lasting silences between us because of something nasty either of us had said to the other. Most of my girlfriends and, from what I overheard, Yvon's friends couldn't make the same claim about their siblings. We saw so much rivalry and jealousy. However, whatever he accomplished or I accomplished we both joyfully celebrated together.

At the moment, both Yvon and I were very excited for Papa. Only a week after he had completed it, Papa sold his new landscape to the captain of a Norwegian merchant ship that had docked after unloading its cargo at the port. Captain Bernt did not bicker about the price. I was secretly hoping Papa would never sell it and we would have it hung on our living-room wall. He had spent weeks on it, driving Mama to an abandoned farm he had discovered on one of his exploratory rides in his red roadster and having her pose for his composition.

Captain Bernt told Monsieur Passard that the farmhouse was eerily identical to the farmhouse in which he had grown up. But he also admitted that it was Mama in the foreground drawing a pail of water from the fieldstone well that gave the picture its special beauty. Somehow Papa had captured her years younger. She looked closer to my age. It precipitated my asking him if he had known her that young and if that was the way he was seeing her at the time he painted it.

We were walking home. I had accompanied him to the gallery to meet Captain Bernt, a man in his late forties, if not in his fifties, whose full beard was almost all gray. He was very nice and very honored to meet Papa. He looked at the picture and then at me and asked if I was the woman in the painting.

"No, no, her mother," Papa told him. "She is the woman in all my works. This is our daughter."

"Your wife is the one in the painting?" He looked at me suspiciously.

"Yes," Papa said firmly.

I was beaming at having been mistaken for her.

"They must be like twins," the captain said.

Yvon was at work, and Mama was making a special dinner and cake to celebrate the picture sale. We hadn't driven down in the roadster. It wasn't far from our house, and Mama had been teasing Papa lately about getting a pouch for a stomach. She told him he was driving the vehicle so much that he wasn't getting enough exercise. She threatened to stop making what had become her famous madeleines. As a joke, he got down on his knees and begged and then promised he would not drive to any place that was less than two kilometers away. "Three," she countered, and he agreed.

"She'll always be that young to me," he replied to my question as we walked home.

"But she's not always that young-looking in other pictures that you've painted with her in them," I said. "The captain really thought I was Mama. I've never heard anyone look at any other of your paintings and say that."

He looked at me askance, with a strange guilty expression, and continued walking silently.

"Why did she come out so much younger-looking in this one, Papa? Why not in the others?"

"It's a mystery," he said, and flashed a smile. He loved keeping his artistic achievements cryptic, making it seem as if something truly spiritual had occurred, something he really couldn't explain himself. But, I thought, this time he was really trying to avoid my question for other reasons. When you grow older, the well of suspicions grows, too. Distrust is something you learn. Monsieur Appert would often tell me we are in the Garden of Eden when we are children, and as we grow, we inherit and see a sea of sins. "Thanks to Eve, of course."

"Neither of you ever say how old you were when you met," I added. "All either of you say is 'old enough.' What's old enough?"

He smiled again. I breathed relief. At least he wasn't getting angry at me for interrogating him, which was what he often called it when I asked a question after an answer to the previous one. Why was there always this tension between us when we asked about or referred to their lives before they had come to France?

"When you fall in love with someone, Marlena, you can never erase how they looked to you at that moment. Maybe it's special for me because I'm an artist and the visual is my life, but if you ask your mother, she'll probably tell you that is how she sees me all the time, too, the way we were." He smiled. "People who are truly in love with each other never age in each other's eyes."

"So she was that young when you first met?"

"To me she was."

"When?" I persisted.

He laughed. "How old am I?" he asked.

"Thirty-seven."

"How old is Yvon?"

"Sixteen."

"Use math."

"But I don't know how long you knew each other before you decided to come to France and get married. Not exactly, anyway."

"Less than a year," he said sharply. "Okay? Enough about that."

He walked faster.

I had never been stung by a bee, but I imagined how I felt at the moment was how I would feel if it had happened. I hurried to catch up. Something had broken free inside me when the ship's captain wondered if I was the woman in the painting. Questions bottled up for years were pouring over my tongue whether I liked it or not.

"Why didn't you stay in America? Wasn't it better for making money on your work?"

He looked at me and continued to walk. I thought he wasn't going to answer.

"I told you that Jean-Paul trained me in doing portraits to make money. We had met by chance. He saw me drawing funny images of people on the boardwalk in New York City, caricatures. You know, like cartoons. It was an easy way to make money to live, and he stood there watching me work. Then he suggested I should do more sophisticated art and invited me to his apartment to see his work. It was all landscapes, but he said he had done portraits to earn a living first, to be able to eat. So I followed his lead, his training, learning how to paint someone and make him or her look better, more handsome, prettier than they were."

"Why prettier or more handsome?"

"Anyone who wants his or her portrait done is somewhat vain, so you flatter them. Okay?"

"But why not stay in America to do the landscapes?" I asked, rushing the question because we were almost home. "There are beautiful places to paint, I'm sure."

"Jean-Paul convinced me that people loved art more here. The greatest artists are from Europe, and artists here have been doing it a lot longer, even though there are some great ones in America. I didn't think we'd stay for the rest of our lives, but . . ." He paused and looked back at the sea. "We fell in love again, this time with this place." He smiled. "Lucky you, right?"

"Oh, yes," I said.

"So stop asking questions as if you're upset about it," he added, unexpectedly roughly.

Was that how I sounded?

"I'm not!" I cried, but he was already yards ahead and almost to the front door.

At least I had learned something, I thought, and later, when

Yvon was home from work, I told him about my conversation with Papa. He looked almost as suspicious as Papa had when I asked the first question.

"Did he tell you where exactly or how exactly he had met Mama?"

"I didn't get to that. He answered quickly and walked fast, but Mama once told us they had met when she had visited an aunt in Charlottesville, Virginia, right?"

"Uh-huh," Yvon said, his eyes shifting from mine.

"He was visiting his cousin. The one who left him some money."

"Right," Yvon said.

"So it couldn't have been in New York City. Did he ever tell you anything different?"

"No."

"Did he tell you something he never told me?"

"No, Marlena. Don't be a woodpecker."

"What?"

"I have to wash up for dinner. We're opening a new bottle of wine to celebrate Papa's sale tonight as well," he said, smiling.

I wasn't sure who was better at changing the topic, Yvon or Papa or Mama. I was about to shout after him, cry out, *You know more than you're telling me, Yvon Hunter!* but I stopped myself when Mama appeared and asked me to help her set the table. Jean-Paul's woman friend, Anne Bise, had already arrived. Papa had gone to pick up Jean-Paul in the roadster.

"I have a roast, and I want you to help with the mashed potatoes and then help set the table," she said. "What was the captain of the ship like?"

"He was very nice." I thought a moment and then quickly said, "He thought I was the one in the picture."

"Did he?" She ran her hand over my hair, smiling. "You are getting very pretty and growing so quickly, I can see him thinking you were older."

"It's not because I'm getting older."

"What?" She tilted her head. "What do you mean?"

"I thought Papa had painted you looking younger in the picture," I said. "He admitted it," I quickly added so she couldn't deny it.

"Did he?" She held her smile, but she looked nervous. I could see it in her eyes.

"Did he draw a funny image of you on the sidewalk in Charlottesville? Is that how you met?"

She stared a moment. "Did he tell you that?"

"He said he used to draw caricatures, used to do that in New York City, and that was how Jean-Paul discovered him."

"Yes, that was how it was."

"And he was doing those funny pictures on the sidewalk in Charlottesville. So did he do one of you?"

She nodded.

"Something like that. Let's go. You know how hungry your father and Jean-Paul can be, especially after they have a few aperitifs. I'll have hors d'oeuvres for them. I'm just finishing that."

I went into the kitchen and said hello to Anne, who was sitting at the table working on string beans. She had long, spidery fingers that seemed to be moving totally on their own. It was obvious to me that she had been a very pretty woman when she was younger, because she had held on to her dainty facial features and youthful light-green eyes. Unlike other women her age, she didn't expand at the hips like a balloon as if some invisible hand was pressing down on her head, turning her into a squash. She had a soft, friendly smile, and her light-brown hair still battled the gray strands. She was quite fond of Yvon and me. She called herself our godmother just because Jean-Paul was our godfather. Neither of us ever contradicted her when she introduced herself to people that way.

"If I don't see Marlena for two days, I think I'm meeting a new girl," she told my mother. "She's growing that fast."

Mama looked at me as if she hadn't noticed, but she didn't smile as I was anticipating.

"Yes, she is growing quickly. Some women leave their childhood as if they are escaping from it. They don't realize what they've lost until it's too late," Mama said.

Her expression made me feel guilty of something.

"I can't help growing up, Mama," I protested, maybe too hard. They both laughed.

"That's the tragedy of it," she said, and Anne nodded.

"Not to me," I insisted. "What was so bad about your leaving childhood, Mama? What did you lose?"

Her smile evaporated so quickly that it couldn't be remembered.

"Just start on the mashed potatoes," she said. She turned away from me and began talking about the new work being done on the port and how more tourists would be coming to our quiet little village.

We heard Papa drive up with Jean-Paul. Yvon went out to help bring him into the house. They sat in the living room, where Papa poured them all an aperitif. Mama sent Anne out to join them, refusing to let her do any more work on dinner preparations. I began to set the table. Mama brought them all a tray of caramelized-onion tarts with olives and anchovies. It was actually something Anne had taught her to make.

Papa described the merchant-ship captain and what he had told us about Norway and the farmhouse back there.

"I think the one you used in the painting originally might have been built by a man from Norway, Beau," Jean-Paul said. "Maybe you sensed the captain was coming and painted the landscape just for him."

"I'm as good as a gypsy fortune-teller, huh?" Papa said.

"Every artist has a little clairvoyance in his soul," Jean-Paul insisted.

For some reason, Papa looked quickly at me when Jean-Paul said that.

"Well, you did when you looked at my early attempts, old friend."

"That didn't take much clairvoyance. Anyone with an ounce of talent and an eye for it could recognize what it was in you to become."

"And what's that exactly?" Papa asked.

"More famous than me, for sure," Jean-Paul said. Everyone but Yvon laughed. Sometimes I thought he loved Jean-Paul as much as he loved Papa and never wanted to hear a negative thing about him. I smiled because it was such a generous and selfless thing for Jean-Paul to say. He was still far more famous.

Papa loved the hors d'oeuvres, and Anne said Mama had made them better than she could. Jean-Paul disagreed, and Anne said he was still flattering her to keep her faithful. Even Yvon laughed at that and especially at how Jean-Paul protested.

"You see, Yvon," Jean-Paul said. "You can never win with a woman, and even if you do, you lose, because they make you feel so terrible that you've won."

Yvon smiled. "I'll keep that in mind," he said. "And never disagree with any woman I like."

"*Bon chance* with that," Jean-Paul said.

"Some things are not left to chance," Yvon said. "And even if they are, it's what you've made of it."

Jean-Paul and Anne laughed.

"So much wisdom packed in so young a body," Jean-Paul said.

Papa looked proud at how well Yvon could hold a conversation. Jean-Paul was right. Yvon was so much older than any other boy his age. There wasn't a man in the village who didn't respect him as a man. *My brother*, I thought, *will always fill me with confidence.* Was it unnatural to love him so?

I went back into the kitchen with Mama to get our dinner ready to serve. She glanced at me and looked very sad for a moment.

"Anything wrong, Mama?"

"I didn't mean to scare you out of your childhood, Marlena," Mama said. "These are just such precious moments for you."

"But they weren't for you?"

"Sometimes they were, but I was in far too much of a rush to become a femme fatale."

"What?"

Hearing her say such a thing about herself was quite shocking. My mother? A femme fatale? I knew what that was from listening in on Anne and her conversations about other village women. And when I mentioned it to Yvon, he went into a long explanation, as if it proved something he always believed. He even said, "All women have a little of that in them," which by implication meant me, too.

But he surely didn't mean Mama, I thought. Now she was admitting to it.

"I was very competitive and very determined to be one. But thankfully, your father came along and saved me."

"When? How? Were you as young as me? Where exactly?" I fired my questions almost in a frenzy.

"Slow down, Marlena."

"I just want to know more. I'm old enough now, aren't I, Mama?"

"Yes, but you should learn everything slowly. Just as it's not wise to rush into your future, it's not wise to rush back to your past. Sometimes that can be tragic," she added. "Let's get this food out before they eat the table," she said. I was disappointed. How could a return to the past be tragic?

"Nevertheless, you will tell me everything about how you fell in love with Papa, won't you, Mama?"

"Of course," she said, then brushed back my hair and kissed me. "But don't expect a fairy tale. It wasn't all that different from how other people fall in love."

I was still excited. No matter how simple the story was, it would be a fairy tale to me. It had to be. How could my parents not be magical?

At dinner, Jean-Paul, who heard about the captain mistaking me for my mother in the landscape, suggested my father might now consider me for some of his future works. I looked at my mother first and then my father. They seemed to have the same expression . . . sadness.

"Perhaps," my father replied cautiously, eyeing my mother. Mama said nothing. Why was my growing up so painful for them to take?

"You're a lucky man to have such beauty available. I remember when I had to talk to some pretty women, convince them to spend the time standing still and—"

"Oh, you had such a hard time," Anne said, shaking her head and clicking her tongue. She looked at us, especially Yvon and me. "Your godfather created the concept of a flirt. I hear that men making movies have the same line he used when they approach a young woman these days."

"What's that?" Yvon asked.

"Did anyone ever tell you that you ought to be in pictures?"

Jean-Paul assumed the expression of someone insulted, and then he laughed. "Well, it used to work," he confessed. "It worked with you, *mon amour.*"

She slapped him playfully on the arm. "I only pretended it did to make you feel better about yourself," she said. "Men and their egos."

We all laughed.

How could my childhood have been any better than this? I thought, and then looked at my mother, who was staring at me. She looked terribly sad, as if she was the one with clairvoyance and not Papa the artist. Maybe she was right to be sad. My childhood was dissolving, and with it all the pretend and magic. How many times had Mama told me that adults don't have time to dance among the stars? Did I push her too hard? Did I wish for something I would regret?

Later that night, after Mama, Anne, and I cleaned up, Papa took Jean-Paul back to his house, and Yvon, being a gentleman, escorted Anne down the hill. I was unaware that Mama had slipped out of the house. I went looking for her and saw her standing on the side of the path to the crest of the hill near our house. She had her arms folded across her waist.

It was a moonless night, with scattered thick clouds, and a little cooler than usual for this time of year. I went back in and fetched Mama's light-blue shawl, slipped on my pink cardigan sweater, and hurried out, but she wasn't there. For a few moments, I thought she might have gone around and reentered the house from the front, but then I saw her silhouette moving toward the crest of the hill. I ran after her.

"Mama!"

She turned and waited for me. I handed her the shawl.

"Thank you, sweetheart," she said.

"Where are you going?"

"Just getting some air. It always seems a little stuffy after we have a big meal and drink a bit too much wine."

She turned and continued to walk toward the crest with her head down. Her voice seemed different, sadder. After having such a good time and Papa making money on his picture, why would there be any sadness?

"Are you all right?" I asked, catching up.

"Oh, yes." She smiled.

"Something made you sad," I insisted.

She nodded.

"What?"

"Seeing you grow up so soon. Sometimes you can't help but wish everyone you love would stay the way they are forever, especially your little girl," she said.

"Did your mother wish that for you?"

She laughed. "Oh, yes. My mother was not in favor of me becoming a woman. She was quite Victorian."

"What was that?"

"Stuffy, prudish. I thought she was afraid of life. She was unable to explain a woman's monthlies to me and hired a nurse to do it. Don't worry. I'll never be a Victorian when it comes to you. Now that I see how much you've grown and how wise you are, you don't have to be afraid to ask me anything when it comes to sex or boys, anything, Marlena."

I nodded. For some reason, hearing her so willing to talk about such things frightened me a bit. Maybe I was growing up too fast.

"Is that why you don't like talking about her very much?"

"I don't have pleasant memories of my childhood and my mother, so I don't like thinking about her. I'd rather imagine I was born on that beach down there," she said. "I grew instantly into a young woman, and the first person I saw was your father. He had been waiting for me, like in a dream."

"Well, what about your father?" I asked, now that she had been this revealing.

"He was a man solely consumed with his banking business. Well, not always that way, but again, I'd rather not think about it. I don't want to relive the pain and disappointment, and I certainly don't want to visit any of it upon you or Yvon."

Pain and disappointment in your father? I couldn't imagine such a thing happening to me.

"What did he do?"

"Hey!" we heard, and looked back at the house. Papa had dropped off Jean-Paul and probably stopped on his way back to get Yvon, who was also on his way back up the hill.

Mama waved.

"We're coming down!" she shouted, so they wouldn't start walking up.

I was disappointed. I wished my father and brother would have stayed away just a while longer. Despite her reluctance, I sensed I could have learned a lot more about her family, her childhood.

"Come," she said, and took my hand. She probably could feel my disappointment. "Let's talk only about happier things, Marlena. Happiness makes us strong."

The moment we returned to the house, we could see that Papa couldn't contain the excitement he had locked away during our dinner celebrating his great sale. He already had been thinking about his next painting, and contrary to his usual secrecy and mystery, he wanted us all to experience his new vision as perfectly as he did. It was going to be that special.

There was a view from the medieval city of Eze that Papa had fixed on. It was high up, and he said he could capture the seaside from our village to Nice and beyond. He had some ideas for how he wanted Mama to stand looking out and down. He surprised us all, but especially Mama, by bringing out a woman's medieval dress, a black Ameline peasant dress with a bodice laced with brace grommets. The skirt was split to show the muslin underdress.

"I thought it would be fun to imagine and create the landscape with you back hundreds of years. So much of the original Eze is there. What do you think?" he asked her, and held up the dress like a bullfighter tempting the bull. "People will think the painting is that old, an original. I'll mix the paint especially to achieve that sense."

"You kept that dress hidden so well?" she asked, surprised. He just smiled.

"Let me see," she said, and went to put on the dress. When she came out, we all thought she looked quite beautiful.

"Yes, beautiful and interesting," Papa added. *"N'est-ce pas,* Yvon?"

"Yes, Papa, but she'll need medieval shoes, too, unless you won't paint her feet."

Papa laughed. "Yvon told me that Monsieur Dufloit has something in his collection, a pair of low black leather boots that will fit your mother," Papa said.

"How long have you been planning this picture?" Mama asked.

Papa looked at Yvon. "Since Yvon and I took a ride up to Eze. About two weeks ago, eh, Yvon?"

"Yes, but it was a very slow ride with all those turns."

"Worth it," Papa insisted. "We'll just start early in the morning. You'll do the preparations for dinner so we don't have to rush back, Marlena. Corrine?"

"Oh, she's quite capable, Beau. I'm sure Yvon will help as well."

"When?" I asked.

"I'll get the boots tomorrow, and we'll begin. Jean-Paul is jealous. He's always meant to do a landscape from that height, but the trip up was too taxing, or it was before I got our roadster. He actually gave me the idea. I drove us up there to see if I agreed. What did you think of the view, Yvon?"

"One of the best, for sure, Papa."

Papa looked at me. "One day, I'll take you up to see it," he promised.

"Your father's mind is always somewhere in the clouds," Mama said. "I'm not surprised he wants to do this."

I was excited about having new responsibilities. Mama left it up to me to decide what we would eat, what I should buy. I didn't even confirm it with Yvon, but no one complained the entire first week.

The work was energizing for both Papa and Mama. Every evening, they returned excited, raving about the scenery and someone or something they had seen during the day. It didn't surprise me that they attracted attention, especially Mama in her medieval dress.

I did more than look after our dinners. I cleaned the house and washed and dried clothes. Sometimes Yvon would come home earlier and do some work around the house. Papa had wanted to paint the wall surrounding our front steps, so Yvon decided to surprise him when he and Mama returned one day. Jean-Paul and Anne came to our dinners on the weekends, Jean-Paul eager to hear about the landscape picture. However, Papa never showed anyone his work now before he was satisfied it was done, not even Jean-Paul.

Being so busy made me happier for another reason. Yvon went into his dark moods far less often. He was even more talkative and had good stories about the customers who came to the shop and the way Monsieur Dufloit treated some of the women he called beldams, women who had whittled their husbands down to baby lambs. His imitation of some of them and Monsieur Dufloit had both Mama and Papa in hysterics. Yvon was so different, looking even older and more mature.

It was his idea to surprise Jean-Paul with a birthday dinner before his birthday, "because he wouldn't approve of it."

He had declared he was not going to celebrate anymore. They reminded him too much of his age. No one believed him, but Yvon loved the idea of a surprise. I wasn't as confident of my baking abilities; however, Yvon encouraged me and promised to be right beside me while I worked. We were so involved in it and the *coq au vin*, a wine and chicken dish I was preparing, that neither of us realized the time until Anne had arrived. She obviously had anticipated Papa driving down to pick up Jean-Paul.

The sight of her shocked us. Mama and Papa knew we were making this special dinner. Papa had said they'd be back much earlier. For a moment, Yvon and I just stared at her standing there.

"Where are your parents?" she asked. "Not back yet?"

She would have seen Papa going down the hill to pick up Jean-Paul, I thought. She knew the answer.

I looked at Yvon, and he put down the spoon he had been using to stir the sauce. He shook his head.

"Artists," Anne said, smiling and shaking her head. "They live in a different time zone. Their clocks have no hands."

I wiped my hands on a towel. Without speaking, Yvon and I looked at each other and then walked past Anne and out to the front of the house. Darkness was in a downpour. The only thing deeper was the silence.

Neither of us spoke, perhaps both afraid of those first few words of fear and concern.

And then, suddenly, I could hear the sound of those horses in my nightmares being driven into a pace so fast their eyes were bulging.

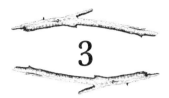

3

There was thunder even though it was a cloudless sky, with stars coming up like air bubbles out of the darkness. They seemed to be rushing in from everywhere, as if they wanted to witness this night. Papa used to call it "a thousand eyes of God opening up to peer down at us."

Maybe I was imagining all these eager stars continually appearing, especially as more time passed and there was still no sign of our parents. Even Anne, who did her best to keep us from worrying, now started to look fretful. Her smiles and reassuring hugs drifted further and further back. They were replaced with signs of her aging, the deeper wrinkles near her eyes, the silvery light bringing out the gray in her hair as she became more and more anxious.

"He must have had engine trouble," Yvon declared as firmly

as he could. He, too, was battling with darker thoughts now. "They're probably walking back."

"They could take hours and hours," I said. "They'll be exhausted!"

He thought a moment and nodded. "I'll go fetch Capitaine Blondeau, who will organize a search. We'll take the police wagon," he said, "so we can pick them up."

"I'll go, too," I said.

"No, you stay," Yvon insisted. "In case they return from some other direction or another way."

"But—"

"Do what your brother says," Anne advised. "I'll stay with you."

Disappointed, I settled into the chair at the rear of the house facing the road that eventually led up to Eze. Yvon was off instantly. Tears were building in my eyes; I couldn't keep them from leaking. I flicked them off as quickly as I could, but Anne saw.

"Now, now, everything will be all right," she said. "I'll pour us both a little wine. It will help keep us calm. See? Parents can be as bad as children."

I said nothing. I simply sat and stared at the road and the way the darkness crept closer to us like approaching fog. What made it unbearably longer was that time seemingly was standing still. The hands of the clock were frozen. It was truly as if the whole world was holding its breath. Anne, trying constantly to keep me from worrying and maybe herself as well, talked about the times she had stayed away from home too long and angered her parents.

"And how often have I sat waiting for Jean-Paul, the food

getting cold? Artists," she said, shaking her head. "They can get lost for hours staring at a strangely twisted branch. I'd yell at him, and he would stand there looking dumbfounded. Eventually, I realized he was like a child when it came to time. Forget schedules or promises, especially the promises he made never to do it again."

"Papa's not like that," I insisted. "He worries more about us than we could ever worry about him. He'd be sure to be back. And don't forget Mama is with him. She would keep close track of time."

Anne was silent. She could see I was too old now, beyond the age when I would cling to hope woven out of fantasy. This was probably what Mama feared when she talked about leaving childhood too fast. You have trouble sugarcoating reality when you get older. A frog could never really be a prince.

I had no idea how much time had passed, but finally we heard the sound of horses and a wagon followed by other men on horses. I stood to see better. Anne stepped up beside me and took my hand. We walked out as they approached. I could see Yvon in the front of the wagon, bent over. The police and the volunteers caught up and gathered around the wagon when it stopped. No one spoke. We walked toward it slowly. Yvon rose and hopped out to greet us.

"You found them?" I quickly asked.

He nodded and looked at Anne. "The roadster went off the road at one of those sharp turns," he said, speaking like someone hypnotized. "We think something happened with the front tire on the right and Papa lost control."

"Where are Papa and Mama?" I cried, after I had panned the wagon seats and the men on horseback.

"They're in the wagon," Yvon said.

"Are they all right?"

"They're in the wagon," he repeated. He wasn't looking at either Anne or me. He was looking beyond us.

I felt as if my chest had become hollow. There was no heartbeat; there was no blood in my veins. In moments, I would crumple like someone whose bones had shattered, and my body would fold and sink to the ground. I didn't feel my feet touch anything as I walked forward. Anne rushed to join and embrace me.

None of the policemen could look at me. Capitaine Blondeau started to speak to another policeman. Anyone between us and the wagon moved aside. When we reached it, I looked in and saw the sheets over Papa and Mama. I had started to lift them away when Yvon was suddenly beside me, grabbing my wrist.

"They were thrown from the roadster onto the rocks below," he said. "They are battered and broken badly, Marlena. They must be taken to the funeral parlor to be prepared. No one can look at them now, especially you."

I was shaking my head, but I had no voice. Somewhere inside me, a loud *NO!* was echoing.

"But I must see them!"

"You don't want to remember them like this," he whispered. "Don't look. Please."

"Remember?" The word refused to be understood. "Mama wants to know about our dinner," I managed, forcing a smile. "I did everything that I promised her."

I didn't realize Yvon had put his arm around my shoulders until he tightened it and drew me hard against him. Capitaine

Blondeau and all his men were staring at me. It was then that I finally managed to scream. My shrill cries rolled down the hill toward the village. I could hear people shouting to each other and rushing up toward us. Yvon was trying to turn me back toward the house. I fought against it, breaking loose for a moment, my small fists pummeling his shoulders and chest as I tried to get past him and back to the wagon. Anne moved forward to help him. I crumpled in her arms, and then Yvon lifted me into his and carried me back into the house.

All I could hear at that moment was the sound of the horses and the wagon continuing on to the funeral parlor and the waves of indistinct words and sobs washing over the house as more and more people gathered. Yvon put me on my bed, and Anne sat beside me, holding my hand. I closed my eyes, and I screamed and screamed until I had no voice. Exhausted, I fell into a well of darkness.

My mother's friends came quickest of all. No one really knew what else to do but cook and bring food. I heard all the sobbing and an occasional cry of disbelief or anger. Anne had given me something Dr. Veil had prescribed. I drifted in and out of sleep, the voices sometimes so mixed they sounded like gibberish. At one point, I told myself that this was all a nightmare, and the next time I woke, it would all be gone. But it wasn't, and eventually I found the strength to get up and go out to the living room, where our neighbors and friends had gathered. It was almost morning now. Sunlight was slowly pushing shadows back to where they slept daily.

Yvon was seated on our smaller settee. He looked up at me sharply when I stepped out, anticipating my screaming and crying more, but I just stared, feeling too drained of any energy to do anything more than breathe. Was I breathing?

He patted the space beside him, and I moved quickly to it.

When I sat, he put his arm around me, and I lowered my head to his shoulder. One of the policemen who had gone looking with Yvon had been talking, describing his theory of the accident. Someone offered the ironic truth that this might be the first automobile fatality in France. The words drifted off, with no one caring to talk any more about it. Even adults liked to pretend that what had happened hadn't, but they couldn't do that and look at each other.

At one point, maybe to break the heavy silence, I asked Yvon if he believed that the policeman's description of the accident was true. I had no idea why that mattered now, but I felt a need to blame someone, something.

"Most likely," he said. "Papa and I often talked about the sharp turns. He was careful. He had become a very good driver. It had to be something going wrong with the car."

I closed my eyes.

What else could I do? Yvon was trying to make sense of it all, but even though I wanted to as well, nothing really mattered to me. How could it? Should I hate the car? Did the devil bring it? Were my parents being punished for something?

Was this Eve's fault?

I expected to hear that from Monsieur Appert when he appeared, but he couldn't look at either of us and didn't stay long.

For days afterward, there were always people at the house. Jean-Paul was brought to see us first thing in the morning and stayed all day. He tried to look brave for Yvon and me, but he was too overwhelmed and often broke down crying. We ended up caring more for him than ourselves, fearful that he would just expire like some candle flickering at its last moments, and we'd have another death with which to contend. His eyes were swimming with pain and brought tears constantly to mine. Both of us made him eat and drink. Anne was the best help when it came to him. Once I overheard her telling him he must be strong for us. "They have no one else," she said.

He looked at her. I was half-listening, but I heard him say, "That's not so."

The words were lost on me for the moment, and I didn't recall them until after Yvon and I had gone to the Clervoy Funeral Parlor. Monsieur Clervoy was someone we kids made fun of rather than ignored, probably because an undertaker could not be ignored. He was a looming presence, a reminder that life was fragile, but he was frightening to confront, because Madame Sorel, a widow who was said to be close to a hundred, told us that he slept with Death. He was tall and lean and always seemed draped in shadows, slinking through the alleyways even though it would take him longer to get where he was going.

"They are *bons amis*. Clervoy must be nice to him to get his business. He looks at me with hungry eyes," she would say, with her eyes scary wide, and then cackle. "But he will die before I do," she promised. "Death is afraid of me. I'll outlive you all."

Usually, we couldn't wait to get away from her. For some reason, she enjoyed frightening us. Maybe she was getting some vengeance on age; she was so jealous of our youth.

Yvon's only comment when we viewed our parents was that

Monsieur Clervoy had made them beautiful again. "There are all kinds of artists," he said.

What he had done was make it so they looked simply asleep.

I dreamed they would wake and it would all be some terrible misunderstanding. But I did not tell Yvon this. I wanted to be as adult as he was and not make a moment more difficult for him. He had his grief, too, and didn't need me wailing at his side, pounding my fists against myself and demanding that this not be true. I would stand quietly with him, tall and regal, and keep my tears and screams under control. I was determined to be the little lady Mama had wanted me to be.

My greatest fear now was what would become of us. That was when Jean-Paul's words to Anne resurfaced in my memory. During our period of mourning, Anne stayed with us, and when he could, Jean-Paul joined her. Whether it was out of pity or not, Monsieur Passard advanced us money he expected to make on Papa's remaining paintings. We didn't need much, because everyone in the village was sending food over daily. I actually didn't want Regine and my other girlfriends visiting, because they were so depressing that I usually retreated to my room to cry. Everyone was bringing flowers until we had to put some outside.

Yvon wasn't that hospitable to his friends, either. It was as if we were both trying to keep grief on the other side of our door. The only people we tolerated at dinner were Anne and Jean-Paul, but he was looking more and more fragile to both of us, falling asleep even at the dinner table. Half the time, we kept a brave face, more to protect him than ourselves, because if he cried, we could see his bones rattle.

My birthday came and went while we waited to do the funeral. I refused to celebrate it or accept a single gift. Everyone understood. Both Mama and Papa had always made a big thing over my birthday. Yvon used to say that to them it was a national holiday. Sometimes he sounded jealous. I didn't even want to think about it. Nevertheless, Anne slipped me a very pretty pearl bracelet.

"For when you can be happy," she said. I started to protest, but she put up her hand. "You will be happy again, Marlena. You don't want to hear it, but it's true."

I put the bracelet away.

Papa and Mama's funeral brought people from out of the village as well. A newspaper from Nice had sent over a reporter to write about a talented artist who was taken too soon from his work, as if his being taken too soon from his children was less important.

When Jean-Paul and Anne came to be with us two days after the funeral, I sensed that something very important was about to be announced. Yvon did, too, although he tried to hide it from me. And it was then that I again remembered the strange thing Jean-Paul had said to Anne before the funeral. I had not told Yvon.

"Both Anne and I would have been honored to take you into our home," Jean-Paul began, after Anne had served the coffee and sat at the table. She nodded, smiling, and reached for my hand.

What did he mean by "would have been"?

"That's fine with us," I said quickly.

To my surprise, Yvon did not instantly agree. He simply stared at Jean-Paul and kept from looking at me, even though

I was looking at him expectantly and wondering why he wasn't enthusiastic about it.

Jean-Paul nodded. "Years ago, when your parents first arrived to begin their lives here, your father gave me some papers to keep for him."

"To keep from my mother," Yvon instantly added. I was quite surprised. How would he know that?

"*Oui*," Jean-Paul said. "To keep from your mother as well. You knew this how?"

Yvon didn't answer. He rose instead and left the room. When he returned, he was clutching what looked like a small pile of letters. He sat and put them on the table.

"What is this?" I asked immediately.

Yvon looked at Jean-Paul. "When did you find these?" Jean-Paul asked.

"Years ago, in a box at the back of my father's closet, but I didn't understand them at first. As I grew older, whenever I could without my parents knowing, I reread them."

Jean-Paul looked at the pile. "From his older sister in Richmond?" he asked Yvon.

"Yes."

"Then you know Hunter is not your father's real name and therefore not yours."

"*Oui*," Yvon said.

"What? What is our real name?" I asked.

Yvon turned to me slowly. "Dawson," he said, "and Papa didn't just have a sister. He had sisters."

"Sisters?"

"There are two."

He looked to Jean-Paul, who nodded. "Effie and Pauline," he said. "Effie is the older. She was younger than your father."

"But why did he change his name?"

Jean-Paul looked at Yvon. From his expression, it was clear to me that he had not learned the answer in the letters.

"Your father wanted a fresh start," Jean-Paul said. "But . . . this terrible thing has changed everything. Your aunts are on their way."

"On their way where?" I asked.

"Here," Jean-Paul said.

"Why didn't Papa ever mention them to us?"

Jean-Paul looked at Yvon. He turned to me slowly. "They— Effie, at least, was angry at him for not doing what their father wanted and working with him in their business. All the responsibilities for that fell on her after their father died, as well as caring for her younger sister. In the letters, she never stops reminding him."

"Your father wanted to be an artist, not a businessman," Jean-Paul said. "That's part of the reason he wanted a fresh start. He wanted to make it clear to his family back home that he did not want to be a part of the family business." Jean-Paul looked again at Yvon, who just stared, not agreeing or disagreeing.

"What was the business?" I asked.

"It still is," Jean-Paul said. "It's a real estate company. They own commercial properties and rent out offices and warehouses in Richmond. They're very wealthy people. Neither Effie nor Pauline ever married and had children. Your father calling himself someone else here doesn't matter. Legally, he was still a Dawson, and so are you. You two are in line to inherit it all. Someday you'll be quite rich in America."

"But we don't live in America," I said. "We live here. Yvon and I will do just fine. Won't we, Yvon?"

No one spoke for a long moment.

Then Anne smiled. "Both of you are quite capable for young people, but you have family who want to care for you."

"Family? People we've never known who have a different name. No, you are our only family," I insisted. The tears that came now were hot, burning. Rage was quickly replacing sorrow. Not once had I screamed out at God for the injustice of my parents' deaths. I didn't pout or snap angrily at anyone. I had yet to be any sort of a burden.

But this was too much. I pushed the pile of letters farther away from me.

"I don't care what these letters say. Papa didn't want us to know any family; otherwise, he wouldn't have changed his name."

"That's not true. Your father left us with instructions should anything ever happen to him and your mother before you were adults," Jean-Paul said. "It was my responsibility as your godfather. He and I talked about his family from time to time, especially after he had received one of those letters. He believed his sister Effie blamed him for her not having a husband and a family."

"How could that be his fault?" I asked. "He wasn't there."

"She says in the letters that he left her with all the business and family responsibilities, and she basically had no personal life," Yvon said.

"That's right," Jean-Paul said.

"I don't believe it. That's just an excuse. Maybe she was too ugly."

"Maybe," Jean-Paul said, shrugging. "You'll find that most people often look to blame someone else for their own failings and mistakes."

"What about his younger sister? Why doesn't she have a family? Does she blame Papa, too?"

Jean-Paul looked at Yvon to see if he was going to answer first, but he looked as confused about that as I was.

"You'll make up your own minds about it, I'm sure," Jean-Paul said cryptically.

"I don't want to make up my mind about any of it. I don't want anything to do with her or her sister. I won't change my name and go to America. I won't!" I said, and stamped my foot.

"Don't punish the earth. It's not its fault," Jean-Paul said, and smiled. It was something he often said after any of my outbursts that ended with pounding the floor. His smile didn't calm me this time.

"Why would we go?" I looked at Yvon. He was too silent.

"You're now their only family, too," Jean-Paul said. "As I said, you two inherit everything someday." He looked more at Yvon. "It's considerable."

"I don't care!" I screamed.

I got up and rushed to my room, slamming the door behind me. And then threw myself on my bed and buried my face in my pillow. I wished I could suffocate myself and be with Mama and Papa. All these secrets were kept from me. I didn't even have a real name.

Minutes passed. I turned over and glared at the ceiling. Why hadn't Yvon ever told me about those letters? Why didn't he ask Papa about them in front of me? Why would he keep it a secret from me? Was this why he was often afraid? I should have known he had a reason for looking so dreadfully thoughtful so often. Why keep all this from me until now? Had he made Mama and Papa a promise that I never knew? I felt so alone, so apart from everyone.

I was as angry at him right now as I was at anything or anyone.

There was a light knock on my door. I tried to ignore it, but he knocked harder.

"What is it?" I yelled. I could be just as pouty and annoying as any of my friends if I wanted to be, and right now, that's all I wanted to be.

Yvon opened the door and entered, closing it softly behind him. For a moment he just stared at me. I turned away, and he came to my bed and sat.

"Recently, when I went for a ride with Papa, he referred to his sisters," he said, "and he told me about his changing our name. He didn't know I had read the letters."

I turned. "Then why wouldn't he tell me as well?"

"He would have eventually. He thought I was old enough to understand it, why he had deserted his family. He asked me to wait for you to be older."

"That's a lie. He wouldn't desert anyone."

"It was the way he put it. I think he was feeling badly about it. He didn't get along with his father. His father had no respect for his artistic talent and dreams. His mother had, but she had died so early in his life, and his sister Effie was always on his father's side. Everyone, even his mother's old friends, was pressuring him to make art his hobby and take on more responsibility for his family business. Eventually, he ran away from home, and that was when he met Jean-Paul."

"It's not fair that you knew everything and I didn't."

"I don't know everything, Marlena. I'm sure there is more, lots more."

"I don't care. I don't want to know it, any of it. I'm not going to America to live with them. I'll run away, too, just like Papa did."

"He was older, and he was a man. A runaway young girl ends up on the streets. Papa would want us to have what he didn't. That's why he left those instructions with Jean-Paul."

I turned away. My lips quivered. I didn't want to cry. Crying and wailing would prove he was right, that I was still too young to hear dreadful news and know how to handle it. Everything inside me twisted and knotted. It was harder to breathe. I had to be more like Yvon. I had to be strong and calm, but oh, how my heart ached. Like bitter frosting spread on a cake of agony, these secrets and revelations choked me. I was being force-fed so much misery that I would surely die. All the sunshine in our lives was being blocked. Without it, like flowers, I would wilt. Yvon would, too, despite his show of strength.

"Why can't we just stay with Jean-Paul and Anne? No one has to know any of this. No one will care."

"Jean-Paul is getting very old. He's barely able to look after himself, but both of them really believe family is first, and fake name or not, they are our real family."

The truth of his words gave them more thunder.

"Why do they want us? Why do they care about two children they've never met? Why would they come so far to get us?"

He shrugged. "As Jean-Paul says, like us now, they have no one else to call family. Families like to leave their wealth to family and not to strangers, too."

His reasonable tone only made the pinpricks of pain and fear sharper.

"Well, I'm not going to feel sorry for them and be their family just because of that," I said, then folded my arms across my breasts and turned my back on him. He didn't move. I spun around again. "You sound like you feel sorrier for them than you do for us."

"I don't," he said. "I feel sorrier for us."

"We'll be just fine if we stay here."

"Will we? In Villefranche-sur-Mer? I haven't woken up one morning without anticipating seeing Mama or hearing her voice. Sometimes I stare at the hill and wait to see Papa appear with his easel. I wake up listening for their laughter. Often, when they were in bed, I could hear that, hear their laughter and their love for each other.

"Everything about and everyone in this place will keep us thinking of them, Marlena. Every street corner she stood on, every person he spoke to, and every scene he painted would keep us in mourning."

"So? We should be always thinking about them, right?"

"But thinking with pain and sorrow? If I didn't leave to be with our aunts, I'd eventually run off myself."

"And leave me?"

"I'd worry about taking you to nothing but trouble."

I was silent. That was horrible to contemplate: Yvon leaving me, too? He saw how I shuddered with the thought and reached for my hand.

"Maybe there's a new life for us in America, Marlena. I know Papa would want that, even Mama, maybe especially Mama."

"But we're leaving them if we go to America," I said, the tears like drops of glue in my eyes.

66

"They're gone. We're not leaving them. We'll take them with us in our hearts, and someday we'll return. Maybe to live here again, but we need to put time and distance between all this and then."

"When we see our aunts, we might hate them," I warned. I hoped.

He shrugged. "They might hate us when they see us. Jean-Paul is always telling us that you can choose your friends, but you can't choose your relatives."

I turned away again. He put his hand on my shoulder for a moment and then got up and walked out. I could hear his muffled conversation with Jean-Paul and Anne, and I realized that good-byes were the longest and most painful words you ever speak, especially when you leave people you will most likely never see again.

A little while later, I got up, scrubbed the resistance out of my face, and returned to the table.

"You must never think that we didn't want you to live with us," Anne said as soon as I sat.

"I don't."

She smiled and then took out another envelope. "Your aunt Effie has sent us information and instructions. They will arrive tomorrow. They stopped in Nice for rest and are continuing here in the morning. They have booked passage for you and them out of Marseilles. Everything, the train to Marseilles, all of it, is organized. She's a rather efficient person, down to the minute."

"What minute? They're coming tomorrow? When does she expect us to leave?" I asked.

"Tomorrow, an hour or so after they arrive, she hopes, expects. Your aunt doesn't say 'I hope.' She says 'I want' or 'We will.'"

"Tomorrow?" I looked at Yvon. "But you'd have to tell Monsieur Dufloit you were leaving and—"

"He's already found someone else."

"Who?"

"Louis."

"Your best friend has taken your job?"

"Better he got it than someone I don't care about," Yvon said.

I sat back. I felt like the whole world was closing in on me, collapsing around us, and so quickly. It was like putting your hands up against the rain.

"In her letter of instructions," Anne said, gazing at the paper, "your aunt advises you to pack very little. She will be buying you what she calls 'more appropriate clothes,' when you arrive in Richmond, Virginia."

"How does she know what we wear isn't appropriate?" I asked. "Mama never bought us inappropriate things."

"Things are different in America," Jean-Paul said. "The Americans always had strange ideas about the French."

"Well, what does she think we are, unsophisticated nincompoops?"

He just smiled. "Let her spend money on you."

"Well, I'm going to pack the dress Mama bought me recently. I might even wear it tomorrow," I said, my voice full of defiance.

"Good idea," Anne said. "Wear what is most precious to you."

"We have lots of people to say good-bye to. We can't leave that quickly," I insisted.

"In a way, it will be easier for you if you don't get to say good-bye," Jean-Paul said. "You can leave letters or notes for anyone you want, anyone you don't see. We'll make sure they get them."

I sat back. Both Anne and Jean-Paul had answers for everything. I felt terribly frustrated and still very angry. We were living all our lives with a false name. No wonder we had no relatives. Yvon was sitting quietly, not complaining about anything. I was growing annoyed with him, even though he was acting mature and I was acting more like a child.

"I'm going for a walk," I declared, and rose.

"Good. Pick up some onions and tomatoes for me," Anne said, and handed me some money.

I looked at Yvon. "Do you want to come?"

He shook his head. "I have some things to do here, a few things I was fixing."

"Yes. Yvon's right," I said, quickly jumping on that. "What about this house?"

"Your aunt has asked us to handle all that for you," Anne said.

"What about Mama's jewelry?"

"You go through it tonight, and take whatever you want, of course. She'd have liked that," Anne said.

I looked at Yvon again. He was just staring, silent.

"There are things of Papa's you'll want, right?"

He looked at me and then looked down. Maybe he wouldn't take anything. He was so afraid of memories.

Without another word, I hurried out of the house and turned to walk down the hill. Yvon was right, I quickly thought, as I gazed out at the bay and the sea. Everything here will constantly remind us of Mama and Papa, and not one day would go by without us, especially me, crying. We'd grow to hate the world we once loved and thought was free of anything ugly and mean. The rain would never say *Excusez-moi* again. It would come hard and cold. I would begin every day at the graveyard, as if I hoped I could draw them up and out and bring them back to us with a miracle.

I lowered my head. I avoided looking at anyone as much as I could. I knew what I would see in their faces: pity and sorrow. It would go on forever. Whenever I walked by, people would begin to whisper. My girlfriends would avoid me for fear I would ruin their fun. Who would want someone with so much grief written on her face? But I would never say good-bye to Mama and Papa. I would never put them aside or mourn them in shadows, especially just to please my friends.

What I anticipated when I went to the fruit and vegetable man, Monsieur Trenet, happened. He quickly packed what I needed, as if I had some infectious disease, and then refused to take any money.

"For your parents," he kept saying. "For your parents."

How could it be for my parents? They were dead; they would never eat again. But I said nothing. I thanked him quickly and practically ran home, taking streets and roads that would keep me from seeing as many people as possible. The moment I arrived and Yvon saw my face, he knew.

"You were right about people, about everything now," I said. I gave Anne the vegetables and went to my room.

Later, even though we all knew it was our last dinner together, none of us mentioned it. To help us think more hopefully about America, Jean-Paul told stories describing where he had lived and the amazing things he had seen and done.

"It's an exciting place for young people," he claimed. "There is more opportunity, even for women. I heard there are even some women doctors, but nursing is a good career, too."

He looked to Anne to support him. She started to smirk but turned it into a smile quickly.

"Marlena can be almost anything she wants," she said. "You'll have much, much more to do in Richmond. You'll have all sorts of new friends. Other girls and especially the boys will be interested in a French girl."

I looked at Yvon, whose eyes narrowed.

"Maybe not for the right reasons," he warned.

Jean-Paul laughed. "Your brother will take care of you. His father taught him well."

"As long as he's not too bossy," I said.

"You'll look after each other," Anne said, smiling. "And when you're ready, you'll come visit us and be full of wonderful stories. And in the meantime, you'll write frequently to tell us everything, won't you?"

"*Oui*," I said softly.

Yvon looked down and moved some food with his fork.

"Special dessert tonight," Anne said. "Marlena's favorite, a custard tart. I made it at home and brought it secretly to surprise you."

I smiled, but the tears were filling my eyes. This was just too many good-byes. We were, in every sense of the words, leaving the only family we had ever known. But we had a false name. We had become like the gypsies, wanderers.

Afterward, I helped Anne clean up while Yvon and Jean-

71

Paul talked about the new construction at the port, as if we were not leaving and we would see it all come to fruition. In fact, we all talked without any mention of tomorrow, of our leaving. I began to hope it wasn't true. Tomorrow would come and go, and nothing would change. Yvon would return to work, and I would be back with my girlfriends.

Jean-Paul, as usual, fell asleep sitting.

Anne looked at me and nodded. "You two have a very big day tomorrow. You need to get your rest."

"I won't sleep," I said defiantly.

"I will," Yvon said. He looked at me. "You will, too."

Anne hugged us both. Before I went to bed, I paused in the doorway of Mama and Papa's bedroom and looked at the picture of the swan. It seemed to be looking back at me, its beauty now in its sadness. I heard Anne come up behind me. She put her hands on my shoulders.

"When you settle into your new home," she said, "I'll package the swan and have it sent to you. I promise."

I said nothing, just nodded and went to my room. Yvon was right, of course. I fought sleep, but it finally took control, and I opened my eyes when sunlight washed over my face and did what I had feared, announced that it was tomorrow.

We had breakfast in relative silence, even though Anne tried her best to get us talking and not be sad. Jean-Paul looked so tired and old. He cupped his coffee with trembling hands. How could the curtain be coming down so soon on the only life we had ever known? Now I was grateful for Yvon's stoic silence. He was my rock. He gave me what little confidence I had left.

But he had to keep himself busy so he could avoid thinking about what was about to happen, too. He tinkered about the house, fixing a doorjamb, adjusting a window. Because we really hadn't told friends we were leaving today, thankfully no one came around. Their good-byes would be salt on a wound, I thought.

Most believed it was better for them and for us to leave us to finishing our mourning. I'm sure they all promised each other they would be there for us soon, hoping the time would come when they wouldn't look at us and feel the need to cry. Who could blame them?

Just before noon, Yvon, who had been watching even though he was doing everything to avoid it or not let us know he was, announced, "A carriage is approaching."

I think I felt my heart stop. I was holding my breath.

Anne went to the front door to look. Jean-Paul, who had been dozing, opened his eyes and then struggled to stand. The four of us gathered in front and watched as the approaching carriage drawn by four strong-looking black horses was brought to a stop. The driver and his sideman, both bearded, smiled at us, and then the driver quickly got down and opened the door, dropping the steps quickly.

Aunt Effie stepped out first, the driver reaching up to assist her. She looked older and in more control. She pulled her arm away from his hand sharply and paused to look out at us. I didn't see any warmth at all in her eyes.

Dressed in a long, black corduroy fitted jacket with high lapels, she looked prepared for much colder weather. The long sleeves had buttoned tabs at the cuffs. Her long matching skirt hid her black shoe boots. Standing at least five foot ten, with wide shoulders for a woman, she peered at us from under her rather plain-looking wide-brimmed hat. Maybe because her clothes were so jet-black, her face looked pale, her copper-brown eyes sinking under a wide forehead rippled with deep wrinkles, perhaps made deeper by her look of disapproval and unhappiness. The journey might have been more difficult than she had anticipated, even with a night's rest.

She pulled in the corners of her bluish pale, thin lips and cleared her throat before speaking. We were all just staring.

"I'm Effie Dawson," she said. "This is the right house, isn't it? This is where my brother . . . resided?"

"Yes, ma'am," Anne said. "I'm Anne Bise, a family friend, and this is your nephew, Yvon, and your niece, Marlena. Jean-Paul is their godfather."

"I know who Jean-Paul is," she said sharply, and glanced at him with stern disapproval. For a moment, that confused me, and then I thought it was Jean-Paul, after all, who had the most to do with Papa becoming an artist and not part of his family business.

Aunt Effie looked us over as if she was here to consider buying us like slaves.

"You're both too thin," she said, "but I suppose that's a French thing."

She took another step forward. Neither of us spoke. I was tempted to break into laughter. Our thinness a French thing?

"Pauline!" she screamed, looking at us. "Get out!"

A woman who looked no taller than I was peered through the opened door fearfully. She had the face of a child, round and soft, with big blue eyes. Her skin was richer, smoother than her sister's. How much younger was she? I wondered.

She clapped her hands. "We're in France," she said.

Aunt Effie turned to look back at her and then looked

at us, shaking her head. "My sister, Pauline, has been my responsibility from the minute our mother passed away. You will realize almost immediately that I have had all the training and experience any mother would. Not that I need anyone's stamp of approval," she added, nodding at Anne and Jean-Paul.

Neither of them spoke, so she turned back to us and then gestured toward Pauline and added, "Well, this is it. This is us. Welcome to your new family."

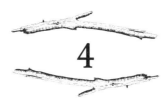

4

Aunt Effie had arrived like a seagull pecking nastily at everything, not to eat it but just to poke it. Before she took another step, she went through a litany of complaints, as if we were responsible for whatever was wrong with the whole country. Her voice was high-pitched, on the doorsteps of a scream. The roads were too bumpy and almost nonexistent in places, the food they were served wasn't fit for beggars on the Richmond streets, and the wind, especially here, surely made this place close to unlivable. Her ears were filled with a constant roar of the sea and the screams of terns. "And," she added, "the number of people who don't know how to speak English is astounding."

"Not more astounding, surely, than the number of Americans who don't speak French," Jean-Paul said.

She hoisted her shoulders as if he had tossed icy cold water on the back of her neck. "We're staying only as long as it takes to leave," she declared in response. Then she turned to Yvon and me. "So please don't dilly-dally. We have train tickets from Nice to Marseilles, and I don't want to miss our scheduled departure for the crossing back to America."

Yvon and I stared with our mouths open, especially when Pauline had emerged and stood beside her, obviously careful to remain a little behind her, like an attendant to a queen. Aunt Effie's light-brown hair was graying at the roots and pulled so severely back her forehead looked stretched. Aunt Pauline, who wore a round blue felt hat that looked a size or so too big, had light-brown hair more loosely pinned. Curled strands fell over her right eyebrow. She was dressed in a drab-looking button-down jacket and a skirt and wore what looked more like men's laced-up shoe boots.

Unlike Aunt Effie, she appeared to be excited with the view of the sea and our surroundings, her eyes bright, looking everywhere, as if she had just been released from some kind of prison. She even clapped her hands and pressed them to her bosom at the sight of a gull soaring over the house toward the sea.

"Hello," she said after her sister had made her long, critical speech. "I'm Pauline Dawson. Effie says I don't have to say my middle name when I introduce myself because it was my mother's maiden name and isn't really mine and people don't remember that anyway. Do you have middle names?"

"Be still, Pauline," Aunt Effie said sharply. "Have you two gathered your necessities for travel?" she asked us. "I assume you two, unlike the rest of the people in this infernal country, speak English well, since your parents were Americans."

"Yes," Yvon said. "We speak English perfectly."

"We'll see about *perfectly*," Aunt Effie said.

Yvon didn't change his expression. Instead, he took a step toward her. "We are pleased to meet you. I'm Yvon Hunter and this is my sister, Marlena." He looked at Pauline. "Like you, we use our mother's maiden name as our middle names," he told her. She beamed, but as soon as Aunt Effie glanced at her, she stopped. Yvon then repeated our names to Aunt Effie as a way of saying to call us by name and not "you two."

Aunt Effie pursed her lips and nodded to herself, as if what she had suspected about us before coming here proved to be true. Whatever that was, it was clear to me that it was certainly not something about which Yvon and I should be proud, not in her eyes.

"First, you are not Yvon Hunter anymore. You are Yvon Dawson, and you," she said, looking at me hard, "are Marlena Dawson. The sooner you refer to yourselves that way, the faster the name will become yours. Now, please give your things to our driver, Maurice, to put in the carriage. I hope you followed my instructions and have little to take."

She turned back to Anne before either of us could respond.

"Would you be so kind as to provide us with some water and a chance to refresh ourselves?" she asked.

"Of course. Let me show you in," Anne said.

"Thank you. Come along, Pauline." She looked at Jean-Paul. "You and I will go over some documents before we leave and be sure that everything I wanted us to arrange is proper and complete."

"*Certainement, mademoiselle*," Jean-Paul said with a little bow.

"That's French," Pauline said instantly. She looked at us. "I can say *oui*, *oui*, and . . . what's the word for good-bye again, Effie?"

"*Au revoir*," I told her.

She smiled. "I remember. *Oh river*."

"Not quite, but I'll help you say it right," I said.

She clapped her hands. "I'd like that. It will be like French lessons, right, Effie?"

"Stop it. There's no time for that nonsense, Pauline. You should go to the bathroom now and wash your face and hands. We have the same long and tedious journey back, and we will not be stopping overnight."

"I'll see after her. Can I offer you something to eat?" Anne asked. She shot me a quick smile before turning back to Aunt Effie. "I assure you it will be better than what would please beggars in Richmond."

"Whatever," Aunt Effie said. Realizing how abrupt she was being, she added, "Very kind of you. Yes."

Anne turned and indicated the doorway. Aunt Effie tugged at Pauline to follow them into the house. I looked at Jean-Paul, but he gazed off to the right. I knew in my heart that our leaving with our aunts was tearing him apart. Perhaps if he were a younger man, he would have put up a fight, but Yvon was right. It was unfair of us to demand anything more of him. For him, every day was a struggle to survive, and Anne certainly had enough to do just looking after him.

I turned to Yvon to see what he was going to do now that we had met our aunts. He couldn't be happy with Aunt Effie. She was nothing like our father. There was barely a resemblance, in fact. Would he tell me to just wait and run off with him? We'd slip away and go to Paris or someplace where we could find our own way. That was my last hope.

But it wasn't to be.

"Let's get our things together, Marlena. We don't want to make it any more difficult for Jean-Paul and Anne. The faster we get our aunt away from them, the better," Yvon said.

"What about away from us?"

"Maybe she'll be the one to decide to run away after she gets to know us better," he said, smiling.

I smiled, too. It was like finally taking a breath. Reluctantly, I followed him into the house. We already had our things packed in our small bags and brought them out of our rooms. Aunt Effie and Aunt Pauline were seated at the table. Aunt Effie looked at us, mostly at me, and stopped drinking and eating. She grimaced. It wasn't going to be difficult to read her thoughts and emotions. They were practically embossed on her wide forehead.

"You can't seriously expect to travel in that dress," she said. "Don't you have something else more substantial for a long journey? It's ridiculous."

"It's not ridiculous. It's a dress my mother gave me. I don't want to leave it," I said firmly. "And I'm quite comfortable traveling in it, no matter how long."

"Young people this age are the same everywhere, irresponsible and unrealistic. I can see I have my work cut out for me."

She shook her head and bit into a piece of fresh bread. I didn't wait for her to say anything more about it. Yvon and I went out and gave our things to the driver. He and his sideman were eating some cheese and bread and drinking some wine. He leaned over to whisper to us.

"A friendly warning. I plan to drive these horses hard and make it a fast trip to Nice and the train station," he said. "If she's what an American woman's like, I feel sorry for you two."

Yvon laughed. "Our mother was an American, and I assure you, she was nothing like our aunt."

"Whatever. I'm not complaining about my woman anymore," he said, and took another swig of wine. "*Vive la France*."

We returned to the house to have some lunch, me thinking this could be the last time I would enter my home.

"Don't give them too much to eat," Aunt Effie told Anne. "I want to leave in ten minutes or so, and I find it best not to put too much into your stomach when making such a dreadful journey. Last thing we need is one of them having to throw up from the rough, long ride ahead. The trains here are prehistoric."

"They're quite used to traveling around here, Miss Dawson," Anne said. "No worries there."

Aunt Effie grunted and then turned to Jean-Paul.

"Let's start on the documents," she said, and reached into a satchel. "I've reviewed them with an attorney and will show you where signatures are needed. My power of attorney is here to show anyone who requires it, and I have signed where necessary."

Jean-Paul nodded but didn't smile.

"Not that I expect much to come of this . . . house and whatever," she said, looking around.

"Your brother's art has become quite valuable," Jean-Paul said. "I wouldn't underestimate the price some of it will bring in the future, either."

"Yes, well, thankfully, none of us will need to depend on it.

I just don't want anyone stealing what is the family's," she emphasized. "Despite the false name."

Yvon, anticipating my reaction, seized my wrist before I could speak. He let go when he thought he had silenced me.

"Jean-Paul and Anne are our family, too," I said as firmly as I could.

Aunt Effie turned slowly to me. Jean-Paul gestured with his fingers lifting on and off the table, indicating that he wanted me to be silent.

"In legal matters, your family is who is a blood relation," she said, with the coldest eyes I had ever seen on a living person. They were like glass for an instant, and then she broke into a smile that came close to suggesting kindness. "But it's understandable you have warm feelings for these people. Orphans cling to whoever shows them any attention."

"Orphans?"

"What else would you call yourselves now? Until I take you off," she added. "You will be better known as Dawsons of Richmond. This is what lies ahead. My experience has always been that it is far more productive and satisfying in the end to face reality. Something your father failed to do," she muttered.

Before I could respond, she turned back to Jean-Paul and began reviewing the documents. I didn't want to listen, but Yvon did, so I left the table and went outside. Anne joined me.

"You mustn't make snap judgments about your aunts, Marlena. I'm sure your aunt Effie is very nervous about all this, and that explains why she seems so stern. She and her sister have apparently had no one else in their lives for so long. It will take time. Once she gets to know the two of you and sees how independent and intelligent you both are, she'll relax."

"I doubt it. As Jean-Paul says about some people, she'll probably nag the undertaker," I said.

Anne laughed.

"Why is her sister, Pauline, so . . . childlike?"

"Jean-Paul told me your father didn't talk that much about her. She seems quite sweet, however. I think she will really like you."

"She was right about the trip. I feel like throwing up already," I muttered.

"You'll be fine. Jean-Paul was right. It's quite exciting, actually, going to America. Maybe someday I'll come to visit you."

"Would you?"

"We'll see," she said, and kissed me. Then she held me at arm's length, her face darkly serious. "Now, I know Yvon is older and more mature than any boy his age here, but you look after him. He's more fragile than he reveals."

"I will," I said.

"Don't cry," she warned when we heard everyone coming out. She winked. "You'll frighten your aunt Pauline."

"More like I'll frighten myself," I said. Yvon, with Jean-Paul holding his arm, joined us.

"Can we please go?" Aunt Effie said to the driver.

"Yes, ma'am," he said. He rushed to open the door and help Aunt Pauline in first. She giggled and turned to wave good-bye as if there was a crowd watching. It provided a little lightness just when both Yvon and I needed it.

Aunt Effie turned to Jean-Paul. "I will anticipate hearing from you soon or . . ." She turned to Anne. "You."

The implication was clear. Jean-Paul might die before the house was sold and any additional payments for Papa's paintings were made.

"Of course, Miss Dawson," Anne said. "Please do not worry about any of it."

"I don't worry. I prepare. Thank you for your hospitality," Aunt Effie said. She looked at Yvon and me and raised her eyebrows. "Please make your good-byes quick. In my experience, that is always the best way."

Yvon turned and embraced Jean-Paul. He held on to him so long that it brought tears to my eyes. Jean-Paul kissed his cheek, and they parted. Yvon then embraced and kissed Anne. He looked at me. Aunt Effie didn't have to tell us to do this quickly. I couldn't stand a moment more. My chest was aching with my effort to keep from sobbing. I hurried to hug Jean-Paul.

"You listen to the soft breeze when it comes in America. You will hear your mama's voice," he whispered.

He kissed me, and I turned quickly to Anne. She held me so tightly that I thought, I hoped, she wouldn't let go, but she did.

"I will come to see you someday," she promised.

Yvon was standing by the steps. Aunt Effie waited just across from him. When she saw I was coming, she got in. Yvon tried to help her, but she moved away from his hand and got in, immediately chastising Aunt Pauline for taking up too much room.

"Let's go," Yvon whispered. I didn't think he could speak much louder without his voice cracking.

I nodded and got in to sit across from Aunt Effie and Aunt Pauline. Yvon followed, and the driver closed the door.

"Everyone's going for a ride with us. Oh, this is so much fun," Pauline said.

"Torture is a more appropriate term," Aunt Effie said.

85

"For us, especially," Yvon said.

She glared at him. I thought she would say something sharp and nasty, but instead, she turned to look out the window.

The carriage started away. I began to lean forward to look out the window facing Anne and Jean-Paul, who were standing next to each other, holding each other and watching us depart, but Yvon put his hand on my arm to keep me from doing so.

"We'll see them again. Just sit back," he said.

I did. I didn't look out. I closed my eyes, and I listened for Mama's voice in the wind. We turned a corner and bounced over the rough road down the hill. I thought about that first ride I had taken with Papa in his new automobile. How happy he was. How happy we all once were.

Yvon could hear my thoughts. I was sure, because out of nowhere, he leaned forward to whisper, "Every time we see one of his paintings, we'll see him."

We made another turn, and we headed away. The sound of the horses galloping was the exact sound I had heard in my nightmares, only this time, I was wide awake. This was really happening. Everything I had known and loved was falling behind. It was truly as if the tide of our lives was being drawn out to sea, never to be washed ashore again.

Almost as soon as we left Villefranche-sur-Mer, Aunt Pauline fell asleep. She sagged against the corner of the seat and closed her eyes, spreading her legs. Her jaw dropped, and even the hard bouncing on some broke road didn't wake her, nor did Aunt Effie pushing her legs closer together roughly. I studied Aunt Pauline's face, searching for the resemblance to Papa, but because her cheeks were so bloated, I saw very little that reminded me of him. The same was true for Aunt Effie. All I could think was that they probably took after their father more than Papa had.

"Tell me about yourselves," Aunt Effie suddenly said. Neither of us spoke quickly. "You're both obviously old enough to be thinking of your futures. Well? What have you done in that regard?"

"I was an apprentice to the village cobbler," Yvon began. "There's really only one in our village and surroundings, so he has always been very busy. Marlena attended school and helped with the house."

"You're fifteen?" she asked me.

"Yes," I said. "Just recently."

"And you're almost seventeen?" she asked Yvon.

He nodded.

"Perfect. You'll both work for our company now," she declared with the authority of a biblical prophet. "You, Marlena," she said, pronouncing my name as if it was difficult to do so, "should have good reading and writing skills. Do you?"

"Yes, ma'am," I said.

"Perhaps in French. It will be different mastering all that in English."

"We've mastered it in English, too," Yvon said. "Our mother tutored us."

"We'll see. What passed for good work here most likely won't in America, but no need to worry. I have excellent people working for me, including someone who can tutor you," she said, nodding at me. "You look well, but I'd like to have my doctor examine you both soon after we arrive. That week, I'll take Marlena to buy some clothes, and my personal assistant, Broderick Simon, will guide Yvon in purchasing what he will need to start an internship at our offices. The expectation is that you will listen and learn and thus be trusted with more and more responsibility, quickly, I hope.

"We own the building I've had named the Dawson Building. We have the top floor, and all the other office space below is rented out. We own five other buildings in downtown Richmond and do the same thing. Choosing the right commercial property to buy is a skill. My father was brilliant at it. We've bought and sold twenty properties since he began. And for considerable sums of profit."

She pressed her lips together hard, so hard that little white spots burst out at the corners, and crossed her arms over her ample bosom.

"It wasn't my dream to become a commercial real estate mogul. There are few, if any, women in my position. The truth is, Broderick stands in for me often, because men resent women holding any high positions of power and authority. I don't imagine it is much different in France, especially in France."

Neither of us spoke. We knew what she was leading up to saying, and neither of us wanted to hear how difficult Papa had made life for her. She looked like she recognized that in our faces and didn't continue for quite a while.

"What did your father tell you about our family?" she demanded.

"That your mother died when he was young and your father died when he was in his teens, maybe not much older than Yvon," I said.

She smiled in her cold way.

"He was older than Yvon. He was already out of our house.

I couldn't reach him for weeks after to tell him the news. I had to hire a private detective to find him. He was still in America, but the news didn't bring him home to the funeral."

Neither of us spoke. Papa wouldn't attend his own father's funeral? I looked at Yvon, but he looked out the window and continued to say nothing.

She turned away, and seemingly minutes passed before she suddenly turned around and almost in a tone of accusation told Yvon, "Perhaps you are meant to step into a more authoritative position with far more responsibility eventually. We'll see. There is nothing special about a man that enables him to do so more than a woman. It takes determination, training, and efficiency, no matter what you are."

She looked more at me. "Your father wasn't up to it for a number of reasons, unfortunately."

I felt Yvon nudge me to keep quiet. Neither of us wanted to get into an argument right now. He sat back and looked out the window again. Aunt Pauline was still quite asleep. As soon as she began to snore, Aunt Effie poked her hard with her elbow. She shuddered, opened her eyes, and then closed them again.

"My sister needs special care and supervision, as I believe you have realized by now. She's been like this from birth, and my mother was quite annoyed with it, so the responsibility fell on my shoulders even when I was no more than eight years old." She turned more to me again. "By the time I was your age, I was capable of managing our home. Necessity is not the mother of invention; it is the mother of self-responsibility. Until now, you both have had someone else carrying your responsibilities. I will provide some of that, but I will expect both of you to begin to do more for yourselves and, by definition, for the Dawson family. Am I clear?"

"*Mais oui,*" I said.

"What?" She grimaced.

"Of course, we will do whatever we can to help you."

"Help me? You will be helping yourself. You are the future. Maybe," she added.

She pursed her lips again and shifted in her seat.

"Another thing. From now on, especially with me and in my house, I do not want to hear either of you speak in French. It will retard your improvements in English, and people might think you were saying nasty things about them," she emphasized. I had no doubt she was thinking about herself. "Also, it will confuse Pauline even more."

"But she said she wanted to learn French."

"She doesn't know what she wants. She's incapable of making mature decisions. By the time we arrive in America, she will have forgotten all about that, I assure you. Don't encourage her.

"Now, I suggest we all relax and rest. This journey hasn't even begun. I have booked you two separate berths on the ship for crossing. Most people are quite exhausted when they arrive, even young people. They spend a great deal of time leaning over the railings, if you get my meaning. I suggest you eat very little, drink a lot of water, and don't wander about too much."

"We've been on the sea many times," Yvon said. "Jean-Paul is a fisherman as well as an artist and has a nice boat, and other village fishermen have taken us both out many times."

"We'll see," she said. She paused, narrowed her eyes, and added, "Arrogance and overconfidence are two of the most dangerous characteristics for anyone, in business especially. Children are born with it, and if their parents are wise, they drive it out of them quickly."

"We aren't overconfident," Yvon said. "We're self-confident."

She smiled. "Spoken like a typical man. Yes, you will fit well in the world you're about to enter. But don't worry. I will make sure you don't make the tragic mistakes." Again, she turned to me. "As your father did."

I wanted to scream and jump out of the carriage, but Yvon put his hand over mine and squeezed it softly.

"Aunt Effie is right," he said. "Let's relax and save our strength for the long journey ahead."

I knew he didn't mean the remainder of the carriage ride and the ocean crossing. He meant what awaited us in Richmond and, probably, the rest of our lives.

Aunt Pauline slept until we reached the train station in Nice. She was as excited about it as would be any small child, so excited, in fact, that Yvon and I laughed. Throughout the trip, Aunt Effie was constantly chastising her for this or that. Aunt Pauline wanted to sit next to me on the train. Yvon offered her his seat, which surprised me, because now he had to sit next to Aunt Effie. But that made Pauline very content. From the moment the train left, she rattled off questions about everything that was happening and everything she saw. Aunt Effie tried to get her to be silent, but I said it was fine. Answering her helped me pass the time, too.

"You'll change your mind about that," Aunt Effie predicted, with the same annoying confidence.

For a while, Aunt Effie closed her eyes and fell asleep. The rattling and shaking had the same effect on both Yvon and me, and when we fell asleep, Aunt Pauline did. I was the first to awake and was shocked to see that the movement of the train had shifted Yvon so that he was leaning against Aunt Effie. He was in a dead sleep. Neither of us had slept well the night before, and the emotional pain of leaving Jean-Paul and Anne added to our exhaustion. Aunt Effie opened her eyes, realized that Yvon was leaning against her shoulder, looked at him for a few moments, and then, to my surprise, closed her eyes again and left him where he was.

An hour or so before we arrived in Marseilles, he woke and was immediately embarrassed, but Aunt Effie said nothing. Instead, she described what we would be doing, how we would be taken to the ship, and what we should do when we got there. She hired a carriage at the train station, and we were quickly off. Pauline began to whine about her aches and pains, as if she was three times her age. Aunt Effie ignored her until she could stand it no longer and snapped at her with words as sharp as whips. She curled up, smothering her sobs.

"As you see," Aunt Effie said, "whatever horrible deed I did before I was born earned me this."

Neither Yvon nor I could believe how cold she was to her sister. We didn't have to imagine much about how cold she would be to us. When we all parted to go to our cabins on the ship, Yvon took my arm and whispered, "We'll see how it is when we get to Richmond. If she's on top of us and everything we do and we find the means to go off . . ."

That was enough of a promise and a hope to get me through the hard days of traveling at sea, but I did have the sense that he was telling me this to keep me from complaining. Grown men were seasick seemingly the whole trip and the food, despite our class of travel, was more like what we fed chickens. We tried not to complain and slept as much as we could. Nevertheless, whenever Aunt Effie said something bitter or mean to either of us, we looked at each other like two who held a deep secret close to their hearts, a secret wrapped in hope. Once we arrived in America, however, we were both far too distracted and amazed to think of much else.

After we disembarked, the train took us directly to Main Street, Richmond, where a tall, stout African man met us.

"Welcome home, Miss Effie," he said, and immediately began carrying Aunt Effie's and Aunt Pauline's things to a big automobile. Yvon was, of course, intrigued.

"This is George," Aunt Effie told us. "These two are our nephew and niece, Yvon and Marlena," she told him, and he tipped his hat.

"Welcome ta Virginia," he said.

Aunt Effie grunted. "Let's go," she said.

"What kind of a car is this?" Yvon asked him.

"It's a Maplehurst, Model 36," he said proudly. "One of the ones holds five passengers."

Aunt Effie got into the front seat when he opened the door for her, and Pauline, Yvon, and I got into the rear, both of us holding our small bags on our laps.

Yvon would never hate cars for the rest of his life, but I couldn't help having a dark, sad feeling when I sat in one. If Papa had still been using a horse and carriage, he and Mama would surely still be alive.

We started away from the station, and in moments, we were on a long, wide street. Having grown up in the small seaside village of Villefranche-sur-Mer, we found the sight of a city with over one hundred thousand people awesome. What we had heard about America seemed every bit true.

The paved wide streets were crowded with pedestrians and what looked to us to be a disorganized combination of automobiles and horse-drawn wagons and carriages. Funny-sounding horns blared everywhere. There was a constant flow of voices, laughter, shouts, bells, and musical instruments, pianos and fiddles. How could Aunt Effie complain about the roar of the sea compared to the bedlam on the city streets of Richmond? Our eyes were stuffed by so many different things we had never seen. It both excited and frightened me. How did anyone, especially a young person, find his or her way through all of this?

There were so many restaurants, stores, and bars. We passed a theater, but what truly amazed me was how many African people there were amassed in some places, while in other places we saw none. We made a turn when we reached a church. It was the first time Aunt Effie told us about anything.

"This is St. John's Episcopal Church," she said. "It's my church and will be yours. It's the oldest church in the city of Richmond. It's where Patrick Henry gave his famous speech."

"Who?" I asked.

She nodded, smirking. "You will need a quick education in American history now that you will become an American," she said.

"I want ice cream," Aunt Pauline said suddenly, and pointed toward a store.

"Not now, Pauline. And don't ask again," Aunt Effie said firmly. Pauline sat back, disappointed.

We continued down what was Broad Street, moving farther away from the busy streets and noise, passing houses but none as large as the one we headed toward. Neither Yvon nor I had seen anything like it. How could our aunts be living in such a place? I thought twenty houses like ours back in France would fit in it.

"This is where you live?" I couldn't help asking as we turned into the drive of pinkish-colored stones that curved in front of the house and then out another way.

"It's the house my father bought and restored," Aunt Effie said, "the house your father grew up in and deserted to live in shacks and closets."

I sat back in awe. Yvon was just staring, as overwhelmed as I was.

It was a two-story rectangular stone building with more windows than in all of Villefranche-sur-Mer.

"Our house has historical architecture," she continued. "Those two high Dutch gables date back to the early seventeenth century. There is a garden terrace on the east side and, as you will see, a two-story cathedral-ceilinged library we call our sitting room."

"Cathedral-ceilinged?" Yvon asked.

"Perfect English, you said." She smirked and then explained. "That means a high ceiling. Someone about to enter the commercial real estate world needs to be able to describe and understand buildings, structure, and fixtures. You will," she predicted as we came to a stop.

Instantly, the front door opened, and two middle-aged women in maids' outfits charged through. We were shocked to see that they were exact twins, identically stout, with wide hips and puffy forearms. They had graying ebony hair and oval faces so alike that they looked like mirror images: small button noses, thin lips, and gray-black eyes.

"These are my maids, Minnie and Emma Brown," Aunt Effie said. "They have been with our family for over twenty years. Show them respect, and never question what they do. They do it because I told them to do it."

The driver opened the door, and the Brown sisters, clutching their hands exactly the same way against their ample bosoms, waited for orders.

"Welcome home, ma'am," the one on the right said.

"Thank you, Minnie. The young girl will go to the Gold Room and the young man to the Green. They don't have much to bring up, so tend only to my and Pauline's things."

"Yes, ma'am," Emma said.

"I'm tired, and I want some chocolate milk," Pauline declared after Aunt Effie stepped out.

"You go to your room and wash and change first, Pauline. You've been in those clothes so long they reek."

"I have not," she protested.

"I'm going to change, too," I said.

She relaxed and, with George's help, got out. She stood there waiting for Yvon and me to get out.

We all stood for a moment, my brother and I still awed by the house.

"This is where you'll live," Aunt Effie said. "It won't be your home until it feels your appreciation and respect. Everything in it, every piece of furniture, must be held in highest esteem." She paused and looked at Yvon. "That means reverence and admiration."

"I know that word," he said. "It comes from *estime* in French." He looked very pleased with himself.

Aunt Effie smiled at him. "Maybe there'll be some benefit

to that French arrogance, but be careful. As I warned you, it can destroy you, too," she said. She turned to Pauline. "Get yourself inside, Pauline, and do what I said. NOW!" she screamed.

Pauline hurried toward the door.

George started the car and drove toward what looked like a small barn.

Aunt Effie turned to us. "You are about to see for yourselves all that your father left behind."

She turned to go in quickly, leaving us behind her. It was as if she was saying, *Sink or swim.*

Yvon reached for my hand. "We'll be just fine," he said. He laughed. "Unless we get lost in there and never see each other again." He looked up at the roof and then off to the right. "Look how well these grounds are kept. Someone cuts the grass with a scissors."

He surprised me by sounding so excited. The idea of our running off was obviously dead for now.

"Maybe it won't be so bad, Marlena. She can't be so hard and mean all the time."

"She'll never love us, Yvon. She'll never think of us as family."

"Her loss," he said. "C'mon, let's see how the rich really live. I'm sure we can survive."

I nodded, but I didn't have his confidence. Hopefully, he had enough for the both of us.

As we walked to the door, carrying our small bags stuffed with the little we had taken from France, I was sure we'd both need more than confidence and new names. We would need new hope.

5

The interior of the house was just as impressive as the outside, if not more so. To use Aunt Effie's terms, the main entrance was a high-ceilinged room with red oak paneling. There was an L-shaped staircase with a scrolled banister in the same oak. Everywhere we looked, there were antiques and paintings, but there was no art like Papa's. Most of it looked like historical scenes, and some depicted biblical ones. It looked more like a history museum. In fact, the floor was composed of gray and black slate squares, something we had seen only in a museum in Nice once. When we stood in this grand entrance, which was more of a lobby to me, the house definitely reminded me more of a government building than a home. Even the portraits of ancestors looked like they belonged more in an encyclopedia. There was no warmth, no personality, in what we were seeing, unless perhaps no personality *was* its personality.

The Brown twins hurried past us with Aunt Effie's and Aunt Pauline's things. They walked in small, quick steps like ducks. Then they paused at the foot of the stairway and looked back at us as if they had just remembered we were there. Both wore the same look of surprise at our not rushing to keep up with them. Why wouldn't we have paused? No one was offering to show us around our new home. How did we know our rooms were upstairs? Aunt Effie had hurried Aunt Pauline in as if she wanted to keep her away from the eyes of the public and put her away in her room as quickly as possible.

"Y'all just follow us up," Minnie said.

"And we'll bring you to your rooms," Emma added.

We started up behind them. They not only looked exactly the same, they moved exactly the same, their gait a bit of a waddle. The steps were wide enough and their coordination so in sync that they could walk up side by side without bumping their hips into each other.

"It's like a body with two heads," Yvon whispered.

"Shh," I said, and slapped him gently, swallowing down a laugh.

"Do you know which room was my father's?" Yvon asked them when we were on the second floor.

"Your sister is in that room," Emma said. "It's called the Gold Room because there is gold trim around the curtains."

"And around the mirror," Minnie added.

"But there is no real gold in it," Emma said.

"Why am I in that room if it was my father's? My brother should be in it. I don't want to be in a man's room."

"We don't decide where people sleep," Emma said.

"This way, please," Minnie said.

I looked at Yvon, anticipating his disappointment.

"It doesn't matter, Marlena. I'm sure any of these rooms is almost as big as our house."

The twins paused at the second door down on the right and turned back to us. The first door down had a lock dangling on a round hook. The key was in it.

"Whose room is this?" I asked, pointing to it.

"That's Miss Pauline's room," Minnie said.

"You're in this one," Emma said.

"Why is there a lock on the outside of her door?" I asked.

They looked at each other, but neither answered.

"You each have a bathroom in your room. The next room is your brother's," Emma said, nodding.

"Let us know if y'all need anything. We have to unpack Miss Effie's things and Miss Pauline's," Minnie said.

"And get back to our other duties," Emma said.

"Dinner will be at seven tonight," Minnie added.

"You're the cooks, too?" I asked.

"Oh, no, miss," Minnie said. "Mrs. Trafalgar is the chef."

"She's been for nearly twenty years now," Emma said. "But we do help serve and clean up."

"Off we go," Minnie sang. She continued down the hallway, but Emma turned and walked back to Pauline's room. She paused to look at us as if she wanted to be sure we didn't follow or look into the room. Then she entered and quickly closed the door behind her. It was instantly followed by the sound of Minnie closing the door to Aunt Effie's room behind her after she had entered. We stood there in silence for a moment.

"Do you think they think the same thoughts at the same time?" Yvon asked.

"Maybe, but I'm not going to ask them, because I'll get the same answer."

He laughed.

"Why did Aunt Effie rush Aunt Pauline in so fast?" I asked.

"I'm not going to start second-guessing why she does what she does, especially regarding Aunt Pauline. I'm tired," Yvon said, yawning. "Let's unpack what we have and get some rest. I have the feeling this place is run by the clock, and General Effie will be having a marching drill or something in an hour."

He headed for his room, and I entered mine. He was right. My bedroom was easily as big as half our house in France, with two large windows that almost reached the ceiling. The bed was at least three times as big as my bed in France. A darker oak had been used for the frame and low bedposts. The pillows were the size of sofa pillows to me, and there was a rich-looking brown comforter. Beside the bed was a small matching dresser with three drawers, and on the left was a large dresser with a square gilded mirror. The windows were draped in a light brown with gold edging. I wondered if Aunt Effie had named it the Gold Room to avoid calling it her brother's.

On my immediate right was a cushioned rocker, but it looked like no one had sat in it since it had been brought here. I sat in it; it was very comfortable. Papa had always enjoyed sitting in Jean-Paul's rocker and talking. I gazed around, studying every detail, looking for something that suggested my father had lived here. There was nothing I could see. Probably Aunt Effie had cleared out any reminder of him and had sold or given away whatever he had left. There were certainly no pictures.

However, there was nothing particularly feminine about the room, so I believed the twins when they said it had been his. There were fresh flowers in a vase on top of the dresser. I looked up at the beautiful teardrop chandelier that sparkled so, making it look brand-new. Probably was, I thought.

The bedroom walls were paneled in a lighter wood, and there were two large paintings of what I imagined were early Richmond streets and homes. That was not the sort of art Papa favored. He would have found them boring. Maybe that's why she had hung them here.

The bathroom was off to the left, where there was a claw-foot tub, a sink, and a toilet. Everything looked spotlessly clean. The floor was covered in large beige tiles with a matching rug at the tub. Thick-looking towels and hand cloths were on a rack, and there was a narrow closet on the right with bathroom accessories and more towels and cloths. I had the feeling that everything in the bathroom was brand-new, too. It couldn't have been like this when Papa was a young boy. In fact, despite the generally masculine feel, now that I saw more of it, I couldn't imagine him living in this room. Even now, I didn't think he would like it, despite how rich and new it all looked. I was convinced that because of how angry she had been at him, Aunt Effie had the room completely redone to remove even a suggestion that he had once been here.

Because of the absence of anything suggesting Papa, Yvon wouldn't be particularly happy about being in his room, either, but if it was anything like mine, I expected he was surely as overwhelmed as I was by the size and the newness of it all. I recalled my mother once telling me that everything in America was bigger, even the teacups.

I decided I would take a bath and change into the few clean clothes I had. My dress did look worn and dirty. Aunt Effie was right about it, of course. It wasn't a dress meant for long travel. I had worn it too many days. There were stains, too, despite my having washed it once on the ship. When I gazed at myself in the bathroom mirror, I saw that my hair looked almost as disheveled as my clothes. Some strands were curling like broken piano strings. I hadn't been able to wash it properly. Mama would be so upset, I thought. She spent so much time brushing my hair and telling me that I must keep after it the way a princess or a queen keeps after her crown. I didn't feel particularly like either right now, but as Mama would tell me, that didn't mean I shouldn't try to.

Everything I would need, even something I rarely had, perfumed bath oils, were on a shelf by the tub. Despite how cold the house felt to me, or maybe because of it, I did feel as if Yvon and I had been brought to a castle. No one, not even the richest person in Villefranche-sur-Mer, had a home like this and everything that came with it. Should I feel like Cinderella? Anything that made me happy made me sad, too. And guilty! Even for an instant, I didn't want any of it to cause me to forget my home, my family, and the world I once knew.

"America will seduce you," Anne had half-jokingly warned.

After I filled the tub and sat in it, soaking and enjoying the bath oils, I washed my hair. Then I fell asleep for a few minutes. When I opened my eyes, I nearly leaped out. Standing there in the doorway and staring at me was Aunt Pauline. Her mouth was oddly twisted, and she had a grip on her dress as if she wanted to pull it apart and off her.

It occurred to me that there was no way to lock my door. But again, I wondered, why was there a lock outside hers?

"I'm supposed to take a bath, too," she said, "but Minnie and Emma are still too busy."

"Can't you take a bath yourself?"

"I once did and almost drowned, so Effie says I can't. Effie doesn't let me do anything much myself, you know," she added in a loud whisper, her eyes on the bedroom door. "Effie is perfect, and I'm not."

"Aunt Effie is not perfect, Aunt Pauline. No one is, but especially not her."

She widened her eyes and then smiled. "If she heard you say that, she'd threaten to put a candle to your lips."

"A candle? You mean a lit candle?"

The strange woman stared without answering.

"She never did that to you, did she?" I asked.

Again, she didn't answer. Her silence was chilling for a moment. I shrugged it off. Surely, this was part of her wild imagination. If Aunt Effie was that cruel to her, someone would have noticed and reported her.

"How did you almost drown?"

"I slipped and slid down under the water and bumped my head when I was ten," she said. "Little kids fall, don't they? Effie says I don't pay attention to the important things. She says I'm always daydreaming and breaking things and hurting myself, which is why I have to be helped all the time. Do you daydream?"

"Everyone daydreams."

"Not Effie."

"*Oui, très probablement pas,*" I said.

"Oooh," she said, bringing her hands to her throat. "That's French in the house, and Effie said we can't hear that."

"I can't help it. Aunt Effie will have to understand. It's my native language." I thought a moment. "You haven't taken a bath yourself since you were ten? Is that what you're saying? That's stupid."

She smiled. "You're upset about it. That's good."

She paused and stared at me, making me feel self-conscious. I covered my budding breasts.

"I forgot who you are," she said. "Exactly, I mean. I remember your name, Marlena."

"I'm your niece, Aunt Pauline. And Yvon is your nephew. My father was your brother, Beau."

"Oooooh, Beau. He disappeared like snow in spring. When it snows and I say Beau is coming back, Effie gets very mad. She shut me in my room for saying it once."

"Is that why there's a lock on your door, so she can shut you in there to punish you?"

"I don't know. Effie gets very angry. Sometimes."

"How old were you when he left?"

She thought. "I have to ask Effie," she said. "I useta ask for him every day until Effie said she'd put me in the cellar forever if I didn't stop."

"Then don't bother to ask her. You'll only get her started."

"Started?"

"Complaining. I think she's an expert."

"What does that mean?"

"She's good at it. Could you hand me my towel, please?"

"Oh. Yes, yes," she said, excited.

She gave it to me, and I wrapped it around myself as I stood to step out of the tub. I reached for another towel and vigorously dried my hair before wrapping it around my head. Pauline stood by, fascinated with everything I was doing.

I wondered if she ever had a friend.

"Did you go to school in Richmond?"

She shook her head.

"Who taught you how to read and write?"

"Effie taught me a little but then stopped. She said the mud between my ears dried up."

"Not a nice thing to say. Maybe I can help you learn now."

She smiled but was obviously more intrigued with how I was drying my hair.

"I could do all that, too, if they let me," she said.

"Of course you can. As soon as I'm dried and dressed, I'll go with you to your room and help run your bath."

"You will?"

"Why not?"

"Did you ask Effie?"

"We'll surprise her," I said. Then I mumbled to myself, "She might need a few of those."

I dressed as quickly as I could and then followed her out to her room. She was behaving as if this was the most exciting thing she had ever done, giggling, with her eyes bright. When we entered her room, I stopped and gazed in awe.

The whole room was still more of a nursery. It was done in pink and blue, and everything I saw on the shelves was something more for a little girl than a woman her age. She couldn't use some of the furniture like a chair and a desk because it was too small. There was a music box on the desk and what looked like coloring books. Her bed was much smaller than mine, and her pinkish-white area rug looked like it had been stained a number of times. It was probably as old as she was, I thought.

On her bed between the pillows was a stubby-looking little doll with most of its hair gone. The skin of the doll looked yellowed like old paper, and there was what appeared to be a bandage over the left knee. One of the feet was in a shoe, and the other wasn't.

"How old is that doll?" I asked her.

"She's only six months old," Pauline said.

"No, I mean . . . never mind," I said.

"She fell and scraped her knee just like I did. Mama was very sick then, so Effie had to help me. She didn't like doing it. She hates looking at blood." She leaned toward me to whisper. "Effie won't drink tomato juice. She says it looks like blood."

"Brilliant," I said. "I don't understand this room," I muttered, mostly to myself.

Off in the corner was surely what had once been her crib, with baby toys still in it. Why did Aunt Effie want to keep all that still here?

"Don't you like my room?" she asked, looking like she might burst into tears. I guess I had a look of disapproval on my face.

"It's very nice," I said, and then noticed a picture in a silver frame pushed a little to the side on the dresser.

"That's Effie and me," she said when I lifted it to look. Aunt Pauline looked no more than four or five. Aunt Effie was already tall, with a face that didn't look much different from how it was now. But Pauline was absolutely beautiful. She looked more like a doll Papa had shown me in a newspaper once. It was called a Kewpie doll, created from a comic strip.

In the picture, Aunt Pauline was beaming with her smile, but Aunt Effie looked like someone had stolen her knickers.

"You were beautiful," I said.

"There are more pictures of me, but they're all in the attic."

"What? Why?"

"I don't know."

I put the picture back. "I think I do," I said, and looked at her bathroom.

Everything in it was older than what was in my bathroom.

The tub was about the same size but had what looked like rust stains. When I turned on the water, the faucet sounded like it would break. It took a lot longer to get the hot water.

Why was her sister treating her so poorly? I thought, but smiled at her. "Do you want me to wash your hair, too?" I asked.

"Oh, yes." She thought a moment. "But I don't know if it's time."

"Time?"

"Effie tells me when it's time to wash my hair and when it's time to cut my nails. Look," she said, and pointed to a calendar on the bathroom wall. I stepped up to it.

Days were marked with an H and an N, and another had an M. H was surely for hair and N for nails.

"What's the M?" I asked, and put my finger on it.

"M means monthlies," she said, and pressed her left hand over her mouth. "Shame on me for saying it," she muttered through her fingers. "Shame, shame, shame."

"What?" I thought a moment. "Oh. But you don't have to be ashamed. All women have monthlies. My mother never made me feel ashamed of it. It's only natural."

"It's Eve's fault," she said.

"What did you say?" My eyes nearly popped. "Who told you that?"

"Effie."

"She must be related to Monsieur Appert. Aunt Effie shouldn't have frightened you about it. It's not a bad thing. It's uncomfortable and sometimes painful, but when you bleed –"

"Oooooh," she moaned, and shook her head. "Don't."

I stared at her. She was absolutely terrified.

"Effie washed my mouth out with soap and put me in the wine closet whenever I said it in front of people until those people left."

She was actually shaking.

"Okay, okay. We won't say it. I promise."

She relaxed and then smiled. "I have to have a dress for dinner," she said. "Effie always tells me what to wear."

"I'll look in your closet and pick something out for you," I said, "while the tub fills up."

From what I could see, there was nothing very new hanging. I sifted through and picked out what I thought was the nicest. When I turned with it, we heard, "What are you doing?"

Aunt Effie was in the doorway, her hands on her hips. With her shoulders hoisted, she looked like she had grown two or three inches.

"I was helping Aunt Pauline get ready for dinner."

"You should be looking after yourself. That's not your job. Minnie and Emma are on their way here."

She crossed to Pauline's closet, practically ripped what I had chosen out of my hand, and hung it up.

"She doesn't need anything that fancy."

"Fancy?" It was hardly that.

"No matter what, she'll spill something on herself. All these clothes have been washed to death," she said, running her hand through the hanging garments. She plucked a dull, faded pink dress off the rack and tossed it onto Pauline's bed. Then her eyes widened. She rushed past me into the bathroom, where Pauline was standing and staring at the water running into the tub. Some of it had already overflowed.

"You idiot!" Aunt Effie cried. "Why are you just standing there?"

She shut the water off just as Emma and Minnie entered.

"Clean all this up, and get her ready for dinner," Aunt Effie ordered. Then she turned to me. "Go back to your room. Go! You've already made extra work for us."

I looked at Pauline, who, despite all the criticism, was smiling.

"I'm sorry," I said. "I was just trying to help."

"I'll tell you what to do and what not to do, and that will be the way you help. Go."

I stepped out quickly.

Yvon was in the hallway, wearing a faded dull brown bathrobe and a pair of old black slippers with a tear on the side of the left one.

"Where did you get that?"

"Hanging in the closet with a few other things. What's all the commotion?"

I described what I saw in Pauline's room and what had happened.

"You'd think I had set the house on fire."

"We'd better tread softly for a while," he said.

"She's very mean to her, Yvon. You saw how she treated her

on the trip. She never says a kind thing to her. No wonder she's the way she is. You know she stopped her learning how to read and write."

"We can't solve everything in days, Marlena. Aunt Effie is right. We have to look after ourselves for a while first. Just let me know if she's ever cruel to you."

"She hasn't exactly been too sweet to either of us," I said. "How is your room?"

He shrugged, so I stepped into it. Unlike in mine, everything in his looked quite old and worn. There were no flowers to brighten it up. It didn't have the rich paneling on the walls, nor were there any area rugs. The curtains that looked like they hadn't been washed for years were a dark green, thus the name for this room. His bathroom looked even worse than Pauline's.

"I don't think anyone's been in here since the house was first built," I said.

"It's fine," he said. "Lots of room."

"It's cold and old and smells a little like seaweed," I muttered. I walked over to the bed. "There are moth holes in this blanket."

"I'll survive. I'm getting hungry. Did they say what we're eating?"

"MARLENA!" we heard Aunt Effie scream.

"Now what did I do?"

I hurried into the hallway.

"What are you doing in there?"

"Just looking at Yvon's room."

"I don't know what you're used to in France, but young men and women, especially young women, don't go into each other's bedrooms unattended." Yvon had stepped out beside me. "He's only wearing a bathrobe."

"Yvon is my brother," I said. "We've taken baths together."

"I don't want to hear any of that!" she cried, putting her hands over her ears for a moment. "Things will change or . . . or else," she added. "You, boy, get dressed. Mr. Simon is waiting for you in the sitting room. He will explain tomorrow's schedule for you and some of your new duties. Be down there in five minutes."

"Where? I don't know the house yet," Yvon said.

"See if you can find it on your own. That will tell me if you are so dull I'd be pursuing failure to place any faith in you. And you," she said to me, "wait in your room. Minnie and Emma will fetch you to walk down to dinner with Pauline."

"Can't I go down now and look at the house?"

"Just do as I ask. The house is not a museum. You will get to know all about it in good time. I will be taking you to buy some clothes after breakfast tomorrow. Do not tell Pauline. I do not want her going along. She will distract us and waste our time."

"From what I saw, she looks like she could use some new clothes."

"When you earn your own income, you can buy her whatever you like. Right now, it would be like opening the window and tossing out money." She looked at Yvon. "Why are you still standing there?"

He glanced at me and went into his room. I watched her go down the stairway and then went into my room and plopped into the rocker. I felt like I should growl. Surely, Yvon was not going to want us to stay here much longer. Now that we were in America, we could find our own way. I dreamed of us getting jobs and having our own apartment. It pained me to think so negatively of Papa's family, but I felt confident I knew why he wasn't heart-broken to leave. Perhaps he felt sorry for Aunt Pauline, but most likely there wasn't anything he could do for her. He certainly couldn't take her with him. It wasn't difficult to imagine how terrible her early life was under Aunt Effie's control.

Now I was curious about his father and mother. When exactly had they turned over Aunt Pauline's daily needs to Aunt Effie? What was their mother like? How sick was she? From what she had already described of their lives, I was confident Aunt Effie took after their father.

What kind of a relationship did Papa have with his mother? All we really knew was that she didn't discourage his art. Was part of the reason he left because she had passed? Did he hate his father that much? Now that we were here, I could under-stand why he didn't want to talk about any of them, especially Aunt Effie. How much happier was our family in France, far poorer but so much happier. Somehow, some way, I was determined to get Aunt Effie to understand and believe that. It would either drive her mad or soften her hard shell of a per-sonality and she would treat everyone better once she stopped thinking ill of Papa and Mama. Was I still a child to believe it was possible?

Emma or Minnie came to my door a while later. How long would it take for me to know the difference? Neither had a mole or a birthmark different from the other.

"It's time to go down to dinner," she announced. "Pauline and Minnie are waiting at the top of the stairs. It's time for us to enter the dining room and y'all to take your seats."

She was talking about it as if this was going to be some royal event. I half-expected music to accompany us. Pauline, looking more put together, her hair brushed and pinned back, smiled as I approached.

"Where's my brother?" I asked.

"Mr. Simon and him is already seated," Minnie said.

"Well, why wouldn't you have told me? I was ready."

"Miss Effie wanted it that way," Emma said.

"Does she tell everyone when to breathe?"

I turned to Aunt Pauline, who obviously either didn't understand or care about what I had been saying.

"We're all so pretty, aren't we?"

"Yes," I said. I smiled gleefully at the twins, who stared like two mannequins.

"Effie always said that. She always said, 'You're the pretty one, Pauline.'"

"I'm sure it wasn't a compliment," I muttered.

"Are you hungry?" Pauline asked. "I'm hungry. It's all right to be hungry."

"If you have food, it is," I said dryly.

Now the twins gaped at me with the same surprise. It was as if they had never heard of anyone not having food.

We began our descent, Minnie walking ahead of Aunt Pauline and Emma behind her and between us. Halfway down, she turned to me and said, "She's fallen down these stairs. Once she broke her ankle."

"And was laid up for weeks," Minnie said, not turning around. It was as if they had rehearsed what they would tell me.

They paraded us to the dining room, where, as I was told, Yvon was already seated next to an elderly man with thinning gray and light-brown hair. He wore a low-cut black waistcoat with a white shirt that had folded-over tips at the collar with a black bow tie. The right corner of his mouth drooped a bit. He looked at me, glanced at Aunt Effie, who sat at the head of the table, and then nodded.

"You're absolutely right, Effie. I do see a little of your mother," he said, staring at me.

"A little," Aunt Effie said. "Pauline, take your seat. Minnie, pull out her chair."

They moved Aunt Pauline quickly to a chair across from Yvon.

"Marlena, this is Mr. Broderick Simon, my personal assistant. You will get to know him better when you begin to work at the offices."

"Hello," I said, and looked at Yvon to get a hint of how he felt about him. He looked indifferent.

"You'll sit next to Mr. Simon," she said, and nodded at the chair.

Emma pulled it out for me, which surprised me. I sat and looked at Mr. Simon. He had gray eyes and a thin nose that made his eyes and his mouth look larger. Along the edge of his jaw and up the sides to his ears was a well-trimmed beard, the color of which was almost totally gray. He still studied me a moment before nodding and smiling. Some of his teeth looked black, almost as if they had died in his mouth.

"It's too soon, I'm sure, but how do you like America?" he asked.

"It's too soon," I replied, and his eyes widened.

He looked at Aunt Effie.

"I fear they are both a little spoiled," she said.

"Perhaps a little too French," he replied, and for the first time since we met her, Aunt Effie actually laughed.

I saw the look of shock and surprise on Aunt Pauline's face. Aunt Effie turned to the twins.

"Serve our dinner," she said. "Don't just stand there gaping at everyone."

"Yes, ma'am," Emma said.

"We will, ma'am," Minnie said, and they walked quickly through a door that I imagined led into the kitchen. I saw how Pauline was still thinking about what had been said. Her forehead crinkled with her confusion. I almost laughed at the intense way she was staring at Aunt Effie, who realized it, rolled her eyes, and looked at her.

"What now, Pauline?"

"You just said 'French,' but you said we can't say French in this house, Effie. You told us."

I couldn't help smiling at Pauline's logic. I turned to Aunt Effie.

The softness that came to her face when she laughed flew off.

"How many times have I told you not to speak at dinner unless I ask you to speak, Pauline? How many times?"

"I don't know. Two hundred?"

Mr. Simon laughed.

"She's not wrong," Aunt Effie said, turning to me mainly. "I said I don't want French spoken." She looked at Aunt Pauline again. "But the word 'French' is all right, Pauline. So is the word 'France.' It's a country." She looked at Yvon and then at me. "Be sure you two obey that rule. Do you understand?"

I couldn't help it. It was bubbling on the edges of my lips.

"*Mais oui, tante* Effie," I said.

Yvon smiled in amazement.

Mr. Simon's jaw dropped.

Pauline bit down so hard on her lower lip I thought she would bleed.

Aunt Effie's face turned ruby first, and then all the color drained, and it was nearly snow-white. Her lips trembled. She slammed her right palm down on the table so hard that the glasses and dishes bounced.

"How insolent!" she muttered. "You are your father's daughter. He was just this way with our father."

I almost smiled in the face of her rage. Any comparison of me to Papa was most welcome, no matter what it was.

"Perhaps to help you remember, you should now go to your room without any dinner," she said. "Go on up to your room."

"If she goes, I go," Yvon quickly said. "French is our mother language. We can't just throw it off in a day, Aunt Effie, and besides, we don't understand why it's to be so forbidden. If we're speaking ill of someone in our presence, anyone can tell by the look on our faces, besides the words. We are not afraid to say what we mean; we've never been."

"The boy has a good point, Effie," Mr. Simon said softly. He, too, tiptoed around our aunt.

She stared at me while the twins began bringing out our food. When they were finished putting a platter in front of everyone, she leaned forward, her elbows on the table, her hands clasped. The anger swirled in her eyes and then faded with her cold smile.

"As long as what you did is out of habit and not insolence. I know the French have a more liberal attitude when it comes to children."

"We've always been taught to respect our elders," I said.

"Yes, maybe, but your father didn't, and I can't imagine the example he would have set."

She puttered around a little at her plate and glass of wine.

"I suggest we all start eating before it gets cold."

Yvon nodded at me. For now, at least, our first major crisis was over.

"I'd like to wear earrings again," Aunt Pauline suddenly said.

Aunt Effie looked at the ceiling and then at her.

"You've lost one of every pair I've ever given you, Pauline."

"I can wear different ones on each ear, can't I?" She looked to me.

"Don't ask her. We're not talking about earrings now, Pauline. Just sit quietly and eat your potatoes."

"But I don't like potatoes."

"We've been through this for decades, Pauline. You eat what I tell you to eat. Who knows better? Well?"

Aunt Pauline looked down. "You do, Effie."

"Good. Mr. Simon will now explain more about our business. You two are here to be part of this family now, and that means our business."

"So, as I tried to explain to Yvon earlier," Mr. Simon began, "there are really four types of real estate companies, goals, and business entities.

"There is residential real estate, commercial real estate, industrial real estate, and land. Your grandfather began with residential, moved to commercial and a little of industrial before he passed away. We are more involved now with industrial, manufacturing buildings and warehouses, but we still manage a number of commercial buildings as well."

"Sounds like a lot," Yvon said.

He turned to him. "There is, as I started to explain, much to learn."

Yvon nodded.

"Explain what it means to bid," Aunt Effie said.

"When something becomes available, we evaluate its value to us and offer a price, sometimes sealed so no one knows what we've offered until the auctioneers or current owners open all the bids and the highest one wins the property. That's why it's very important to learn how to value a property, square feet, fixtures, location, and access to roads. You'll see. I hope it will be interesting to you."

"Of course it will be interesting to him," Aunt Effie said, "especially when he hears the sums involved. One of our commercial properties provides the company ten thousand dollars a month."

"A month?" Yvon asked.

She smiled.

"We have five such properties," Mr. Simon said. "A great deal of our work has to do with banks. We have relationships with the two biggest in the state, actually."

"Your grandfather on your mother's side ran a bank," Aunt Effie said. "Did she ever tell you about that, about him?"

"Not much," Yvon said before I could respond. She had told me.

"That bank was acquired by a much bigger enterprise," Mr. Simon said. "It was close to failure."

"Perhaps you didn't inherit your maternal grandfather's poor business sense," Aunt Effie said. Yvon's face reddened. "I'm not surprised she avoided talking about him."

Yvon and I exchanged looks. I had never really described

Mama's feelings about her father and mother, what she had revealed to me that night.

"He's a smart young man. I'm sure he'll do well, Effie."

She grunted and then paused again to look at Yvon when she spoke.

"Now tell them who our biggest competitor is these days," she said.

"Garland Foxworth," he said, "and his young son, Malcolm, especially in the industrial sector."

Neither Yvon nor I said anything.

"Does that name mean anything to either of you?" Aunt Effie asked. Her eyes seemed to narrow in anticipation of our answers.

I shook my head.

"Why would it?" Yvon said. "We've not been here twenty-four hours. We don't know any big American businessmen."

"Neither of your parents ever mentioned the name?"

"No," Yvon said quickly.

She looked at me.

"No," I said.

"Neither your father nor your mother?" she pursued.

"Neither mentioned the name, no," Yvon said. He looked down quickly. I thought his reaction was strange. It seemed like he wanted to get the questions over with. Why would the name Foxworth matter to us?

Aunt Effie tapped the table with the tips of her fingers and looked at Mr. Simon.

"Well, it will mean something to you," she predicted. I thought she was looking more at Yvon. "A good businessman knows as much about his competitors as he does about himself."

"Well said, Effie," Mr. Simon commented. "Your aunt is quite well known for her business acumen. You have as much to learn from her as you do from me," he told Yvon.

He didn't say anything. Then he looked at me for a moment before gazing down at his food again.

"Can I talk now, Effie?" Aunt Pauline asked.

"What is it, Pauline?" she replied, her eyelids fluttering with annoyance.

"I think I should have a new dress and new shoes."

"Why?"

"Aren't we going to have a party?"

"What? Why would we have a party, Pauline?"

Pauline smiled as if she knew something Aunt Effie didn't know.

"Our nephew and our niece have come to live with us."

"I'm surprised you remember who they are."

"Marlena told me, didn't you, Marlena?"

I looked up quickly at Aunt Effie. Why that would make me feel guilty and afraid, I didn't know, but it did.

"We'll see if you remember tomorrow," Aunt Effie said. She seemed to enjoy mocking her sister.

"I will. And do you know why?" Aunt Pauline said.

"No, Pauline, pray tell us why."

"It's like Beau's come home," she said.

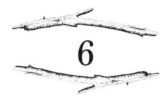

6

After dinner, Aunt Effie told the twins to take Pauline to her room before they did any of their other chores. I wondered why it would take the two of them to escort Pauline to her room, until I saw how Pauline pouted and, like a little girl, refused to move. Still, I wondered if one twin always needed the other beside her for every task Aunt Effie assigned. Did they go to the bathroom together?

"I can take Aunt Pauline up to her room," I said.

"NO," Aunt Effie said, so firmly both Yvon and I stepped back as if she had belched smoke. "You are incapable of knowing or doing what is required. Don't assume because you've traveled with your aunt for days that you have any idea what her needs are. Concern yourself with your own right now. Go on up, Pauline."

"I don't want to go to bed yet. I don't wanna!" Pauline cried. Each twin took an arm. Before she could resist, Aunt Effie stepped toward her. She was only a few inches taller, but because of the way she held herself, she looked like she towered over her sister, who stopped resisting immediately and gagged on her tears, her shoulders jerking up and down.

"You know that you have to go to bed when I tell you, Pauline," Aunt Effie said in a softly controlled voice. She smiled with a syrupy sweet grin. "You know when you don't get your proper rest, you mope about and don't have any fun. I always think of what's best for you, don't I?"

"But . . . I wanna have fun now, too."

"No one's having any fun now, Pauline. We are all preparing ourselves for a good night's rest." Her syrupy smile flew off her face. "I happen to be tired, too. Don't just think of yourself. Have you forgotten how far we have traveled to fetch these two, what an ordeal it's been?"

"I don't care," Aunt Pauline said. "I don't care about deals."

"Ordeals, not deals. Oh, for God's sake. I swear you'll drive me into an early grave. Would you like that? Would you? Then where would you be? Well?"

Pauline shook her head and looked down.

"Do what I say, then, and do it now," Aunt Effie snapped, and nodded at the twins. They practically lifted Aunt Pauline off the floor, turned her, and marched her out.

As soon as they started away, Aunt Effie stepped toward me. She looked like she was about to slap me, but I didn't cringe. I screwed my courage tightly and stared back at her.

"Never interfere when I order Pauline to do something. Never."

"I didn't interfere. I only tried to help."

"Help," she practically spit. She thought a moment. "Did you tell her that?"

"Tell who what?"

"Did you tell her your coming here was like your father returning?"

"No, Aunt Effie. I did not. I don't think our father ever wanted to return to Richmond or to this house. The truth is, he never mentioned you, either of you, to Yvon or me. All our lives, we thought he was an only child."

She continued to stare at me with a cold smile, her eyes taking on that glassy look more at home with the dead. Maybe she was dead inside. I was frightened, but I wasn't going to let her know.

I looked at Yvon. "That's the truth, *n'est-ce pas*, Yvon?"

"*Oui.* It's the truth."

"I don't doubt it," Aunt Effie said, not taking her eyes off me. "That is the way he lived, like an only child. He was never grateful for what he had, what he had inherited. In the end, he ran from his familial responsibilities, the act of a coward, not a son and brother."

"He did not," Yvon said, stepping toward us. "He did the exact opposite and assumed those familial responsibilities, providing for us and our mother. We were a family, too."

She nodded. "Maybe he thought that was the way to redeem himself."

"For what?" Yvon snapped back. "Pursuing his own dreams and the woman he loved?"

"For what he did to his own family by deserting us when he was most needed here." She smiled at him. "I'm not surprised

125

at your reaction and refusal to see it. In the Bible, it says the sins of the father will rest on the head of the son or heads of the sons. You'll feel the burden. This is your opportunity."

"For what?"

"To redeem him."

"And exactly how will I do that?"

"Eventually, you will assume those responsibilities he abandoned. You will study and learn our business and relieve me of the burdens that belong on a man's shoulders, not a woman's. That is your true inheritance," she said. She seemed to soften, her body relaxing. "In time, you will not only realize all this but welcome it. Back where you were, in the life you had, becoming a cobbler might have been sufficient, but before you reach another birthday, you will look back on it as if that was a pebble on the beach."

Yvon looked at me. He seemed at a loss for words. I had never seen him cower to anyone, especially a woman. I was waiting for him to give it back to her, to continue to defend Papa.

"I know who you really are inside," she continued. "You're not simply arrogant, you are competitive, hungry. You're a wolf, not a sheep. You would have died early in your shoes being a cobbler. There was simply not enough of a challenge to it for a young man like you."

To my surprise, Yvon continued to be silent. She was belittling what we were, what we had, but for some reason, he didn't look upset. On the contrary, he was looking back at her as if he really did like the picture she was painting.

She turned back to me.

"As to your comments about what your father wanted and didn't want . . . in the end, I cannot believe your father was

126

anything but ashamed of himself, ashamed at how weak he had become, at how weak he was."

Yvon seemed to snap back with those words. He stepped closer to her. His eyes finally filled with the pride and outrage he easily called upon back in France.

"Ashamed? He was very proud of what he was accomplishing. He was far from weak. He was becoming a well-known artist in France, and his work was getting more and more attention and money. Jean-Paul told you so."

"I'm not thinking of that. In his heart, he was surely ashamed of what he had done to us. You say he never mentioned us," she continued, looking at me now. "You don't mention what you are embarrassed to mention. You're old enough to know that's true. You either pretend it never happened or ignore it. That's human nature. Some have too much of it."

I looked to Yvon again to say something.

"He wanted to be an artist" was all he could think of at the moment.

"Right. I wanted to be queen of England." She stood straighter. "You heard a little about the financial empire we have built and are building. You will soon see firsthand that whatever your father was earning or could have earned was a pittance when compared to our financial worth as Dawson Enterprises. He enabled you to be a cobbler's apprentice. I will enable you to become a major real estate entrepreneur. There's a French word for you," she said, with that smile I was beginning to hate. "Entrepreneur. Embrace it. Eventually, that's who and what you will be."

She stabbed him in the chest with her long, bony right forefinger. He winced, but he didn't utter a sound.

"In your heart, that's who you want to be."

She relaxed. I had nothing more to say, and apparently, neither did Yvon. The truth was, I was tired of arguing, here in the hallway, her shrill voice echoing off these cold, tall walls. We both looked quite wiped out.

"Good. Now, my advice to you and your sister is to follow Pauline to bed. Tomorrow is a big day for both of you, and both Mr. Simon and I will need you two to be alert. You both have a lot to learn."

She turned back to me.

"I don't want to see or hear that you have encouraged Pauline any more."

"About what?"

"Anything," she said, and joined Mr. Simon, who had stood quietly by to continue to the library. We stood there side by side looking after them.

"We can't stay here, Yvon. She hates us because she hated Papa. She'll make our lives as miserable as she has made Aunt Pauline's."

His silence encouraged me.

"We'll sneak out of here tonight," I suggested. "Pack what we have and go."

"Will we? How much money do you have?" he asked.

"Money? None, of course."

"Then be realistic, Marlena. I have none, either. We're in America. We know no one. We don't even know where we would go."

"I have Mama's jewelry."

"So? You'd sell it?"

I was quiet. He was right. I couldn't do that.

"Besides," he said, continuing to look after Aunt Effie and Mr. Simon, who turned into the library, "I wouldn't want to give her the satisfaction. She'd only tell people, especially Jean-Paul and Anne, that we inherited Papa's irresponsibility or something and like two frightened children ran off into the night. She'd feel she had done all she could for us. Her knotted, rotted conscience would be satisfied. I won't let her get away with it."

"But . . . what will we do?"

He smiled. "Maybe I will learn whatever I have to learn about the business and eventually, as she predicts, take over Dawson Enterprises or whatever it's called. Who wouldn't want to be filthy rich? Look around you. Look at all she has and what could be ours. When you have all this, you really have control of your life."

"I hate all this, Yvon. I hate being here. I want it to be back to the way it was."

"Well, it can't be, Marlena. There's no time to be a child bathed in fantasies anymore. Maybe right now it feels like we took a trip down into hell, and maybe," he said, looking around, "this is hell in a way, but we're not going to suffer anymore. I promise."

"She frightens me, Yvon."

"She's mostly talk. Don't you see what she wants or what she thinks she wants? We might be what she sees as her vengeance, some sort of way to punish Papa. For a while, we will feel like her slaves doing her bidding. You probably don't remember because you were too young, but Jean-Paul had taken us out on his fishing boat, and we sat and talked about how sad some people in the village always were, like Monsieur Charcot, always complaining, blaming fate."

"I remember he was always drunk."

"Exactly. It did seem like fate was hurting him all the time, the failures, the losses. I asked Jean-Paul if he wasn't right. What control did he have of his life, the sickness in his family, the loss of his business in that flood? 'You can't blame him,' I said, and Jean-Paul said, 'Yes, you can. He still had control of his life.'"

"How?" I asked.

"He was like a man caught in a wild current of bad luck. He couldn't get out of it, but what he could do, Jean-Paul said, is swim faster in the current. Keep his pride that way, and eventually, he would enjoy life again. That's what Jean-Paul told me. I'm going to do the same thing."

"How?"

"I'm going to be a good student of this business, learn everything, and master this current we're in, and when I do, and take over the way she wanted Papa to do, my first action will be to retire her to some home for the mean-spirited," he said. His eyes brightened with the vision. "She'd regret the first day she decided to use me to get back at Papa. The twins will be taking *her* up to bed someday."

I envied him. He had found a purpose, a goal. I had no idea where I was, what I would do, and what I would become. I had more in common with Aunt Pauline at the moment.

"But what will I do? How do I swim in this current?"

"You'll learn the skills she wants you to learn and eventually be right at my side. You'll see. We'll always be a team, Marlena. We'll be as strong as Mama and Papa would expect us to be."

"Do you really think so?"

"*Oui*," Yvon said, holding out his arm. "Enjoy tomorrow. Let

130

her buy you new clothes and shoes, and learn how to be an American girl."

It surprised me how quickly he seemed to be able to adjust to this new life. Could Aunt Effie be right about him, his ambition? Should I be upset? But then again, he was right. Who wouldn't want to be rich, especially in America? Yvon always knew the right thing for us to do. He probably did here as well. Our mama and papa were gone. We had only ourselves now, and his wisdom was what I had to believe in and follow.

I took his arm, and we headed for the stairway. We paused to listen to a ripple of Aunt Effie's laughter coming from the library.

"Do you think those two are lovers?" I asked.

"Please," he said. "Aunt Effie making love to someone? I just ate."

I smiled. My brother was truly like our mother. When he wanted to, he could make anyone feel better about him- or herself. We continued ascending the stairway. After we reached the second floor, we paused to watch the twins come toward us quickly.

"How's Pauline?" I asked.

"She's snugly in bed," Minnie said.

"Almost asleep already," Emma added. "Miss Effie was right to send her up."

They walked past us to the stairway, but as soon as we reached Pauline's room, I shouted for them. Both came back up quickly.

"What is it?" Emma asked.

"Why are you shouting outside her door? You'll get her disturbed," Minnie added.

"Why did you lock her in her room?" I nodded at the lock that had been snapped shut.

"We have to lock her in her room," Minnie said.

"It's not something we want to do. Miss Effie wants us to do it," Emma explained.

"Why?" Yvon demanded, stepping toward them.

"She walks in her sleep," Minnie said.

"The last time she did that, she fell down the stairs and broke her ankle," Emma said. "Remember? We told you."

"You didn't say she walked in her sleep. Even so . . . this is horrible," I muttered, and looked at Yvon. He shook his head and shrugged. "No one should be locked up like this, no matter what. Tell them, Yvon."

"What can we do about it, Marlena? Maybe it's the right thing to do," Yvon said. "We don't want her to hurt herself."

I looked at the lock. "There could be a fire," I said quickly. "She might not get out in time."

"Miss Effie would save her," Minnie said.

"Before she would save herself," Emma added, nodding.

"Right. And there's really a Santa Claus," I told them.

They both looked terribly confused. They started away, walking so closely they rubbed shoulders.

"C'mon," Yvon said. "Let's go to bed before she has them lock us in, too."

He stopped with me at my doorway, and I realized how far we were from the home we loved in a small village that now seemed like a fantasy. My heart ached so. We hadn't only lost our parents; we had lost an entire world, and our aunt from some island in hell was redesigning who we were and who we would be.

"What's happened to us, Yvon? It's like we're stuck in a nightmare."

He shook his head. "We either fell into a hole full of hate or one full of gold coins. We'll see," he said. "Try to get some sleep. Buying clothes with Aunt Effie will exhaust you. Anything with Aunt Effie will exhaust you. Maybe you can exhaust her."

"Me? I don't think she is capable of feeling anything but anger and hate, and that gives her energy."

"Then we'll watch her rot," he said. "Don't worry. She won't harm a hair on your head with me nearby."

"I know."

He hugged me.

"I'm going to write a letter to Jean-Paul and Anne before I go to sleep," I told him. "I'm going to tell them everything. It will be a book, not a letter."

"You'll be up all night if you start," he said. He started away, then stopped. "But if you do, give them my love."

I watched him enter his room, and then I entered mine. It wasn't until I sat to write that I realized damn Aunt Effie was right. I was exhausted. The letter would have to wait another day. Instead, I prepared for my first night in what had once been my father's home. How I wished I could feel something warm and loving for it like I did for our small house in Villefranche-sur-Mer. I was afraid I would start crying, so I stopped thinking about it. Instead, I listened to the creaks and moans in the walls as the wind swept over the mansion. Somewhere nearby, I heard the sound of one of those funny automobile horns. To me it resembled the cry of a sick bird.

The shadows seemed to shift and shake with the movement

133

of clouds blocking and then floating away from the half-moon. A breeze stirred the curtains and tinkled the chandelier. A house this big with rooms this large encouraged loneliness, I thought. How I missed the sound of the sea and getting up to glance out at the water to be comforted by the light of stars dancing on the calm waves. With his art, Papa had made our world cozy and safe. Unlike my friends, I took none of it for granted but always looked for and was excited by the beauty. Every day was a surprise. The only surprise I envisioned here was a cobweb in some corner the twins missed when they cleaned.

Thinking about living in a city this big with all those people walking the streets was even more frightening. How do you begin a new life in such a place? No one would know us when we walked these streets. Who would say *"Bonjour"* and smile because the sight of us helped him or her get through their day? Where would we find real aunts and uncles, *grand-pères* and *grand-mères* in a world full of strangers? How would I meet any new friends?

The only education Aunt Effie had suggested for me was learning secretarial skills so I could be of some use to the family business. We were indentured servants, committed and condemned because of her hunger for vengeance. Both of us, Yvon and I, could feel the determination she had to make us pay for what she believed Papa had done. Our parents' deaths came like a gift to her. What a terribly mean way to be! She had pounced on us like two lost and helpless baby birds that had fallen out of their nest.

"The sins of the fathers," I muttered. "What about her sins?"

I turned over and hugged my pillow. I was truly exhausted. It wasn't only the travel; it was all these emotions flowing in and out around us like the incoming tide. Would we drown in them?

I felt myself drifting. Sometime during the night, I awoke to what I thought was the sound of Pauline's door being pulled and pushed against that lock. It stopped, and I wondered if I had dreamed it. I was asleep again in moments, not waking again until the sunlight exploded on the walls to announce our first morning in America.

Before I had a chance to get out of bed, the door was thrust open. Aunt Effie stood there in a dark-gray dress with a double-layered skirt, the fuller top skirt a mini crinoline, fur-trimmed. I had seen a drawing and a picture of a dress like it in a magazine on the ship. She held her hat in her right hand. But being stylish did nothing for her. She still looked dark and withered by her unhappiness.

Live in anger, and you die in pain, Jean-Paul would tell us.

"Why aren't you up and dressed?" Aunt Effie demanded. I looked about and realized there was no clock.

"I don't know what time it is. I was tired. I . . ."

"Get up, and put on that ridiculous dress you wore for now so we can organize the day. I'll have you in something proper in less than two hours, and we'll finish our shopping before lunch. Mr. Simon is arranging for you to have a tutor. He'll be here this afternoon and begin your work to develop your necessary social and secretarial skills. I will not send you to some fancy girls' school to prepare you for some arranged marriage. This is a different time from your mother's, when girls who came from families with means were pampered."

"My mother's? What do you know about my mother's family?"

"Enough to make me sick if I think too hard about it. Get moving."

"I don't understand."

"I'm not asking you to. Just do what I ask."

"Is Yvon up?"

"Yvon is up, had his breakfast, and has been taken to the offices," she said. "And don't bother inquiring about Pauline. I decided to avoid her whining when she sees we're going out to shop and had her breakfast brought to her. She'll remain in her room."

"Yvon left?" I muttered.

I couldn't believe it. Why wouldn't he have looked in on me first?

She smiled at my surprise. "Perhaps you don't know your brother as well as I do," she said.

"What's that mean? How could that be? We've been with you only a short time. You can't know who we are."

"I'm not saying I know who you are, but a man's a man. I don't have to be with one long to know what I need to know about him. You'll learn to be the same way if you listen to my advice and do what I tell you," she said. "Now, no more of this chitchat. Get up and come down for some breakfast. I intend to leave within the hour."

She closed the door.

Be the same way? I wouldn't want to be anything like her, I thought. I rose and dressed and hurried down. Aunt Effie was standing and talking to an African woman with stark gray hair, which, although it would indicate age, looked in stark contrast to her beautifully smooth face, with the most sparkling ebony eyes I had ever seen. Papa would surely have liked to paint her,

I thought. Wearing a light-green apron that reached the hem of her skirt, she had to be Mrs. Trafalgar. I hadn't expected her to be an African woman. She was a little taller than Aunt Effie and much slimmer.

"Sit down. Mrs. Trafalgar will bring you your breakfast," Aunt Effie said. "You are never to call her anything but Mrs. Trafalgar."

Mrs. Trafalgar gave me the warmest smile I had yet to see in America and immediately put me at ease.

"She has made you some oatmeal and some toast with jelly. Drink that orange juice, and don't dilly-dally," Aunt Effie ordered. "I will organize our transportation with George. I expect to leave in twenty-five minutes."

"Mornin', darlin'," Mrs. Trafalgar said, as if Aunt Effie hadn't spoken. "It's comin' right up," she added, turned, and went into the kitchen.

Aunt Effie looked at me for a long moment, long enough for me to ask, "What?"

"You have your father's eyes. Hopefully, you'll see the world and your responsibilities more clearly," she quickly added, like someone who realized she had just acted human. "I'll see to our transportation."

I watched her move quickly out of the room, wondering to myself if it would be at all possible to think of her someday as my aunt. Maybe the longer we lived here, the closer we would become. She would think more of us and soften, although from the way she treated her sister, it was hard to imagine her saying anything kind to anyone. I suspected she was a bitter person from the day she could utter a sarcastic or outright nasty remark.

Some people are born with warts on their tongues, Jean-Paul would tell us. *The most painful thing you can do to them is feel sorry for them. They hate being pitied.*

That was probably very true for Aunt Effie, I thought. Perhaps that was exactly what I would do, tell her I felt sorry for her. I could exact some revenge as well as she could.

Mrs. Trafalgar brought out my food on a little silver tray.

"I could have fetched it myself," I said. I didn't think I'd ever get used to being waited upon hand and foot.

She smiled and put it before me. "There's goin' ta be plenty of time for ya ta do chores," she said. "Give yerself a chance to get useta being here first. A newly planted flower needs ta get acquainted with its new soil 'fore it can grow again. So sorry ta hear about yer trouble."

"Trouble?"

"Yer daddy and mama."

"Oh. Thank you. Do you live here, too, Mrs. Trafalgar?"

"Oh, no, missy. Ma husband, George, and I live in the Jackson Ward district of the city. Many of ma people are there."

"Who are your people?" I asked.

She laughed but didn't really answer me. "Y'all really from France?" she asked instead.

"Yes, ma'am," I said. "*Je suis née en France.*"

"Oh, ma goodness, French itself. Means?"

"I was born in France."

"Oh, sure." She smiled. "Ya as pretty as a French girl supposed ta be." She looked at the doorway to the hall. "Better finish yer breakfast. Yer auntie went to fetch ma husband, George. They'll be comin' along."

"Where is he?"

"Oh, he works the house, looks after it all," she said. "You met my brother, Yvon, this morning?"

"Yes, I did. He didn't say much, but he's a handsome young man. I'm sure he will do well. George took him ta the offices." She looked at the door. "Finish up now like yer auntie told ya."

She hurried out as if she was afraid Aunt Effie would catch us talking.

Almost as soon I finished eating, Aunt Effie was at the door.

"Put this on," she said, holding out a light-blue wool shawl. "It's a bit on the cool side this morning."

"Thank you."

I followed her to the door. George was waiting at the automobile. He opened the door for us, and Aunt Effie got in, with me right behind her.

"Don't slouch when you sit. A young lady always is cognizant of her posture. Do you know what that means?"

"Yes. I don't slouch."

"You are now," she insisted. "You haven't been taught what good posture means. Shoulders back, head high, and fold your hands in your lap, and don't lean against the automobile door. I suggest you watch how I comport myself in public. You will in time be meeting many people, and first impressions usually stick. You understand?"

I wanted to say, *My first impression of you nearly turned my stomach.* Instead, I simply nodded. I looked out the window at the people and stores, but my gaze was clouded with the tears that seemed to ice over my eyes.

"My mother did not live long enough for her to teach me everything I needed to know about conducting myself properly in society, mainly because I was stuck at home caring for your aunt Pauline, but when the time came for me to join my father because he no longer had any hopes of passing on his success to his son, I had to watch and learn."

Then, in a softer tone, she added, "Much like you, I was a fish in a bowl tossed into the sea to find her way amongst the schools of other fish."

I looked at her. Did she really see some resemblance between us? Was this a note of compassion and understanding?

"If you do what I tell you and listen carefully to my instructions, you will survive."

"Survive?"

"This is a dog-eat-dog world. That includes the women in it. Those whom you meet out there," she said, nodding toward the street, "will see you as a threat. You are going to be very attractive, and you will have the Dawson name and power behind you eventually. I expect most men will make fools of themselves trying to attract your interest. It's in the nature of men," she added, speaking as though she was chewing on a rotten egg. "I doubt that your mother had a chance to educate you in all this or that it mattered, living in that village," she added, pronouncing "village" as if it were a profanity.

"My mother taught me what I needed to know."

"Did she? How much about her own youth did she tell you?"

I looked at her and then down, my heart beginning to race. Did she know that Mama had kept most of her youth a secret from both Yvon and me? Except for that day she suggested she had been a femme fatale once, she said little more and didn't want to talk about that at all.

"How do you know so much about her?"

She smiled and looked out her window. "I know," she said, "what I had to know. My father and I used the services of a private investigator to discover why his son, my brother, would give up so much for this silly pursuit of art and then a woman. When you're old enough, I will tell you what you need to know."

"You're a liar. You're just trying to get me . . . to hate what my life and my family were so I'll do whatever you say."

"You'll see for yourself," she said, surprisingly and disturbingly calmly. What would I see? "We're here."

We stopped in front of a store with large windows. Printed over them was the name THALHIMERS. George stepped out to open the door for us and help us out. My eyes went everywhere. It seemed like an explosion of people coming and going, some walking very fast, others involved in conversations as they went along. Groups of women were going in and out of the store. When we entered, I couldn't believe all the different things that were being sold in one place.

"Is this a street fair?" I said.

"Hardly. This is one of the first department stores. We'll be going to the ladies' clothing department," she said, just as a tall woman with dark hair spun into what looked like a beehive approached us.

"Miss Dawson, welcome," she said. "Everything is ready for you."

"Thank you. This is my niece, Marlena."

"What a pretty girl. Please. Follow me," she said.

I looked at my aunt.

"It's all right to say thank you when someone gives you a compliment."

"She said it so fast and turned. I know how to say thank you."

Rather than get annoyed with my response, she looked pleased. "Perhaps you did inherit enough from your mother to survive," she said.

I had no idea why she had decided to weave this web of mystery around my mother's past, but it was annoying me. Every time I wanted to snap back at her, however, I thought about Yvon. He wanted us to be clever and do what she asked for now. He was right, of course. We didn't have much choice. It was just that by the time I was finished swallowing down my rage, my throat would ache and my stomach would want to explode.

All that anger flew out of my thinking when we began to look at the clothes. I didn't have much to say about it, but I was overwhelmed by how much she was buying for me. She ordered dozens of this and dozens of that, as if stockings, undergarments, blouses, and skirts, even hats, were like potatoes and tomatoes. Once I tried something on and she liked the way it fit, she bought two. Everything was to be wrapped and boxed and delivered, except for the dress she wanted me to wear now.

"Take what she came in and burn it," she told the saleslady.

"No," I said. "My mother gave me that dress."

She thought a moment and then told her to put it in a separate bag so it didn't touch anything new, not even a pair of stockings.

As we headed for women's accessories, she said, "You'll find that sentiment is a weakness in this world, especially in the business world. Your cutthroat competition will take advantage of it every time."

"I have only pity for them," I said.

She smiled. "I do look forward to having this discussion after your brother and you have been fully dipped in the new world, perhaps a year from now."

From accessories, she took me to shoes and boots. Never once did I hear her say this or that was too much, no matter what the price. Since everything was in American money, I wasn't sure how expensive things were, but because of the sheer amount of what she was buying me, I knew she was spending a lot of money.

"Why are we buying so much?" I finally asked her.

"We?"

"You."

"I don't intend to have to do this again for some time. Caring for you today is taking me away from business. Although I have Mr. Simon, I must approve most everything we do. I expect you to be self-sufficient as quickly as possible. One helpless soul around my ankles is quite enough," she added.

We left with me in new undergarments and a new dress, stockings, and shoes, but we took little of what she had bought me. It was all to be delivered later today.

"When we return home, you will wait for the arrival of Mr. Donald. He has been hired to tutor you in all things and not only the secretarial skills you will be required to have. He is what we call a *professional gentleman*. From time to time, you, as well as your brother, of course, will be required to attend formal dinners, business dinners, and I want you both to be proper and impressive. You are Dawsons now, the Dawsons of Richmond.

"You've never lived under the umbrella of our family's reputation and success. You have no idea what it means to be in elegant society. You are no longer a French girl walking barefoot on some beach, Marlena. You are my niece, a Dawson, and so must be thought of as such. Mr. Donald will show you how a young lady comports herself in society, how you will eat and speak. I have given him free rein. Mr. Simon will personally attend to your brother. I expect that what you learn from Mr. Donald you will practice at our home immediately, and when I feel you are ready, I will introduce you to other families and permit you to work for the Dawson company.

"In time," she said with confidence, "you will be reborn."

"I will never forget my home, my parents, and the life I had," I said defiantly.

She nodded softly. "We'll see," she said, and looked out her window as we motored back to the mansion that at this moment seemed more like a prison.

I was beginning to appreciate what poor Aunt Pauline had endured her whole life.

What if she was right? I thought—I feared.

What if I forgot my family back in France and became just like her?

7

When we arrived, I saw another motorcar, smaller and less impressive, parked near the barn, which my aunt made a point of telling me was not a barn but a garage. I was happy to inform her that this was another English word born in a French mouth. When we entered the house, a short, stout man with a well-trimmed auburn goatee stepped out of the sitting room to greet us. His eyes widened and brightened at the sight of me, which I would ordinarily feel was something nice, but the way his thick lips folded and unfolded, showing the tip of his pale pink tongue, made me hesitate. I did not return his smile.

He stepped forward, rubbing his palms together as if he had just washed his hands and was drying them. His nose was thick at the bridge, which made his hazel eyes smaller. I had seen pictures of men dressed the way he was, dressed to meet the king. He was wearing a black cotton frock coat and a black brushed cotton vest with a flat front and a notched lapel. There was a gold pocket watch, the chain attached to the third button of his vest. He had a stand-up-collar dress shirt and a gray ascot.

"Sorry to keep you waiting, Mr. Donald, but shopping these days takes longer than it used to."

"Most things do, Miss Dawson, most things do. And this, I assume, is our Marlena."

"Yes. Our Marlena," she said, sounding like pronouncing my name stung her tongue. "Marlena, this is Mr. Donald, your tutor."

She waited. I saw the way her eyes went from me to him and back to me.

"Very pleased to meet you," I said. I reluctantly held out my hand.

He nearly jumped forward to take it and held it in his stumpy, thick fingers as he widened his smile and nodded at my aunt. "Nicely done. Maybe our work won't be so difficult," he told her.

Nicely done? What did I do? From where did she tell him I had come? Some uncivilized part of the world? He kept my hand a few moments longer. When he felt me pulling it back, he finally let go.

"I wish it were so, Mr. Donald, but I suspect you'll earn every penny I pay you."

He laughed. "Do you need to take a few minutes to freshen up?" he asked me. "Or should we begin and get acquainted as quickly as we can?"

"She can freshen up on her own time," Aunt Effie said.

"Please get started. I have a few things to do before I go to the offices."

She turned to me.

"I'm leaving you in very capable hands, Marlena. Devote your full attention to Mr. Donald, and treat him with the utmost respect. I will inform Minnie and Emma, my maids, to set the table for a formal lunch experience," she told Mr. Donald.

"Thank you, Miss Dawson. Shall we?" he asked me, and gestured at the sitting room. "I have some papers and books to introduce you to as a way of beginning our work."

My moment of hesitation raised my aunt's eyebrows, so I walked quickly into the sitting room. The books and papers he had described were on the dark-cherrywood table, and the table had been moved closer to the Wedgwood-blue settee.

"Let's sit there," he said, indicating the settee. "You must tell me all about yourself first. I'm intrigued. Brought up in France and almost overnight becoming an American. Quite an experience for one so young, I'm sure."

I sat. He stood there for a few moments looking down at me, perhaps anticipating an excited *thank you*.

"I would give anything, Monsieur Donald, not to be here," I said, with a fixed glare that wiped the intended friendly smile off his face.

He turned those lips into his mouth as he had done when I first entered the house. His eyes lost any twinkle they had, and his puffy cheeks hardened.

"Yes, of course. I am sorry about the circumstances. But," he added after a brief pause, "we must make the best of it now. One look at you tells me you have the strength to do so and have the potential to be a fine young lady."

"My mama and papa always told me I already was."

"Of course," he said, his eyes shifting everywhere as he struggled to find the perfect words. "I'm here to put the finishing touch on you, nothing more and certainly nothing less." He glanced at the doorway and then back at me. "So, your aunt envisions you working at your family company," he continued quickly, and waddled his way around the table to sit beside me. I shifted on the settee as far as I could to my right, because his leg was right up against mine. He reached for one of the papers.

"I have here a sort of test of your English skills so we can determine where best to put our energies. You do read English?" he asked suddenly, his face fearful as the possibility of his truly starting from scratch occurred to him. Obviously, Aunt Effie had told him little about me.

"My mama and papa were Americans. Mama taught both my brother, Yvon, and me how to read, write, and speak in English. My papa was usually off painting, but we all read aloud at night from their favorite books sometimes, and once in a while, Papa got an American newspaper off a ship that docked in Villefranche-sur-Mer. We all read it."

"Amazing," he said, but breathed in obvious relief.

"Not so amazing to us. Learning, whether it was languages or anything else, was never something we feared or avoided."

He laughed nervously, frequently glancing at the doorway. "Quite so, quite so."

This close, I could smell what I recognized as some sort of whiskey. His nervousness and excitement created dots of spittle at the corners of his mouth.

"Well, I do believe you, but let's let you fill out the questions as best you can anyway. Okay?"

148

I took the paper and the pen and sat back. None of the questions looked difficult.

"Is this all of it?" I asked.

He widened his eyes at the way I had asked, making it seem like nothing challenging. My confidence both surprised and pleased him.

"For now," he said. "Yes. Please." He lowered his eyes to the paper and then looked at me.

I sat forward and began answering the questions. I could feel his eyes fixed intently on me, but I concentrated on the test. It took only a few minutes. When I handed the papers back to him, he smiled but looked skeptical. He leaned back and began to review my answers and then smiled again.

"One hundred percent correct. Well, you do have the basic skills," he said. "We'll move right on to more elevated information. And then we'll spend time on your necessary social skills. I can see you are a sophisticated young French girl, but many more eyes will be on you and on you critically because you are a Dawson. That will be something you'll have to get used to."

"I'm quite used to people looking at me, sir. We come from a small village where everyone was like my aunt and uncle or my grandparents."

"I'm sure," he said, and cleared his throat. "But my job is to give you the grace to look your part here."

"My part here? What is that?"

"You're a Dawson of Richmond," he said, as if I was in line for the crown. A Dawson of Richmond? Would I ever get used to being that?

He reached for one of the books and flipped through some

pages before leaning in to show me what he wanted me to read. There were topics like "How to Write a Proper Business Letter," "How to Write a Proper Thank-You Note," "How to Write a Proper Meeting Invitation," and the like. Everything was preceded by the word "proper."

"However," he said, sitting as closely as he could to me, "at your aunt's request, my main task after we have mastered all this will be to help you learn something called stenography. Have you ever heard of that?"

I shook my head. "What is it?"

"A method of shorthand when you're taking notes. By the time we're finished, you will be able to write as quickly as someone speaks. Later, you will translate it back to the person's actual words. Doesn't that sound exciting and wonderful? Any young woman today who can master that is of great value in business and legal matters."

He sat back. I didn't think he appreciated my indifference, but reciting back what someone had just said certainly did not sound more exciting than merely strolling through Villefranche or walking on the beach.

"As you can see, your aunt has very high hopes and goals for you. You should be appreciative. You'll be head and shoulders above most young women and," he said, leaning toward me so that his lips were only inches from my face, "many young men."

His breath made my stomach churn.

He put his hand on my leg, just above my knee, and patted me. "How's that all sound?"

"*Je ne sais pas,*" I said.

"Pardon?"

"I don't know. It's all too new to me."

He stared a moment and then brightened. "Oh, you said something in French." He smiled so widely now that I could see some teeth were gone in the back of his mouth on the right side. "Perhaps you'll teach me as I teach you. I've always wanted to speak French."

"Why?"

"Why? It's a beautiful language, and someday I intend to travel there. I'm hoping you'll tell me all about it. I'm hoping we'll be more than simply a teacher and a student."

"In what way?"

"What way?" He laughed. "Why, we'll be friends. You'd like that, wouldn't you?" His eyes twinkled with whatever he was imagining behind them.

Before I could respond, the twins appeared in the doorway.

"Miss Effie asked us to tell you when lunch was ready," Minnie said.

"The table is set," Emma added.

"Well, then. Let's begin the enjoyable dining lessons," Mr. Donald said, standing instantly. "I am somewhat hungry." He turned and offered me his hand. "Mademoiselle Dawson, *s'il vous plaît?*"

I took it and stood.

"See? I know a few words here and there. Good pronunciation?"

I nodded, even though it wasn't.

"Shall we walk in together properly? Every little thing we do together is a lesson of one sort or another. Men will want to escort you all the time, and you'll want it to look . . ."

"Proper?"

"Exactly." He offered his arm and then took my hand. "Now, you don't want to hang on their arms like some lady of the street. You want it to look natural, like you're quite accustomed to it. Keep your posture," he said, putting his hand on the small of my back, "and just be firm."

He tugged gently at my hand so my arm threaded through his.

"There, that's good," he said, patting my hand.

The twins stood there looking at us, neither smiling, and then turned and left for the dining room. We started out.

"Have you ever attended a formal dinner or lunch?" he asked as we left the sitting room.

"Not formal lunches or dinners. Only delicious ones," I replied, and he laughed so loudly Aunt Effie, who was coming down the stairs, stopped and looked at us in astonishment.

"I see you're getting along. That's good," she said, continuing down.

"Have you changed your mind? Are you joining us?" he asked.

"No, I'm off to work and to see how young Mr. Dawson is doing. How are her English skills?"

"Quite good, actually. She'll move right on to the more elaborate lessons. I venture to say you'll have a stenographer available sooner than you think."

"Both she and her brother have good reason to succeed," Aunt Effie said.

Mr. Donald nodded, even though he had no idea what she meant.

"Enjoy your lunch," she told me. "And listen to and do whatever Mr. Donald instructs you to do."

"Where's Aunt Pauline?" I asked quickly.

"Worry about yourself for now," she replied, and started for the front entrance.

We continued to the dining room. He moved ahead to pull out my chair when I had let go of his arm and stepped forward.

"Oh, don't sit like that," he said quickly. "You're not getting on a horse. You must be graceful in all things, even sitting. And you must let me bring your chair closer to the table. It's not very ladylike to tug your own seat like that. You wait because you expect to be treated like a lady. Now, shift a bit," he said, putting the palm of his hand on my hip a little lower than I expected. I moved quickly. "There, now slowly sit and keep your hands in your lap until I sit and the service begins. Patience . . . patience is a sign of elegance, expectation, and self-respect."

He nodded at the twins.

"I will start by explaining the silverware," he continued when he sat.

Even though I was hungry, his comments about my every move, every bite, slowly drove my appetite away. My mouth was open too much when I chewed, and I chewed too quickly. I kept forgetting my posture, and when I drank, I gulped. I was happy when lunch ended, even though it meant we'd return to the sitting room. To get away from him for a while and catch my breath, I went to the bathroom. I remained in there as long as I could. I wasn't afraid of the work, but the tenseness throughout my body was exhausting me.

On my way back to the sitting room, I stopped in the dining room again and asked the Brown twins about Aunt Pauline.

"When does she have her lunch?"

"Oh, we brought it up to her earlier," Minnie said.

"Miss Effie wants her to stay in her room and not get in your and Mr. Donald's way."

"In her room? Are you saying she's been there all day?"

They both nodded.

I thought about it a moment. "I think she's better off right now," I muttered.

They looked at each other as if one was waiting to see if the other would laugh.

Mr. Donald rose as soon as I entered the sitting room.

"I have samples of the proper business letter to show you and explain," he said. He patted the space beside him. "Are you okay?" he asked when I didn't move.

"Yes," I said.

"Did you enjoy your lunch?"

"Is honesty part of being socially acceptable?" I replied.

He looked stunned for a moment and then laughed. He laughed like someone who was trying not to laugh, tightening his lips and snorting. It brought a crimson tint to his bubbled cheeks.

"A lady," he said, "is very stingy with the truth. You use it only when it offers an advantage. I'll teach you how to disguise your true feelings."

"That will be your biggest challenge, Mr. Donald," I said, and he tried to stuff back his laugh again, this time coughing and holding his stomach.

"You're quite the clever young lady. I must say you live up to my image of a pretty French girl. Please," he said, indicating the settee and stepping aside so I could get to where I had been on the settee. "We'll put clever repertoire on the back burner. One thing at a time. For now, business letters."

I sat, and he began to explain the letter format. He went on in a dull monotone, sounding less interested in it than I was. My mind began to drift, the memories of the sea returning, Mama's beautiful laugh, Papa's smile, and the four of us heading to the village on a Sunday morning. Every vision squeezed my heart. Suddenly, he surprised me with his hand on my thigh, his fingers closing gently.

"You must give me your full attention," he said. He kept his hand on my thigh and moved his tongue over his lower lip as he fixed his gaze intently on me. "I asked you a question twice."

"Sorry," I said.

His fingers moved a little toward my knee, and then he shifted uncomfortably in the settee. I really hadn't paid attention to his words and looks. He had moved closer, and I had no more room to shift on the settee.

"Excuse me," he said, standing a little and leaning over me to reach for some papers on the table to my right. As he did so, I felt his crotch move against my shoulder. When I glanced down, my heart thumped. The sight of the bulge sent thornlike shivers through my breasts. He moved as if he was struggling to reach the papers, rubbing against me side to side. I had no doubt what I was feeling. I hadn't realized that he had brought the table even closer to the settee. There was barely room for me to stand. Panic was like a tern opening its wings inside my stomach.

I pushed him back and turned to stand, shoving the table a few inches so I could slip around it.

"Marlena!" he cried.

"I feel a little sick," I said, without looking back.

I rushed out of the room. His cry of surprise, shouting my

name again, fell quickly behind me. In moments, I was up the stairway. When I entered my room, I shut the door and threw myself onto my bed, clutching the blanket and pulling it around me. My shivering didn't stop. I brushed at my shoulder where he had pressed himself against me, feeling I should take soap and water to it. My stomach was still churning, all the food I had eaten at lunch threatening to rush back up my throat. I lay back and closed my eyes.

A little while later, there was a knock on my door.

"What is it?" I cried. Did he dare come up to my room? If he entered, I would scream and scream. There was no lock on my door.

"Are you all right?" Minnie or Emma asked. Their voices were too similar to distinguish which one had spoken from behind a door.

"Mr. Donald is very concerned."

"Tell him I have an upset stomach, and I'm sorry but I can't come down," I said.

"Can we help?"

"Yes. Leave me alone," I said. "That's how you can help."

I heard them walk off. And then I lay back again, closed my eyes, and, surely from the emotional terror, fell asleep. I woke hours later to the sound of knocking again. The twins were back, but they had returned to bring in the packages that had been delivered from the department store. I let them in to hang garments and put things away in drawers. They worked quickly, neither looking at me.

"Has Mr. Donald left?" I asked.

"Oh, yes, ma'am," Minnie said. "Quite a while ago."

"He said he would return tomorrow," Emma added.

"He left your work in the sitting room and said he hoped you'd be better quickly," Minnie said.

I nodded and left them in my room. As I passed Aunt Pauline's door, I saw that it was still locked. I listened, but I didn't hear her, and I was afraid to call to her. I couldn't let her out, and she would surely beg me to do so. I went on to the stairway.

It was quiet downstairs. Yvon and Aunt Effie had not returned. To keep myself occupied, I decided to walk through that part of the house we had yet to see. Just past the entrance to the kitchen, there was a door on the left. I opened it and looked in at what was obviously an office. The large dark-cherrywood desk and chair were against the far wall. To the right were file cabinets and a table with papers neatly stacked. There was a rocking chair on the left, with a small table beside it, and in front of the desk was a soft-cushioned chair. The floor was a dark wood with a light-gray area rug.

The portrait above the desk and chair had to be my grandfather's portrait, I thought. I could see resemblances to Papa in the shape of his eyes and chin. His father had a broader forehead. Truthfully, he looked more like Aunt Effie, or she like him, especially around their mouths, their jaws and cheeks. I knew that people who did have their portraits painted or their pictures taken did not believe in smiling in those days.

Papa told me people used to believe only the poor, the lewd, drunks, or foolish innocents would smile in pictures. Smiling, they believed, took away from the authority and strength of their faces.

"My job, especially when I'm capturing your mother, is to get her softness and beautiful spirit suggested in her face. Just a slight turn in the lips, the glint in the eyes, the way you have your subject hold her head, can make a difference."

In his portrait above the desk, Grandfather Dawson looked like he was peering down with scrutiny, searching for something to disapprove. Sitting under that painting would cause anyone to question every little decision she had made. There were other pictures on the walls but none that had captured my grandmother or my father and his sisters. Where were those pictures? Why wouldn't a father be proud to hang them on his office wall?

I went farther into the office and looked at the titles of some of the papers stacked on the table. They were all about various properties in Richmond, with drawings, pictures, and comments. How would I ever get excited about any of this? Would Yvon?

The desk was so organized and immaculate that I was afraid to touch it, but the bottom right drawer was slightly open, so I pulled it out farther and looked inside it at a folder under a paperweight with the image of a heart. My curiosity was overwhelming. I looked at the door, listened, and then slowly lifted off the paperweight and opened the folder. There was finally a picture. It was obviously my grandfather, somewhat younger. Standing on his right side was a little girl who was obviously Aunt Pauline, and on the other side was Aunt Effie, older, thinner, but just as serious and hard-looking, with her hair tightly woven in a bun.

Aunt Pauline had pretty hair brushed down to her shoulders with a bow at the top. There were no colors, of course, but her eyes still looked quite striking. No one was smiling. When I looked closer at Aunt Effie's hands at her sides, I saw that they looked somewhat clenched, almost like claws. She wasn't enjoying being photographed, that was for sure. I stared at the picture for a while and then slipped it back in the folder and looked to see what else was in the drawer.

There was nothing. How odd not to see a picture of my father or my grandmother, too. I closed the drawer and was about to step away from the desk when an envelope caught my attention because I recognized the handwriting. It was Anne's.

My fingers were trembling when I picked it up. I was so afraid it was something terrible about Jean-Paul. Very carefully, I pulled out the folded paper and sat in the leather desk chair. The letter within was quite short.

Dear Miss Dawson,

I can reassure you that the children have a very limited knowledge of their family roots in America and will, as you request, leave the familiarizing them with it all entirely in your hands.

Neither Jean-Paul nor myself would assume such responsibility. There is no reason for your threats. We want only what is best for Yvon and Marlena.

Yours sincerely,

Anne Bise

I refolded the letter and put it back into the envelope. Why would Aunt Effie threaten them? Threaten them with what? What was she afraid Anne or Jean-Paul would tell us about our own family? Did this have to do with her anger at Papa? Why was it important for her to know that we had very limited knowledge of our family roots? Was she afraid we wouldn't want to come back here with her to America?

I turned and looked up at my grandfather, who now seemed to be glaring angrily down at me.

"Was this about you? Did you kill someone or something?"

I was tempted to start exploring what was in the file cabinets and had risen to do so when I heard the sounds of someone entering the house. I hurried back down the hallway.

It was Yvon. He was heading directly to the stairway. I called to him, and he paused on the steps.

"Hey," he called back. He reached for my hand. "C'mon upstairs with me. I want to tell you all about my day at the offices."

He looked very excited, but what made my heart cringe a little was how pleased he looked as well.

"Yvon," I said as he closed his hand around mine.

He tugged me to follow him up quickly.

"She'll yell at you for bringing me into your room," I warned.

"She won't be back for a while. Don't pay attention to that, anyway."

I followed him in and first realized how good his new dark-blue business suit with his new shoes, tie, and shirt looked on him. He had never worn a suit in France.

Before I could tell him anything, he rattled on with his great excitement.

"Wait until you see our offices. And the view, amazing! We're very high up and can see practically the whole city of Richmond. I like Mr. Simon, too. He's very patient and nice to work with. Before the day ended, I understood all the major concepts in real estate, and I even sat in on a discussion involving a bidding on a new property. There are seven other young men working there, two for nearly five years and the rest three or four. All were very nice to me. I think they know I'll eventually have more to say and do, and one day . . ."

He paused.

"What's wrong? You look a little upset. Didn't you have a good day with the tutor?"

I skipped all the minor things about Mr. Donald that I hated and went right to the incident. He stared at me and then sat on his bed.

"Why would she bring such a man here?"

"Maybe she doesn't know what he's really like," I said. "He's returning tomorrow."

"Like hell he is," Yvon said, and stood up as if he had just sat on hot coals. He pushed up his sleeve and looked at a watch.

"Where did you get that?"

"She told Mr. Simon to have one for me at the offices. It's not very expensive, but it's expensive enough. My first watch," he said, proudly showing it to me. "Okay, she should be home any minute. You wait in your room."

"But . . ."

"Just do what I say," he said.

I nodded. "You know, Aunt Pauline has been shut up in her room all day. The twins told me Aunt Effie left orders. She's like a prisoner. It's a horrible way to treat your own sister."

"One crisis at a time," Yvon said. He looked very angry again. "Let's go. You go to your room for now."

We walked out and stopped at my door.

"I'll come get you when I need you," he said. I watched him go to the stairway and then went into my room to wait.

Less than twenty minutes later, I heard him come running up the stairs. "C'mon," he said after opening the door. "She doesn't believe what I'm telling her. Maybe she doesn't want to believe it."

"She won't believe me, either, Yvon," I said, walking to the door. I felt myself trembling.

"You don't lie, Marlena. If she can't see that, she's stupid."

We walked down and went into the sitting room, where Aunt Effie waited. The twins left just before we stepped in. I had the feeling she had interrogated them about Mr. Donald already.

"Mr. Donald is a man of high regard," she began before we were fully in the room. "Accusations like the one you're making are very serious and if proven untrue will hurt you deeply, hurt this family deeply."

"I'm not lying," I said. "What Yvon told you is the truth."

"Describe it in detail," she challenged, folded her arms across her bosom, and sat back. "A girl your age should not be as aware of such things, anyway, and many girls your age, especially where you come from, I imagine, fantasize."

"Maybe in America," Yvon said. "Girls from France are not that ignorant of things of a sexual nature and don't have to fantasize."

"I imagine with your parents, that's very true."

"What?" Yvon said. His face reddened. "What does that mean?"

"Please. Hold down the dramatics. Go on," she ordered me.

I described every touch before I got to what he had done up against my body.

"The man could have had a pen in his pocket or—"

"The bulge was not there when he first sat beside me, and there is not a pocket between his legs. Do I have to tell you what's there exactly for you to believe me?"

It was her turn for her face to turn crimson and then a

shade more like purple after she had swallowed the lump in her throat.

"He wasn't just leaning over and pressing himself against me," I continued, seeing her skepticism fading. "He was rubbing from side to side and—"

"Enough," she said, and waved at us as if she was shooing flies.

"It's not enough," Yvon said. "If he goes near my sister again . . ."

She looked down and then nodded. "I have a very good woman friend who ran a school for girls designed to ready them for secretarial work. She retired over a year ago, but I will ask her to take his place. You wouldn't learn anything from him now whether or not he was innocent. Her name is Ella Cornfield. She never married, and she lives alone. Her older siblings have passed away. She doesn't live far from here. I will go to see her after dinner. I'm sure she will be happy to fill her time bringing a country girl up to snuff."

"I'm not a country girl," I said.

She looked up quickly. "No. You're not, are you? Why, when I saw you two, was Mr. Donald laughing and you were on his arm? You didn't look afraid or abused."

"He was showing me how to be escorted, and he was laughing after he asked me if I had attended formal lunches or dinners and I said only delicious ones. I didn't mean it to be funny. I meant it to be true."

She nodded slowly. "You're right, Yvon," she told him, her eyes narrowing. "People your age do grow up faster in France when they have parents like yours, perhaps."

She put up her hand before he could respond.

"I have to go up to see about my sister. I'm hoping her experience today will cause her to behave and listen to me when I tell her something. She's very spoiled, you see. It was the way she was brought up, not that she is really very brought up. I did my best, but both my parents babied her. Now look at the result. Right now, she's showing off for you two. That will end, or I'll keep her in her room for weeks."

She stood.

"I've done it before," she said, and left us.

"Do you believe she had no idea that man was like that?" I asked Yvon.

"Yes, I believe that. In the end, when she had to accept that what you were saying was the truth, she looked quite sick about it. Whatever. You'll have a different tutor, and you'll learn what you need to know. We're going to do this, Marlena. We're going to take over this company someday and be powerful and rich. We'll do what we have to in order to belong here and get the respect we deserve. When you think of it, who else does she have but us? Who is all this for now? She won't live forever, and why should strangers benefit? Perhaps Papa didn't want it, but that didn't mean he would never want it for us."

His ambition surprised me, but he was so determined that I didn't dare challenge it. Perhaps America was changing him faster than it was me, or perhaps it was always in him to be this way.

I nodded. "Okay, Yvon. I'll do what I have to do."

He smiled. "I'm going up to change out of my monkey suit," he said, smiling. "Let's enjoy our dinner."

"Wait," I said. He paused. "There's something else, something more serious."

"What?"

"I wandered into Aunt Effie's office, the one that was surely our grandfather's."

"And?"

"There was a letter on her desk from Anne."

"Anne? And? Jean-Paul?"

"No. It's about . . . us . . . some family secret Anne promised never to reveal, promised only Aunt Effie could reveal it," I said.

He looked up the stairway to be sure Aunt Effie was occupied. "Show me."

After we went to her office, I did. He read it and then put it back in the envelope.

"What do you think it means?" I asked.

He shook his head, his eyes shifting. "I don't know. I wouldn't believe anything she said about us, anyway, Marlena. Ignore it."

"Wait," I said, and opened the bottom drawer. He stepped beside me as I opened the folder and showed him the picture.

"Aunt Pauline was a very pretty girl, and Aunt Effie looks unchanged. I didn't find any pictures of Papa."

"Stop snooping," he said firmly. "She'll find out and be very, very upset. When she wants to show us something, she will. Let's get ready for dinner."

He started out.

When she wants to show us something, she will? Maybe there was never a picture of Papa.

Never a picture of Papa? Even young?

Yvon kept things from me. I knew that.

But he never deliberately lied.

Until now.

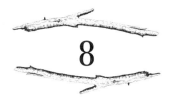

8

For the moment, at least, Aunt Effie had gotten what she had wanted from her sister.

Aunt Pauline was quite subdued and obedient at dinner. She kept her eyes on her food and didn't speak unless Aunt Effie said something to her like "Take your elbows off the table, Pauline" or "Don't chew with your mouth open, Pauline."

"I'm sorry," she said reflexively. I imagined that was something she had said thousands of times, especially to Aunt Effie.

"Pretty soon, Marlena will help you do things properly, Pauline. And I won't be the only one nagging you."

"She will?" Aunt Pauline looked at me with a smile slowly forming. Then she looked down quickly, as if a smile was forbidden at the dinner table.

"She will be learning herself, and she can share what she

learns with you. That," Aunt Effie said, looking at me, "will help reduce my burden. Won't you be happy to share your new social graces and knowledge with Pauline, Marlena?" she asked, her voice syrupy sweet.

Aunt Pauline looked up at me expectantly.

"Yes," I said. "Of course. I'd be happy to help in any way I can."

Yvon's eyes brightened. It was as if my friendly response had opened the floodgates. He immediately began to talk about the business and asked questions. I saw from her reaction that Aunt Effie liked that. I felt oddly forgotten while they talked. It was as if she was shifting Aunt Pauline and me off to the side.

And Yvon didn't look at me once the entire time. He didn't hide how fascinated he was with Aunt Effie's elaboration on his questions. He dropped in unveiled compliments. It was plainly obvious how hard he was trying to please and impress her, and although I knew what he was doing, I couldn't help being annoyed and disappointed. Back in France, Yvon was never one to try to be liked. If you didn't like him as he was, it was too bad. I admired him for his self-confidence and tried to be just like him.

After dinner, he and I were alone in the sitting room. Aunt Effie had gone to see Ella Cornfield, and the twins had brought Aunt Pauline up to her room to prepare for sleep.

"You sounded like you really like her now, Yvon," I said, flopping into the accent chair. He had a commercial real estate brochure in his hand and sat on the settee. He acted like he had not heard me and opened the cover of the brochure.

"I'm surprised at how pleasant you were to her at dinner," I said. "She wasn't particularly nicer to you than she was to me coming here. You can't possibly like her this quickly."

He looked up as if he had just realized I was with him. He shrugged.

"Whether I like her or not doesn't matter. She wants us to be family, Marlena. We'll let her believe whatever she wants, and if you do help her with Pauline now, she'll be more obligated to us. It's all just . . . just good business," he said. "And," he added when I didn't smile with encouragement or satisfaction, "it's not like we have any choice. We talked about this. It's get along or get out, and then what?"

Even though I knew in my heart that he was right, he didn't sound or even look like the brother with whom I had left France. But then again, Mrs. Trafalgar might be absolutely correct, I thought. You can't grow again once you were transplanted until you became well acquainted with the new soil that would nourish you. How could I blame him for doing just that? In his own way, he was still protecting me by accepting and adjusting.

The question bouncing around in my head was, could I do the same thing? Could I ever be anything like the way he was now? Would I ever be able to put our past lives, our beautiful memories, on some shelf while I went on pretending I was happy here? Despite all we had and where we were, I couldn't believe, maybe refused to believe, that we would be happier.

I saw the look of disappointment on his face when I didn't readily agree.

"If you act like a child, she'll treat you like one, Marlena. Being an adult means doing things that are unpleasant for you sometimes. You have to think of the bigger picture. That's something poor Aunt Pauline is incapable of doing," he added. "Don't become like her."

I felt the blood rush into my cheeks. He sounded more like Aunt Effie than like my brother.

"I'm ready to go to sleep," I said. "She can surprise me in the morning with the news of whether Miss Cornfield will be my new tutor or not."

He nodded, but he didn't get up to accompany me. He continued to read the brochure describing some property. Nevertheless, I thought he would realize how disturbed I was the moment I walked away. I expected him to come after me. The French Yvon would, but he didn't. I paused and looked back at the sitting-room doorway. The whole house looked darker. Lights flickered, and shadows began to close in from all corners. Once again, I felt how cold the world we were in was. Tonight it seemed even colder, perhaps because Yvon was moving faster and closer toward thinking of it as our new home.

I turned and continued up. Exhausted from what had been an emotional roller coaster of a day for me, I was happy to go to bed. This particular evening, I felt as if I was sinking into sleep rather than drifting to it. If either Yvon or Aunt Effie had come to my room later to tell me about my new tutor, I did not notice or hear a word.

I tried to get up as early as Yvon did so I could have breakfast with him before he went to the offices, but he was gone by the time I descended. This morning, Aunt Pauline was there, and Aunt Effie, rushing out herself, paused to tell me that Ella Cornfield would be here in an hour to do what Mr. Donald was apparently incapable of doing.

"Don't you have to be here to introduce us?" I asked when she started away.

"For over twenty years, Ella Cornfield ran a school to train girls for business opportunities. She doesn't need to be formally introduced to a new student. She is quite capable of getting you to know who she is quickly and formulating your curriculum. Just be cooperative. If she's a problem, you have a problem," she said with the sharpness of a good fisherman's knife.

"What about Mr. Donald?"

"What about him?"

"What if he shows up?" I asked.

"He won't show up. I had George go to him with an envelope full of money after he took your brother to the office. I paid him what he would have gotten if he had completed the assignment."

"Why? You still don't believe me?"

"Believing you has nothing to do with it. You will learn that whether you are right or not, gossip and accusations always come back at you threefold. No one in Richmond knows who you are yet, Marlena. Many know Mr. Donald."

"Then they should know what he really is," I insisted.

She shrugged. "Perhaps. What they choose to do about it is their business, not ours. Pauline, you stay out of everyone's hair today. It's a very nice day. Emma and Minnie will take you for a walk to the park while Marlena has her lessons. Be sure you go to the bathroom first and listen to what they tell you. Do not go anywhere without their permission. Understood?"

Aunt Pauline didn't speak. She stared at her plate.

"Did you hear me, Pauline?"

"Okay, Effie," she said meekly.

Aunt Effie stared at her a moment and then looked at me.

"She's wandered off and had to be found. One time, I had to get the help of the police. Where she thought she was going I'll never know."

"To see Daddy," Aunt Pauline said quickly.

"You can't see someone who is dead, Pauline. I've explained that to you a thousand times if I've explained it once."

Aunt Pauline looked down again.

Aunt Effie took a deep breath, closed and opened her eyes, and then left. She did look like she was tiring and aging from dealing with her sister. Did I have an ounce of compassion? Right now, I didn't think so. I didn't believe I ever would feel sorry for Aunt Effie.

"What made you think you could see your father, Aunt Pauline?" I asked her as she scooped up the remainder of her scrambled eggs.

She stared aimlessly for a moment. I thought her eyes were as striking as Papa's. Right now, they were the wondrous and innocent eyes of the little girl I had seen in the photograph.

"Daddy told me to go to him whenever I needed something," she said.

"But you know he's passed away, don't you, Aunt Pauline?"

She shook her head and smiled at me, as if I was the one who needed to be handled like a child and not her.

"He's still here," she said. She looked toward the kitchen. The twins had gone in and were talking with Mrs. Trafalgar. "When they lock me in my room, he comes in," she said. "I never tell them," she whispered.

She scooped up the last of her eggs and daintily patted her lips with her napkin.

"Effie didn't tell me to do this," she said, proud of herself for using her napkin correctly. "Daddy did."

"Did you tell Effie that your father comes into your room at night?"

She nodded.

"What did she say?"

"She said . . ." She raised her chin and looked at the ceiling, like someone who wanted to recall the exact words. "She said, 'I'm glad he doesn't come into mine.'"

I stared at her for a moment. She played with her fork and knife and looked at her empty plate. The twins came back in and told her she had to go up to change and reminded her to go to the bathroom so she could go for a walk in the park soon.

"Can Marlena come, too?" she asked.

"No, she has to stay to do her lessons," Minnie said.

"With none of us disturbing her," Emma said. "Mrs. Trafalgar is packing sandwiches for us. We'll have a picnic in the park. You like that."

She looked at them and then turned sharply to me, for a moment looking more like Aunt Effie.

"You come to the picnic," she said. She did sound like Aunt Effie giving orders, but her imitating her sister was almost comical.

"I think I have to stay here and have lunch with Miss Cornfield," I said. "Maybe another time."

Aunt Pauline folded her arms tightly under her bosom and looked like she was going to pout.

I touched her shoulder. "I promise," I said.

She eyed me suspiciously. "I don't like promises," she said. "As Daddy says, 'Promises ain't worth the words you use to make them.'"

"When I promise something, I mean it," I said, smiling. "That's what my mama and papa taught me."

"My brother Beau and his wife," she said, nodding.

"Yes."

She relaxed. The twins began to clear the table quickly. They looked like they were afraid to hear anything else I might say, especially about my parents.

It made me wonder for a moment. Do they or would they spy for Aunt Effie?

Exactly an hour after Aunt Effie had told me she would arrive, Ella Cornfield appeared at the front door. The twins were still upstairs with Aunt Pauline, and Mrs. Trafalgar, who I didn't think did much more than prepare meals anyway, did not come out of the kitchen when the doorbell sounded. It was up to me to greet my new tutor. Was this meant to be my first new test?

I was surprised at how small she was. Ella Cornfield was just an inch or so taller than me. Anyone looking at her from behind would surely mistake her for a young girl. She wore a pair of wire-rimmed glasses with round lenses that were set just a trifle below the bridge of her small but distinctly sharp nose. Standing there with her lips pressed together, she looked like she had a knife slice of a mouth. Her grayish-white complexion brought out the sparkle of her light-green eyes. The wrinkles at the sides of them webbed and ran deep. Her graying dark-brown hair was swept up in a bun. She wore a tailored ruby jacket tight at the hips and a matching long, flared skirt. I admired her stylish high ankle boots. She was carrying a black leather briefcase.

She cleared her throat, more to stop me from staring at her than anything, and said in sharp, clear diction, "I am Miss Cornfield. I suspect you are Marlena, Effie Dawson's niece?"

"Yes, ma'am," I said, and why I did it, I don't know. It was her forceful presence, perhaps, but I curtsied and then stepped back.

When I didn't move in any direction, she raised her eyebrows, in which there were invading gray hairs. "We're not going to work in a hallway, are we?" she said.

"Oh. My aunt has designated the sitting room to be my classroom."

"Then let's get started. My first lesson is to respect time," she said firmly.

"Yes, ma'am."

I led the way. She paused in the doorway and looked about. "You take the settee," she said, nodding at it.

Most everything she said and I suspected she would say sounded more like a command than a request. Unlike Mr. Donald, she didn't ask me any personal questions. She was all business, having me go through some tests to determine my skills. Her tests were a little longer and more elaborate but were still not a major challenge for me, even though she made me very nervous because of the way she stared and watched me, as if she could see my thoughts.

When she stepped closer to me, I could smell the scent of fresh strawberries. Whatever the perfume was, it was strong, as if she had squeezed the juice out of the berries and let it streak down her neck. I wouldn't have noticed it as much if it didn't remind me of strawberries back in France. Mama and I would pick the wild ones, and she would make jam.

"Did you go to a formal school for English?" she asked when she looked over my responses.

"No, ma'am. My mama taught my brother and me how to read and write English."

She nodded and then began the first lessons in various business correspondence formats.

Just when I hoped we would break for lunch, she sat in the upholstered antique oak accent chair that she had moved closer to the table and pressed her fingertips together in cathedral fashion.

"You have been taught well," she said, sounding more like someone making a conclusion than giving my mother a compliment. "I think we can move you along to the necessary skills to begin an internship quickly. You understand what that means?"

"Yes, ma'am. My aunt has told me what she plans for me to do."

I waited for her to say more and then smiled when she didn't. She looked like she was thinking very hard about what to say next.

"I understand you suffered some indignities yesterday."

My first thought was, Aunt Effie told her? Didn't that mean she did believe me? Why did she refuse to show me she did and then go tell Miss Cornfield?

"Yes, I did. It was very unpleasant for me."

"Actually, that was good," she said.

"Pardon, ma'am?"

She finally smiled. "A young girl, a young woman, I should say, with your physical attributes will suffer and endure similar experiences when she enters what is a man's kingdom. I can't teach you the skills necessary to counter and avoid. That is something you have to find in yourself. My only advice is to contain your outrage, be unafraid, and do what is expedient."

"Expedient?"

"Necessary to survive. Make yourself valuable, and you'll have a better chance to do that. Let's continue," she said.

She was clearly not interested in lunch, and Mrs. Trafalgar

did not appear in the doorway to tell us anything was prepared and ready. I did get hungry and was on the verge of asking her about it, when she surprised me by suddenly standing up and declaring that today's lessons were over. She outlined our schedule for the weeks ahead, gave me my homework, mainly in grammar exercises and spelling, and then started out. I followed her to the door.

"I thought you were going to have lunch with me and go through the dining etiquette," I said. Perhaps I sounded too disappointed or critical.

She stepped back and drew the corners of her mouth back so hard that it looked like the knife that cut the image of her mouth had continued into her cheeks. Her eyebrows were up and her eyes wide.

"I didn't mean to sound like I was complaining," I immediately added.

"I'm an academic. I'm here for one purpose: to prepare you for work, not social events. Miss Dawson will either instruct you in what she feels necessary or find some . . . someone else for that. However, I will have Miss Dawson arrange for us to have something to eat informally in the future. Do the work I have outlined for you so we can move ahead rapidly. Any other questions?"

"No, ma'am."

She almost smiled. Then she looked up at the entryway ceiling and chandelier and nodded. "I remember your grandfather. He gave me the impossible task of trying to educate your aunt Pauline. But he was the sort of man who wouldn't accept failure. He'd rather ignore it. I don't know you at all well enough to be sure," she continued, "but I don't think you'll be anything like him."

She started toward her car and driver. I backed into the house and closed the door.

Yes, I thought, *I won't be like my grandfather, but I'm not sure I can say the same for my brother.*

As if they had been watching the house from somewhere across the way, the twins brought Aunt Pauline home a minute or so after Miss Cornfield had left.

Mrs. Trafalgar had left a platter of cheeses, tomatoes, lettuce, and bread with a jug of fresh cold water on the formally set dining-room table, so I sat down and began eating. The twins looked surprised that I was by myself, but Pauline was so excited she wanted to eat another lunch. They tried to get her to leave and let me eat.

"It's fine," I told them, and they went into the kitchen. "How was your picnic, Aunt Pauline?" I asked her. She did still act hungry.

"I didn't like it," she said.

"Why not?"

"I wanted to get up and go to the pond, but they wouldn't let me go. They thought I'd get wet. They sat beside me so I couldn't just get up and run away."

"Oh? Why would you want to run away?"

She looked angrily at the doorway to the kitchen and then leaned over to whisper. "Daddy was there. He waved to me and wanted me to take a walk with him."

I stared at her. She was so confident of what she was saying that a part of me was wondering if I should believe her.

"Did you tell Emma or Minnie?"

She sat back. "Many times," she said. "They never believe me when I tell them I saw Daddy."

"Well, next time you see your father, you tell me," I said, and patted her hand.

"I will," she said, smiling. She looked overjoyed with the possibility.

I wished I was as easy to please.

Later, when Yvon came home, he hurried to ask me how my new tutor was. He looked just as excited as he had the day before, anxious to get me to talk so he could describe his day.

"It went well," I said. "I'm finishing the homework she gave me. I don't think it's easy to do, but I managed to like her."

"Why isn't it easy to like her?"

"She's all business."

"Time is money to these people. We can't argue with that," he said.

I told him what she had advised me and what she had said about our grandfather.

He thought a moment. "Well," he said, "I don't think he ignored what he had to do to make a successful business. He was a leader in this industry. Do you know they have his picture in the city hall, among those of other very important businessmen who helped build this city into what it is and is becoming? We have a lot to be proud of, Marlena. People could be jealous or upset that he didn't think highly enough of them. I'm sure he was very selective about whom he chose as friends. I've only been there two days, but I can tell you this . . . you either make friends or make profit. That's the American way."

"And you like that?"

"I'm going to do what I have to do to make sure you and I have the best of everything. That's what I like. But I am making new friends at the company who might be of some advantage to me.

I might go out with a couple of them one night. We share a lot in common now. It's not a bad life to have, Marlena. You'll see."

It wasn't only that Yvon sounded different; he looked different. It was as if he had found a way to make good use of his anger and his skepticism. He was in a world that put value on all that, a world that made those things seem more like strength to admire than behavior and feelings to pity.

"Why did Papa walk away from it all, then, Yvon? Why couldn't he do both, paint and be in business?"

He looked like he was going to say something and then shifted his eyes to look away.

"Do you have any idea?"

"I don't know exactly. What difference does it make now? We're here; we have no place else to go."

"We could go home," I said. "That's my dream."

"Go home? Where I could be a cobbler and you could be a seamstress, maybe marry a fisherman and have children draining you of your youth and hope?"

"That didn't happen to Mama and Papa, did it?"

"They were special. It happens to most. Let's not argue about it. We're both on the right paths. I can't wait for you to be working at our company." He smiled. "Then you'll understand everything."

"Our company," I muttered.

"That's what it is, what it will be, Marlena." He smiled again. "Find a way to get used to being rich." He waited for me to smile.

"There's something else happening here, Yvon. There's something . . . that might hurt us," I predicted.

He pulled himself back, a look of dissatisfaction filling his face before I could say anything else. "*Oui*," he said. "I know."

"You do? What?"

"Failure," he said, and went up to change for dinner.

I watched him ascend, feeling a new emptiness inside. With Yvon finding friends, I'd have only poor Aunt Pauline. How would I deal with such loneliness? Whether I liked it or not now, I had to become part of the business, become part of something besides myself.

I heard the front door opening and turned to see Aunt Effie enter.

"Well?" she asked without a hello.

I knew what she wanted to hear. "I think I'll learn quickly with her," I said.

She nodded. "Of course you will. I didn't think it would take long for you and your brother to realize what you have to do. I can't wait for when I don't have to be the one to convince you," she added. "How is my sister?"

It was on the tip of my tongue to tell her about her references to their father so I could see what her reaction truly was, but for now that felt like a betrayal.

"She had a second lunch with me. Miss Cornfield did not want to work on dining etiquette. She said—"

"I know, I know. It was hard enough to get her to come out of retirement to do what she is doing with you. We'll worry about social events later."

She started away and then paused.

"Your father was a very good student, too," she said. I was about to smile when she added, "What a waste."

Before I could give her a sharp reply, she turned and started up the stairs.

I almost didn't tell Yvon what she had said. I anticipated

him saying something like *Ignore her. Let's just lay claim to what is ours.* He didn't say that when I told him, but he didn't say anything nasty about her, either. He just nodded as if he had expected it.

Expecting was one thing, but tolerating was another. Something important between us was slipping away. I didn't know exactly what it was, but I could feel it, feel the widening gap. I tried not to think about it during the weeks that followed.

Miss Cornfield adhered to my aunt's plan for me and began an intense concentration on my learning shorthand. For hours over the next few weeks, she would pace the room and read from business manuals and texts while I scrambled to keep up with her. She wasn't nasty or unpleasant about my mistakes or my failing to keep up. Instead, she slowed down, explained, and kept me concentrating so hard that I was truly exhausted at the end of the day's lessons. Teaching me the symbols and abbreviations for words and common phrases surprisingly brought me to the point where I was writing as quickly as she spoke.

Meanwhile, as time passed, Yvon was given more and more responsibility at the company office. He began to accompany the other agents to evaluate properties. One night after dinner, when he went on and on excitedly about a building in Richmond that was perfect for offices to rent, I sat with my pen in hand and practiced shorthand, copying down each and every word he had said. At one point, he stopped talking and accused me of ignoring him.

"You don't realize how important something like this is, Marlena."

I looked up at him. "Yes, I do, Yvon," I said, and then read off my notepad, reciting back to him every word he had said. Aunt Pauline, who had been sitting with us as she often did, began laughing when Yvon did, even though she had no idea why she should.

"That's amazing," he said. "Does Aunt Effie know how far you've come, what you can do?"

"I'm sure Miss Cornfield is keeping her up on my progress," I said.

Weeks later, after we had finished our main course at dinner, Aunt Effie put her silverware down, clasped her hands, and announced that Miss Cornfield thought I was doing "exceedingly well," and that it wouldn't be that much longer before I was ready to intern at the offices. "You will start to earn a small salary, and that will improve as you gain more experience," she said.

"That's wonderful," Yvon said, and looked at me, urging me with his eyes to sound appreciative and excited.

"Yes, thank you," I said, more to please Yvon than my aunt Effie.

Then I looked at Aunt Pauline. She understood that something significant was happening, but she wasn't quite sure what it was. I had made it a point to spend most of my free time with her, reading to her from novels and listening to music on the new disc-playing machine Aunt Effie had bought. Sometimes Pauline would sing along, and she soon began to be able to sing all by herself if I started one of the songs we had heard repeatedly.

I had told Aunt Effie and Yvon how beautiful Aunt Pauline's voice was and how she had the ability to mimic the recordings.

"Maybe Aunt Pauline can sing something for us to celebrate," I said.

Aunt Pauline did look confused but excited.

"Her best one is 'Sweet Adeline,'" I said. "Aunt Pauline, would you sing that for us?"

"Really," Aunt Effie said dryly, but as if I had pushed a button, Aunt Pauline sat back and began to sing.

Yvon smiled, but Aunt Effie looked at her in the strangest way. It wasn't with any sisterly pride, nor was it embarrassment. It was more like pity, which was at least some show of real feeling for her, I thought.

When she was finished, Yvon and I clapped.

It was very quiet for a moment, and then Aunt Effie said, "She used to sing for our father."

Aunt Pauline's eyes lit up. "I still do, Effie," she said.

Aunt Effie looked at the ceiling, turned her head, sighed deeply, and stood.

Before she could leave, I spoke up. "I'd like to take Aunt Pauline for a picnic tomorrow if the weather permits," I said. "I promised her I would."

"Take her," Aunt Effie said. She said it as if she was saying, *Take her away forever, for all I care.*

She left. Yvon smiled and reached for my hand.

"We're going to make it in America," he said.

I wished I could be half as happy about that as he was, but all I could do was flash a smile, a smile that I sensed in the deepest place in my heart was destined to fade.

Perhaps forever.

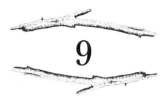

9

The ugliness that hid in the dark shadows of our new home began to emerge. Mama once told me that we spend most of our early lives fighting off sad endings. It was better to end with a laugh than a cry. But laughter does wear thin as you grow older. It seemed that maturity called for less optimism, more realism.

When I spent time recalling our lives in Villefranche and saw myself in my memory, I saw someone with so much vulnerability. How oblivious I was, innocent and protected. Maybe Yvon should have been more forceful and shattered the bubble in which I lived and played. Perhaps he shouldn't have sheltered me so well. I would have been better prepared for what was to come.

Now that I thought more about it, I realized that was what

Mama and Papa had been doing. Perhaps Papa, who created his own world on canvas, thought he could do the same with our lives. They both thought they could keep the dark secrets in their coffins forever. Maybe they were still dreamers, too.

If our new home was anything, it was a house without dreams. There was ambition, ruthless ambition, but that wasn't the same thing. Ambition swam in the sea of reality; dreams floated above it, secure in your imagination. It was what let you see yourself as being prettier, happier, and more loved. Aunt Effie never dreamed; she planned and plotted and, in the end, demanded.

Right from the start, she had given me, if not Yvon, the impression that she thought we were too protected, too insulated. We were long overdue to be sent out naked and alone. Maybe she was jealous and wished she, too, could have simply picked up and run off to some fairy-tale world like Papa had. In time, I would see that inside she was as knotted and as twisted as the ugly truths she hoped would stay buried in the darkness. Reluctantly, I'd have to admit that she was a victim as well, but she lived in self-denial. It was her own fault.

In her way, she would teach me one very important truth: before you could survive in the adult world, you had to master how to lie to yourself. Otherwise, it was all too much, and you would crumble under the weight. That crumbling would begin today.

After breakfast Saturday morning, Aunt Pauline and I helped Mrs. Trafalgar prepare our picnic lunch. She fried some chicken, made some potato salad, wrapped up some home-made biscuits and some chocolate chip cookies. She put apple juice in some jars and made sure we had enough napkins, knives, and forks. While she worked with her thin, vein-ribbed hands, she told us about her family picnics and how much she and her five sisters and brothers looked forward to them on weekends.

She paused and in a dreamy voice expressed her thoughts more to herself than to us when she said, "We wasn't just gettin' out of the house; we was gettin' out of the world we was in. For a few hours, at least, we could be as happy as new bluebirds."

Neither Aunt Pauline nor I said anything. Mrs. Trafalgar looked like she was going to cry, but then she snapped out of her musing quickly and smiled.

"Not the same thing for y'all. Y'all just have fun."

The twins were busy with Saturday housecleaning. Aunt Effie was in her office with the door closed as usual. Yvon went off to meet some of the other young men and, I suspected, women from the company, to go cycling and have their own bought picnic lunch somewhere just outside Richmond. Either it never occurred to him to ask me along, or he felt I couldn't leave Aunt Pauline after promising to take her on a picnic. Maybe he thought I was still too young for them. Whatever his reasons, I did anticipate him saying something more about it than simply "I'll be meeting some friends." But he said nothing else and left before we did.

I went up to Aunt Pauline's room to help her choose the right clothes to wear and pin her hair back. She was obviously more excited than she had been when she was going to the park with Minnie and Emma.

"Didn't Aunt Effie ever take you to the park, Aunt Pauline?" I asked her as I finished with her hair. "Or my father?"

She paused to think about it and shook her head.

"Effie doesn't like the park. She doesn't like bugs or sitting on the grass. She thinks it's a waste of time, and Beau had friends to be with all the time."

"Aunt Effie didn't think it was a waste of time when she was younger, too, did she?"

She gave me that look that often made me wonder if she was smarter than she pretended to be, the look that said, *What a silly question.*

"Effie was never younger," she said. I didn't know whether to laugh or not. She looked so deadly serious. Then she leaned in to whisper, even though we were up in her room alone. "Effie never had a doll."

She put on her gored light-blue skirt and what I had chosen as her best blouse, a two-tone striped floral embroidered cotton. The skirt looked quite faded, creased, and even a little stained, but it was the only one of those she had that I thought she should wear to go to the park.

"I don't have to wear a corset," she said proudly. "But Effie does."

I smiled, but I was still thinking about what she had said. "Aunt Effie never had a doll?"

"I wanted to give her one of mine, but she wouldn't take it. She said dolls were silly. She told me we have to be with real people and not talk to something that only talks back in your head. Why have a toy tea set when you could have real tea in real cups?"

"Didn't your mother and father give her any toys?"

"Daddy said it would be a waste of money. But not for me. He gave me all my toys and dolls. When Mommy was sick, Daddy had to be Mommy and give me whatever she would and do whatever she would do. That's why he worked at home or took me with him sometimes."

"What about Effie? Didn't she help? She did tell us she did."

"She didn't like to do anything but give orders. Daddy said if women could be soldiers, she'd be a general."

I smiled. It was amazing just how many things her father had said that she had committed to memory. He must have been a very impressive man, I thought.

"I have to get my park hat," she said, and went to her closet.

Although it was well worn, I was surprised she had such a fancy hat. It had a large wired brim with two layers of stiff, shiny net with black straw stitched edging. Faded and well-beaten-down pink and cream flowers were woven through.

"Who gave you that hat?"

"Daddy gave me this when I was twelve," she said. "Because I was crying."

"Why were you crying?"

"I got my monthlies, and it hurt and hurt. The hat was once my mother's. Effie thought she should have it, but he gave it to me. Effie said she didn't cry when she got her monthlies. Effie never cries."

"Not that you can see," I muttered.

She stood at attention like someone ready for inspection. "Am I ready?" she asked when she put on her hat.

"What? Oh, yes. Let's go. You'll have to show me the way."

"I will?" She clapped. "Minnie and Emma never let me."

"Well, I want you to," I said, and we left her room, descended, picked up our lunch basket from Mrs. Trafalgar, and started out.

Aunt Effie finally appeared. She called to us as I opened the door. "If you lose her, you'll have to find her yourself or not come home," she warned. Then she returned to her office.

I stood there for a moment wondering if I had taken on too much.

"We won't get lost," Aunt Pauline said. "Daddy will watch over us."

We started out. I was relieved to see that Aunt Pauline actually did know the way. As we walked, she recited rules that had been driven into her, rules about crossing streets, talking to strangers, and picking things off the sidewalk and street. She related them in a singsong way, as if they had all been told to her in a nursery rhyme.

When we reached the park, she directed us to a small knoll that looked out over the pond. She said her father once told her it was their spot, the Dawson spot. It was quite perfect, with a nice wave of shade cast by the nearby hemlock tree. The fall day was a little warmer than I had anticipated, but there was a slight cool breeze occasionally coming across the water. Elongated clouds looked like floating cotton. There were birds everywhere. The fall scene was still bursting with life. It was more like the start of spring.

"It's not as big as the ocean," Aunt Pauline said when I had spread out the blanket and we both sat.

People were dressed in fancy day clothes, strolling alongside the water, women with parasols, men with top hats. Families with little children all holding hands reminded me of the four of us taking our walks along the shore.

"No, it's not. You can't see across the ocean, and there are waves."

"It's better by the ocean, even though Effie didn't like it."

"Yes, I think so. Did Aunt Effie at least go for walks with you and your father when you were both older?"

"No," she said. "It was just Daddy and me. Sometimes I fell asleep on his lap right here," she said. She gazed around as if she was really looking for him.

"And what was Aunt Effie doing while you were out with your father?"

"She was reading at home."

"Your father didn't make her come, at least for fresh air?"

She shook her head.

"Daddy didn't have to make Effie do anything. He said she did everything right all by herself since she was four years old. Anyway, she was too bossy and told him what he should do all the time. She even told him what to wear before he went to work. Sometimes he did, and sometimes he didn't. That's why he liked me more."

"I bet," I said. "And my father, your brother, Beau. He was always with friends? He never walked with your father and you?"

She looked away. I didn't think she had heard me, but before I could ask again, she said, "Beau ran away and never came back."

"Why did he run away?"

She turned away and threaded her opened fingers through the grass, breaking a blade and putting it between her lips.

"Daddy showed me how to do this," she said, and made it sing.

"Yes, I used to do that, too."

"Oh, you did? How smart. Who taught you?"

V. C. Andrews

"My father. Your brother, Beau. Why did he run away and never come back?"

She leaned back and looked up at the sky. "I'm not supposed to say."

"I think that means say to strangers, but I'm your niece and Beau was my father, so you can tell me."

She looked at me and decided. "He saw Daddy giving me a bath, and he got very angry. He screamed at Daddy and shook his fists. Daddy screamed back at him, and they almost had a fight."

"Why?"

She didn't answer. I thought a moment.

"Do you remember how old you were?"

"It was after my monthlies," she said, nodding.

I felt the heat rise into my face. "Why did your father have to give you a bath when you were that old?"

She started to play with the blade of grass again and then stopped. "Because he wanted me to be pretty," she said. "And he had to teach me what Mommy would have taught me if she was still alive, because Effie wouldn't."

"About what?" I asked, my voice just a little above a whisper.

She looked around to be sure no one could hear her and then leaned toward me to whisper. "About sex and sin," she said. My heart stopped and started. "Oh, no!" she cried.

"What?"

She put her hands over her face and then drew them down slowly as she looked off to the right.

"What is it, Aunt Pauline?"

"Daddy. He's mad that I told you," she said. "He looked at me, shook his head, and then rushed away. What if he doesn't come back?"

192

He very well might not, I thought.

Was that a good thing or a bad thing for her? I was suddenly very frightened.

For both of us.

Even though what she had told me hovered over every thought and word I said, I talked about other things, things I had loved doing in Villefranche. I made it all sound like fairy tales and had her rapt attention. *Do anything, say anything*, I told myself, *to keep her from saying any more about my grandfather*. I didn't want to hear any of those details. My imagination was off and running as it was. Now I thought I understood why Papa wouldn't want to return for his own father's funeral. How amazing it was that he was able to keep all this buried inside him. He never let it turn him bitter. I felt guilty for pushing and pursuing him to tell me more about his father and mother.

The worst thing was that I was terribly conflicted about what Aunt Pauline had revealed. Should I tell Yvon this? Should I ask Aunt Effie about it? How angry would she get? Could Aunt Pauline have made it up? And yet, could I keep this buried? Wouldn't Yvon realize something when he looked at my face? He usually read my thoughts well. Why did I ask so many questions? he would say. This was my own fault, and yet I felt I understood more about Papa now and why he didn't want to talk at all about his family. Yvon should be grateful that I'd learned all this.

However, I had no doubt that if the roles were reversed, he wouldn't tell me. He'd still be protecting me. Maybe he never would tell. Was that wrong, even though his motives were drawn out of his love for me?

"I'm hungry," Aunt Pauline said when I was too quiet.

193

"Oh, me, too," I said, even though I had no appetite. I began taking out our food.

She was very occupied with it and watching young children playing on the grass. If one tumbled, she laughed and told me she would always do that, too. I watched her when she looked at them, smiling at her own memories. She had such a pretty face, the face of a child. It was as if time had not touched it. Maybe because her mind had stopped growing, her face, which was the window to her thoughts, had stopped changing as well. Put a child's bonnet on her, take her picture from the neck up, and you couldn't tell her age.

Whereas aging wasn't very kind to Aunt Effie. Maybe that was because she lived a life more or less modeled on her father now. I hoped Yvon understood that rich people could have twisted and troubled lives, too, maybe even more so. He had become so infatuated with wealth, but the more you had, the more you had to protect, especially when it came to being admired and respected. Kings don't often blush, but when they do, I imagined it surely looks like every ounce of blood has gone to their cheeks.

Aunt Pauline lay back, resting her head on my lap. It surprised me, but I didn't move. I stroked her hair and watched her drift into a soft repose. Someone had a toy sailboat on the pond, and someone else was trying to get a kite into the wind. I heard children laughing, saw how happy and loving their parents were, and I wondered why the world was full of happiness all around us, right beside such sadness.

When Aunt Pauline woke and had to go to the bathroom, I found her a public one, and then I told her we had to start for home. The clouds had been gathering anyway, and the air had become cooler, with a stiffer breeze. For a moment, she looked confused about the route, but fortunately, I recalled it all. Aunt Effie's threat had loomed the whole way, so I mentally tied a red ribbon around some things to look for.

The house was quiet when we arrived, but the twins came quickly from the kitchen.

"Miss Effie wanted us to take her for her bath," Minnie said.

"As soon as she returned from the park," Emma added. "Come along, now, Miss Pauline."

"Don't want you to," Aunt Pauline told her, and pulled her arm out of Emma's hand. "Marlena will help me with my bath."

"Oh, dear," Minnie said, bringing her hand to her mouth.

"Dear, dear," Emma said. "She's never like this."

"It's not a major crisis, Emma. I'm glad to help her."

"But . . . Miss Effie's orders . . ." Minnie said. "She had to go on an errand and told us before she left that we must do it as we usually do."

"Blame it on me," I said, and directed Aunt Pauline to the stairs. "Your sister is an ogre," I muttered. "No wonder your father thought she was bossy as a child, and no wonder she's never found a husband."

Aunt Pauline giggled. "You're just like your father," she said. "He would say the same thing about Effie."

Comparing me to my father was the best thing she had done all day.

The Brown twins didn't tell Aunt Effie, and she didn't ask them. She was too impressed with my efficiency spending the day with Aunt Pauline and then seeing her dressed for dinner, her hair brushed and very neatly pinned, and in the sitting room, where I was reading to her from *The Camp Fire Girls in the Outside World.*

"Well," Aunt Effie said from the doorway, "I see today was successful. She didn't get lost."

It was on the tip of my tongue to say, *Oh, yes, it was very successful. I learned why my father ran away from home.* But I thought I should wait for Yvon.

"It was a pleasant day for both of us."

"Your brother is not back yet?"

"No," I said.

She didn't look upset about it. She looked pleased. "I hope you are able to make friends through the company as quickly as he has when you start working there," she said. "We'll have dinner shortly."

She left, but I still stared at the doorway.

"Don't stop reading because Effie came home," Aunt Pauline said.

"No. I won't," I said, smiling, and started to read again.

Yvon did not come home for dinner. If Aunt Effie was upset about that, she didn't show it. In fact, she was in a particularly good mood. She revealed something about a good deal on a building she had wanted the company to sell for quite a while.

"It's the first deal your brother had anything to do with," she told me. "Now that he has a taste for it, we'll see what he can accomplish. I am hoping that after this week's lessons in shorthand, et cetera, Miss Cornfield will decide you're ready to start your internship. It will be a little more involved than working with your aunt Pauline," she said.

I had yet to see her look at her younger sister with any feeling of love. If it wasn't pity, it was disgust.

"I think she'll be upset when I'm not here," I suggested.

Aunt Pauline wasn't really listening and didn't know we were talking about her.

"What of it? I didn't bring you to America to be a babysitter."

"But at dinner you said you wanted help with Aunt Pauline."

I wondered if she could be jealous of how Aunt Pauline had attached herself to me. I was more like the older sister that Aunt Effie was supposed to be.

"I don't mind you doing what you can while you're learning, but I could hire any young woman for wages slightly above a street cleaner's for that if I felt it was necessary. You're here to assume some of the responsibility I had to assume at the company when I was even younger than you are now. That's why I'm spending so much on your business education. Why would I need Ella Cornfield to train you to babysit?"

It took all my self-control to keep from saying anything about Aunt Pauline's revelations. She wanted us to eat faster so I would continue reading to her.

"You eat the way I taught you to eat, Pauline. You don't gobble your food," Aunt Effie said.

"The general," Aunt Pauline muttered.

I did all that I could to keep from laughing aloud.

"What's that?" Aunt Effie said.

Aunt Pauline was silent. Aunt Effie looked at me with suspicious eyes, and then we all just ate in silence.

It wasn't until a good two hours or so later that Yvon came home. His face was red from being in the sun so much, and his eyes were filled with excitement. I hadn't seen him like this since he had driven Papa's new car. Pauline had been brought up to bed. I wasn't sure where Aunt Effie was. I was in the sitting room reading *Anne of Green Gables*. I looked up when he stepped in. He had his jacket folded over his right arm and his shirt opened at the collar. His hair was a little wild, like it would be if he had been caught in the wind.

"I think I cycled fifty miles today," he began. "We found this beautiful mountainside from which you could look down on all of Richmond city. And Daniel Thomas brought along some great apple cider."

I didn't react. I was simply staring at him. He saw the look on my face that I was hoping he would see.

"What happened? Didn't you get to go out with Aunt Pauline?"

"Yes, I did. You had better come in and sit, Yvon. I have things to tell you."

"Did Aunt Effie do something mean again?" He grimaced in anticipation.

"No. At least, not to me today."

"Then what is it?" he asked, sounding more annoyed than curious.

"Please," I said, nodding at the chair. He looked back and then came in and flopped on the chair.

"So?"

"I think I know now why Papa changed his name. Aunt Pauline told me why Papa ran away from his family."

He smirked and pulled his head back. "Aunt Pauline? She would forget to put on her second stocking if it weren't for the Brown twins. How could you believe anything she said?"

"I believed her, Yvon. She didn't want to tell me. I had to convince her to do so."

He sighed and leaned forward. "Okay, what did she tell you?"

I described the scene Papa had witnessed, quoting Aunt Pauline's terms, *sex and sin*.

He stared at me blankly for a moment. "That's disgusting, Marlena."

"I know."

"She had to have imagined it or had some sort of dream or something. Our grandfather? He was a giant in the business world here."

"That wouldn't have anything to do with what he did to her. It helps us understand why Papa ran away from his family, why he brought Mama to France, and why he couldn't stand his name."

"That's not the reason," he said quickly, and then pressed his lips together as if he hadn't wanted those words to come out of his mouth.

"Well, what is it, then?"

"It's not that, I'm sure. That's ridiculous," he insisted, and stood. "I hope you didn't mention this to Aunt Effie."

"No. I wanted to tell you first."

"Good. Forget it."

"But—"

"After what you told her about Mr. Donald, she's going to think you're a bit weird."

"What? I didn't make up any of it."

"I know. I know. It's what she might think."

"Who cares about what she might think? Didn't you hear what I said?"

He sighed deeply. "What would we do about it now, anyway, Marlena? He's dead, and so is Papa. You think if we told people, it would help Pauline. If people heard that, they'd look at her as more of a freak."

"She's not a freak, Yvon."

"I know she's not a freak, but it's how people see her."

"It's how Aunt Effie sees her, but how do you know how other people see her? Mrs. Trafalgar doesn't treat her as if she's a freak."

"I learned it from some of the other employees, the questions they ask, things they say. Mr. Simon certainly does," he emphasized.

"You and I should ask Aunt Effie to meet with us and tell us the truth," I said. "If you ask, too, she won't be able to ignore it."

He thought a moment.

"Not now. Maybe after some time goes by and we're more part of everything . . ."

"You mean part of the business. What are you afraid of? You think if we reveal we know the truth, she'll rather we leave?"

He was silent. "We don't know the truth," he finally said. "Be patient, and for now, do what she asks."

"*Tu avez changé,*" I said. "You've changed."

"Yes, I have," he said. "I've grown up. I'm going to get something to eat and go to bed."

I watched him walk out and then let myself sink back on the settee.

This house, I thought, *this house and all the secrets in it are possessing us.*

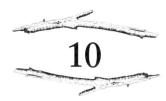

10

Sometimes I would catch Aunt Effie staring at me, and I'd think she realized I knew something. Her eyes would take on that narrow, suspicious look, and when I looked back at her, she quickly would shift them to gaze at something else. Each time, I was tempted to ask her, *Did I do something wrong? Is something wrong?* I hoped that would start a conversation that would lead to what Aunt Pauline had told me. But Yvon's warnings about not upsetting things were stronger than my curiosity. He was all I had. I didn't want to disappoint him so deeply.

I also wondered if Aunt Pauline, either innocently or because she felt it was necessary, had told Aunt Effie about the things she had said to me and done with me. For most of her life, Aunt Pauline was under Aunt Effie's total control. Did she fear her or love her more? Did she love her at all? What was love to someone like Aunt Pauline? Was she capable of having feelings for a man? Did my grandfather destroy that? I knew she was fond of me and wanted to be with me, but could she ever love me as family? Could Aunt Effie?

What made everything more difficult for me, and I supposed Yvon, was coming from a world of love to this dark place in which money and power were held to be more important than affection. Aunt Effie never made an effort to hug or kiss her sister, and Aunt Pauline seemed too frightened of the idea. It was as if we came from a world where flowers bloomed to a world where only weeds could grow. Would we brighten up this home or bitterly add more darkness to it?

My lessons with Ella Cornfield continued for another two weeks. Yvon began going out more often with his friends, which I gradually realized had narrowed down to Daniel Thomas's sister Karen. She didn't work at the company. She helped their mother and father in their bakery business on West Broad Street. I first knew he was seeing her when he brought home a bag of cupcakes and then told me all about how they had met through Daniel and how delightful she was.

"You've gone out with her?"

"Yes, and picnics, too."

"Only with her?"

"And the bees and bugs," he said, laughing.

"Is she prettier than Marion Veil?" I asked him.

"In a different way," he said.

"How can a girl be prettier in a different way?"

He thought a moment and said, "She's not as obvious about it. Her good looks sneak up on you."

"Sounds like you're making excuses for her not being prettier," I said. I couldn't help being annoyed. He had developed this relationship without my having the slightest hint.

"Marion always was sure to let you know she was pretty, Marlena. She was, but that was what really kept me from being as crazy about her as everyone expected I should be, even you. Mama taught us why vanity is really weakness and leads to sin and unhappiness. Did you forget that already?" he snapped back at me.

"No."

"Then why do you have to be so snippy and critical? You haven't even met her."

"I'm sorry," I said. "Will I ever meet her?"

"Of course you will. I'll take you for an ice cream soda this weekend, and we'll stop at their bakery."

"Will we take Aunt Pauline, too?"

"Maybe," he said. He thought a moment and then said, "But I don't want you getting her talking about the bath incident. Can you imagine if she brought that up in front of strangers?"

"I won't. I haven't mentioned it to her, and she hasn't mentioned it since."

"Good." He looked a little guilty for a moment and then said, "It's not that I don't care about her. Just the opposite. It could be painful for her, even though she might not show it. Maybe those nightmares are sleeping, and you or anyone bringing her back to the memories would revive them." He nodded, agreeing with himself. "There's no value in our forcing her to relive it. Grandfather Dawson is dead and gone. There's no one to punish except the person he victimized. Right?"

Before I could respond, he said, "Good. Happier things are ahead, anyway. For everyone," he added, and hugged me.

At dinners now, he and Aunt Effie talked a lot of business. I tried to be as interested and even asked a question when I thought of one. Yvon enjoyed answering it, but Aunt Effie looked more upset than happy about my interrupting to ask what I'm sure she considered simple things.

But shouldn't I? Why was she having me trained to work at the company if she didn't want me that interested? My thoughts and opinions didn't matter. The more I listened to her, the more I realized she had the attitude of a man when it came to giving women more responsibility. At times, I wondered if she didn't resent herself.

Later, I told Yvon what I thought, and he tilted his head, considered the idea, and nodded.

"Could be," he said. "She certainly lets Mr. Simon speak for her most of the time, as if she realizes everyone will listen more to a man. Sometimes she doesn't come out of her office all day." He considered it a little more and smiled. "That's why she's pushing me to take on more and more, maybe. Good for us."

"Does she know you have a girlfriend?"

"I don't doubt it. She seems to know everything that goes on around her."

"And?"

"She hasn't said anything. It's almost as if she expects it, Marlena."

"Why would she expect it?"

He didn't answer.

"Yvon?"

"I don't know. It's the way she thinks about me," he said quickly, irritably. "Stop inventing new worries."

But it was a new worry. Would Aunt Effie design his life? Would she do the same to me?

That weekend, I did meet Karen Thomas and almost reluctantly felt myself agree with Yvon about her good looks and humility. We had gone out without Aunt Pauline, who Aunt Effie had decided should help the twins with washing clothes.

"If she has no basic skills at all, she'll continue to be a lump on everyone's back" was her justification.

At the time, I was more interested in meeting Yvon's girlfriend than starting a new argument. Anyway, Aunt Pauline actually looked happy that she would be doing something. They didn't even permit her to go into the kitchen and butter a piece of bread. She had to ask for it. Suddenly, now Aunt Effie wanted her to develop some independence. Was it because we were here and we could see how poorly she treated her?

Yvon stopped first to buy me an ice cream soda, just so he could prepare me for meeting Karen.

"She doesn't know all that much about us yet," he explained. "I mean, she knows what happened to Mama and Papa, but she doesn't know that Papa ran away from his family, none of that." He was silent a moment. I knew he was hesitating to add something.

"What?"

"She thinks I really wanted to come here and be an American businessman."

"I'd believe it now," I said.

He looked at me curiously and then laughed. "Don't make it sound like I was planning a murder. We can't help becoming rich, Marlena. It's not a sin."

Maybe it wasn't, but for reasons I did not understand, it often felt like it.

The bakery was only a short walk from where we had our sodas. Karen had just finished with a customer. Her face exploded in a smile when she realized Yvon had brought me to meet her. She was pretty, with her velvety black hair and almond-shaped gray eyes. She had a small, perfect nose, soft-looking puffy lips, and a dazzlingly bright smile. She was about my height. She blushed when Yvon complimented her by saying she looked perfectly at home among delicious sweet things. I was quite surprised at his gushing. It was so uncharacteristic of the Yvon I knew in France.

Karen insisted I taste her father's new chocolate almond cookie and seemed very interested in my opinion.

"It's fantastic," I said.

"Thank you. My father will be so pleased to hear that. He says the opinion of younger people is more important when it comes to cookies and cakes." She laughed. "It's true. They drag their parents in and make them buy more than they normally would."

"That's perfect," Yvon said. "And guys my age would be drawn in to have you serve them."

"Oh, go on with you, Yvon Dawson," she said, but smiled at me.

She then brought her father out front to meet us. He had been in the back baking and still wore his apron. I saw she had inherited his eyes and hair color. He was as tall as Papa, with as friendly a smile. I was surprised at how much he knew about France, until he revealed he had been in the navy when he was younger and been stationed in Marseilles for a while.

"Never quite got as far down the coast as I wanted, but I could see it was very beautiful."

Later, on the way home, Yvon talked continually about Karen and how well read she was. He said she knew all the famous novels and kept up with what was popular today.

"You love to read, so you'll enjoy spending time with her, and when you do, you'll learn a lot about Richmond, too. She and Daniel were born here. There were so many changes while she was growing up, and she remembers it all." He went on and on singing her praises. He had never talked about any girl in France, including Marion, as enthusiastically. As Jean-Paul would say, *He sounds love-smacked.*

"You don't have to convince me anymore, Yvon. She's very nice, nicer than Marion Veil."

He laughed. I couldn't help being happy for him. It was just that I couldn't completely drown out the fear I had about one day losing him completely to someone else. As usual, he read my thoughts and feelings.

"Someday, maybe sooner than you think, you'll have a boyfriend, Marlena. When you start working, earning a little money, buying yourself nicer things, meeting more people . . . it's all out there waiting for you.

"We're going to have a good life here," he concluded with almost angry determination.

Maybe he was right, I thought. Maybe I should stop thinking about what we had lost and instead, like him, think of what we will have gained.

The following week, Miss Cornfield and Aunt Effie decided I was ready to go to work at the company. My assignment was to shadow Daniel Thomas's secretary, Doris Munday, who was a twenty-year-old woman married to an electric-trolley-car operator. I had no way of knowing at the time, but Aunt Effie, who made it her business to know all the details of her employees, down to when they washed their hands and faces, knew that Doris was almost three months pregnant and would probably be gone in four, if not sooner. She had no mother or mother-in-law or older siblings to care for their baby, and the cost to hire someone so she could work as a secretary for the wages she earned would be impossible.

Daniel wasn't so keen about her, either. She was a plain-looking woman with tired, dull brown eyes and unremarkable stiff brown hair that always seemed a bit unruly, strands popping out and curling over her forehead and temples. Even before she began work, she had ink stains on her fingers, and her clothes looked as if she had slept in them the previous night. She was clearly not the secretary for Daniel. I saw pretty quickly that he was too much of a flirt, and she was clearly of no interest to him. If anything, he simply tolerated her because Aunt Effie had hired her.

I suppose the first hint of his flirtatious nature came when Yvon told me Daniel had told him that I looked at least five years older than I was. It was clearly his justification for staring at me, winking, and finding excuses to talk with me. My first thought was that Yvon would be angry at him, but he surprised me when I mentioned it all to him.

"Daniel's doing well here," he told me. It actually gave me a little chill to hear the way he was praising him. He was clearly trying to convince me I should be flattered by Daniel's attention. He had never done that regarding any boy. "Right now, he's Dawson Enterprises' top salesman. I've learned a lot from him."

"You learned about his sister," I countered, and for the first time I could recall, my brother blushed. When I laughed, he didn't get angry or embarrassed. He just shrugged, as if to say, *What's true is true.*

However, although Daniel Thomas obviously had the outgoing personality to enable him to be a good promoter of their properties, he was not what I would even generously call a good-looking man. His best quality was his green eyes, but they were set too closely together, which to me emphasized his slightly crooked nose and thin lips. He had an almost square jaw and prominent jawbones. However, he was loquacious and friendly. Everyone did like him. He had a new joke to tell almost daily and dressed sharply, his clothes always looking right off the rack. With wide shoulders and a height of almost six feet, he could overcome his plain looks and make a good impression on anyone, I thought. He was dedicating a lot of his time to me to do just that.

Even though I complained to her about him, Doris Munday was careful about what she said about Daniel. Nevertheless, I would have had to be made of stone not to realize how much she disliked working for him. She was the only person he talked down to. He pounced on any error she made, no matter how small, to the point one day of complaining about a comma that should have been a period in a letter he had dictated to a prospective buyer. He made it seem as if the buyer would reject his sales pitch because of that punctuation mistake. I found her off in a corner crying about it. I had duplicated her translation of the shorthand and not made that error. He hadn't failed to point that out. Lately, he was contrasting her more and more with me, which only made me feel terribly guilty. I debated deliberately making mistakes to help her look better.

After I had calmed her down, I marched into Daniel's office, just the way Mama would have to express her indignation. As beautiful as she was, she could draw in the heat of the devil and put a fire behind her eyes that would singe the face of anyone, no matter how powerful and important he or she was in the village.

He looked up from his desk with that twinkle in his eyes and smiled. Before he could say a word, I began.

"What you did to Doris just now was not only beneath the behavior of a real gentleman, it was cruel and deplorable. You know she is pregnant and sensitive. Your parents and your sister will be ashamed of you. Your actions betray a streak of meanness that would make a shark jealous," I said, turned, and walked out before he could respond.

My heart was pounding, and my face felt like it was on fire. I hurried into the ladies' powder room to escape. Although I had put on a good show and felt justified in doing so, I was trembling. Daniel would surely go to Yvon to complain. Or he might even go right to Aunt Effie!

I buried my face in my hands and sat, looking up when I heard the door open and close.

Here it goes, I thought.

Doris appeared before me. Had Aunt Effie punished me by firing her?

"You won't believe what just happened," she said.

"What?" I asked softly, tightening myself for an ugly blow.

"Daniel Thomas apologized for yelling at me. I was so shocked that I couldn't speak. I could only nod. He said I could leave an hour earlier today, and once again he apologized. He said he had no excuse except a slight tummy ache that had made him unfairly irritable."

"Tummy ache?" She nodded. I couldn't help it. I started to laugh.

"What?" she asked, smiling.

"Men," I said.

She lifted her eyebrows, waiting for the rest of it, but all I did was shake my head.

"Are you all right?" she asked.

"Yes, yes, I am."

When we stepped out, we saw that all the salesmen were in a meeting with Mr. Simon and Aunt Effie. Later, Daniel approached me while Doris was busy writing another letter.

"Thank you," he said, and walked away before I could respond.

It wasn't until we were on our way home that Yvon told me Daniel had told him I was even more beautiful when I was angry. That was something we both remembered was true about Mama.

"He asked me if he could continue to make it up to you by taking you to the real estate convention at the Jefferson Hotel Saturday night. I'd take you with Karen, but I forgot about it and have already bought us tickets to a play."

"A convention?"

"Well, it's a buffet dinner with a couple of speakers talking about the future of Richmond property development. Not the most exciting thing, but you'll learn a lot. I told him he could ask you as long as he promises not to permit you to drink hard liquor. You could buy a new dress for it," he added.

"You want me to go with him?"

"He's harmless," Yvon said, laughing. "Give him another chance."

Why was Yvon pushing Daniel on me like this? I wondered. Was he thinking more seriously about Karen? Everything seemed to be happening so fast, but one of the things Aunt Effie had told us on the trip here was that in America things happen a lot faster. Did he then think if I was occupied with someone, especially Daniel, I wouldn't mind his becoming seriously involved with his sister Karen?

"I don't know," I said.

A buffet dinner? All those executives? Dropping me into Richmond's business society like this was like dropping a baby into the ocean to teach her to swim. What if I said stupid things and everyone started laughing at me?

"I don't know," I said again, but with more hesitation in my voice.

"You should get out now, Marlena," Yvon said firmly. "I don't like it that you spend all your free time with Aunt Pauline. It's very nice of you to care for her and all, but you have yourself to look after, too. We're an important family here," he continued, now actually sounding like Aunt Effie and not only repeating her words. "We'll be involved in charity events, openings of businesses, chamber of commerce events, and whatever. This is no time to be hiding yourself away."

"I'm not hiding myself away, Yvon."

"You're afraid of this city. I know it. It's all so big compared to Villefranche, but we're just as important as anyone else here, including our royal aunt. I'd like to feel you will be okay, too."

He paused and took my hand.

"Let's take control of our own lives, Marlena. I can't do all this if I don't think you'll be happy." He looked into my eyes with such urgency.

"Okay, Yvon. I'll go with him."

"And buy a new dress with new shoes, too. Do you want me to go along with you?"

"If you want, but I doubt you know anything about women's clothing."

He laughed. "I have a better idea," he suddenly said. "I'll ask Karen to go with you. You'd like that, right?"

"Of course," I said.

"I'm giving you money, too. You haven't made enough to get the kind of dress you need, and I don't want us to go hat in hand to Aunt Effie."

"*Oui*, Yvon." I hugged him. *Surely, he's right again*, I thought. *He knows so much more than I do. And he's only doing what Mama and Papa would have wanted him to do, look after me.*

Two days later, I met Karen at Miller & Rhoads.

"Let's not pick the first thing we see for you or the first thing the saleslady shows us," she declared. She was more excited than I was, and she didn't want this to end quickly.

We went through the rack of new dresses, holding some up, laughing and spinning around with one or another in hand, which we could see was annoying the two salesladies hovering around us. Finally, I pulled out a dress of rich sequined silk in what the saleslady called Copenhagen blue. It was a one-piece with a shallow lace yoke and collar. The back and front of the waist were finished with groups of fine pin tucks. It had long sleeves and trimmed cuffs with an invisible side closing. The gathered skirt had a wide button-trimmed self-belt.

When I came out of the dressing room wearing it, Karen's eyes widened with glee.

"It's beautiful on you and so in style."

I turned to look at myself. I could hear Mama whispering in my ear: *Vanity leads to disaster, Marlena. Humility keeps us safe.*

"I guess it will do," I said, as if it were little more than a sack.

"Will do? You'll command every young man's eye," Karen said. "I'm going to want to borrow that."

"Absolutely," I said, laughing. I really liked her and understood why Yvon did, too.

The saleslady showed us the matching high-heeled shoes. They added at least two inches to my height. I did appear to be much older than I was. However, when I looked at what I would be spending, I saw it ate up everything Yvon had given me less a few pennies. I really felt guilty about it, but I think Karen would have been heartbroken if I decided not to spend it.

"I wish," she whispered as we were leaving, "that Yvon had forgotten about his play tickets and we were going together. But," she sang with a wave of her right hand, "there will be plenty of other times, for sure. *N'est-ce pas?*"

"French?"

"I've been studying it. For Yvon," she said. "I'm going to need your help from time to time."

"*Absolument*," I said.

We hugged when we parted, and I headed back to Dawson House.

Although Aunt Effie claimed she was our legal guardian now, I did not feel I needed her permission to go to the business buffet dinner with Daniel. However, before I could even consider that, she stopped at my bedroom while I was putting away the dress and shoes to tell me she had heard I was attending the convention with Daniel.

How had she heard? Yvon wouldn't have asked her permission or told her, would he? It had to be Daniel. But why did everyone at the company believe that Aunt Effie had to know their personal business, too?

She let me know why it was necessary for her to know by saying, "You realize, of course, that when you are out at social events, especially ones involving government people and businesspeople, you represent Dawson Enterprises, the Dawson family. In fact, whenever you're in public, even a walk to that park, you are a Dawson."

"I've never done anything that embarrassed my family," I said.

She smirked. "You've never had the opportunity. Misbehaving in a backward little French village would hardly qualify. I don't know what little indiscretions you've committed, and frankly, I don't care. That's in the past. The present and the future are what we must concern ourselves with."

She pulled her shoulders up and stood more erect to continue.

"You are not to drink hard liquor. You may have a glass of champagne, but only one, and you are not to smoke. If you are asked any questions about our business, you are to say, 'I haven't been working there long enough to know.' Period. Understood?"

For a few moments, I regretted agreeing to go. She made it sound like I'd be navigating through a swamp. Maybe she was hoping to discourage me from going, I thought.

She surprised me, however, when she added, "I'd like to see you in your new dress and shoes. I'm not saying I have to approve anything," she added before I could protest. "I'm just curious as to what you chose. Can you do that?" she asked when I just stared.

"Yes," I said.

"Good. I'll return in ten minutes or so. I look forward to it."

She walked off. Was the shell she had so successfully built around herself beginning to crack? I still couldn't imagine myself feeling anything like family to her, but for the first time since I had met her, I sensed some pain in her. Either no one had offered to take her, or she was ashamed to go by herself. Her life had surely been quite empty, the business not being enough, and perhaps, just perhaps, she saw both Yvon and me as a path to some deeper feelings, not only for us but for herself.

Give a little, I could hear Mama say. *Let out a little more line, and let the timid fish begin to nibble.*

I put on the new dress and even repaired my hair somewhat. While I was gazing at myself in the mirror, she returned. I hadn't heard her come in. I was doing the forbidden thing. I was admiring myself.

"Quite appropriate," I heard her say. "The color is perfect for you."

I turned. She continued to look at me and nod.

"You look more like your mother," she said. I almost exploded with surprise.

"How do you know what my mother looked like? Did you meet her? Did my father introduce you?"

"All in good time," she said. Before I could ask another question, she walked out.

I couldn't wait to share her comment with Yvon. When I heard him coming up the stairs, I rushed out to greet him, wearing my new dress.

"Wow," he said. "Maybe I should not have been so quick to give Daniel permission."

"Forget this for a moment," I said, practically gasping, and then I told him what Aunt Effie had said.

He stared at me, not looking surprised, curious, or upset.

"Well?" I coaxed.

He shrugged. "Maybe there was a wedding picture back then. Maybe they met before he left. The dress is beautiful on you. You do look like Mama," he said. He started away, but I reached out to seize his hand.

"Papa was angry at her for what happened to Aunt Pauline and the way she had accepted it. He wouldn't have introduced Mama to her."

"We don't know that, Marlena. We don't know any of that. You only have the babbling of an—"

"She wasn't babbling. I forced it out of her."

He sighed deeply. "Stop tormenting yourself. Just enjoy what we have now," he said, and continued on.

"But—"

"I don't have any answer for you. Forget it," he ordered.

"I don't believe you," I whispered, more to myself, as he walked away. I watched him go into his room, and then I returned to mine.

Every day, I felt the light expanding in the Dawson house, inching and creeping toward those shadows.

Right now, it terrified me to realize they would soon be gone.

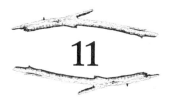

11

I had read about them in the newspapers that came to
Villefranche from Paris, but I had never seen or attended
a real gala held in a ballroom, with everyone formally dressed,
the men in tuxedos and the women in gowns bedecked with
jewels, many wearing tiaras. There were big street parties, of
course, but nothing like this in our small village. People would
bake and cook their own food. It was as if we were all one big
family.

If I had any doubt that this would be a glamorous event,
it was ended when late in the afternoon, hours before he was
going to pick me up, Daniel Thomas had a wrist corsage of
white roses delivered to the Dawson house, with a card that
said, "Please help these flowers look beautiful. Daniel." I
couldn't help but be excited.

For the first time since we had arrived here, Aunt Effie looked pleasantly amused. The way she gazed at the corsage gave me the feeling she was dreaming some man had sent it for her or perhaps recalling a time when one had. I wondered if I could venture to ask her if she had ever gone to a gala, even had a formal date, but I was too afraid she would tell me it was none of my business and insert an ugly blotch into this bright and exciting moment.

Yvon kidded about it. "Well, he's not as clumsy around women as he appears to be."

Aunt Pauline thought it was all so fascinating. She was more excited about it than I was, so I let her carry the corsage box up to my room to watch me prepare to go out.

"I once almost had a boyfriend," she suddenly said.

"Really? How old were you?"

She thought a moment and then smiled.

"As old as you."

"Well, who was he? How did you meet him? What do you mean by 'almost'?"

"His name was Edgar Fish. He took care of my father's horses, Belle and Poppy. He slept in the barn and was sent on errands to get this or that. I wanted to go with him into the city, but I wasn't allowed. And he wasn't allowed to stay in the house long, just long enough to get his orders, deliver whatever it was, and then he had to go. But he always made sure to smile at me first and say, 'G'day, Miss Pauline. How are you, Miss Pauline?'

"I'd sneak around and watch him care for Belle and Poppy, brush them down and feed them. Sometimes he let me brush them, and while I watched him, he told me stories about where he grew up. He said when his sister was eleven, she had to go live and work in a house in Alexandria. There were too many mouths to feed.

"When I came back into the house, Effie said I smelled from the horses and told my father what I had been doing, and then my father sent him away and hired an older man, Mr. Longstreet, who was old enough to be Edgar's father. He could have been," she said, nodding. "He was African, too."

I turned. "Edgar was an African boy?"

"I liked his eyes. They were like candles sometimes."

I laughed to myself imagining Aunt Effie's fears and outrage. What would happen to the precious Dawson name?

"The man I'm going with is not exactly my boyfriend, Aunt Pauline. He's okay," I said, "but he's not what I want in a boyfriend, a real boyfriend."

"Oh," Aunt Pauline said. She laughed. "I know what you want."

"What's that, Aunt Pauline?"

"You want someone with sweet lips," she said. Her eyes were wide and bright with the idea.

I started to laugh and then stopped. "Did Edgar have sweet lips?"

"Yes," she said.

"Did you tell Aunt Effie that?"

"No. Effie doesn't know what sweet lips are."

I laughed. "I think you're right," I said.

I decided to wear Mama's pearl necklace and matching earrings. I hadn't taken them out of the small sack I had put them in the day we left Villefranche. I was afraid that once I looked at them or touched them, I would start to cry uncontrollably. But the jewelry did seem to highlight what I was wearing.

Aunt Pauline thought I looked like a princess when I was fully dressed and slipped the corsage over my wrist. Then she followed me down like a lady in waiting. Yvon had already left to pick up Karen for their show. Aunt Effie stepped out of the sitting room and stood there inspecting me. I saw pleasure and appreciation in her eyes, but then they quickly became stern and cold again.

"Where did you get those pearls?"

"They were my mother's. Where else would I have gotten them?"

"Don't be snippy with me," she warned, and then straightened her shoulders. "In my experience and observation, I can tell you that most women squander their beauty and waste it on men who are self-centered and will enjoy them as they would some ornament. Once their women show the first signs of age, they will treat them as more of a burden than a wife. Beware of them," she said. "That's the only advice I will give you. I doubt your mother gave any similar guidance."

"Because I was too young," I said. "She was denied the opportunity. And she wouldn't know a man who would treat her like that."

She gave me her now famous cold smile. "Denied the opportunity? Not know such men? Do that. Cling to your fantasies. As you grow older, they fade, and the truth pokes in its unfortunately ugly face, and you're sorry you pretended."

"Is that what happened to you?" I asked in a tone that I was sure was confusing. It was a cross between caring and accusing. She stiffened, but she had put a cold hand on the back of my neck. "Is that why you never married?"

"No, that is not why," she said. Before she could continue, we heard the door knocker.

"Oh, your young man is here!" Aunt Pauline said.

The twins came out of the dining room.

Aunt Effie turned on them sharply. "We don't need you. Return to your dinner preparations."

"Yes, ma'am," they said simultaneously, and hurried back into the dining room.

Aunt Effie turned back to me. "Remember how I told you to behave," she said, and looked at Aunt Pauline. "Come into the sitting room, Pauline. I want you to calm down before we have dinner."

"I want to see how her boyfriend is dressed."

"Come into the sitting room," Aunt Effie said with more sharpness and authority.

Aunt Pauline looked at me and then followed Aunt Effie's command.

"At least read to her," I said before she turned fully away.

Then I opened the door to greet Daniel.

"Is this my secretary in training?" he joked. "I'm sorry, miss. I'm here to pick up Marlena Dawson."

"You look very nice yourself," I said. "Wait," I said, after taking a step toward him. "Were you saying Marlena Dawson wasn't this pretty?"

He threw his head back and laughed. "You definitely belong to Effie Dawson," he said.

I almost took another step back and closed the door. "I'm Beau Dawson and Corrine Dawson's daughter," I said. "No one else can lay claim to me except Yvon. And I am nothing like my aunt."

"Aye, aye, my ladyship," he said, saluting. Then he held out his arm. "I have my father's car tonight."

He nodded at the vehicle. Thanks to Yvon pointing out cars just about every time we walked the streets of Richmond together, I knew it was a Ford Model T. The black two-seater had white tires and looked like it had just come out of the factory.

"Very nice," I said. "It looks brand-new."

"I was working on it all day. I washed it and polished it, and then I took a cotton ball to get at the hard-to-reach places."

He helped me step up to the running board and then into the vehicle.

"Hope it starts. It's a long walk to the Jefferson," he joked as he walked around to get in.

I looked back at the windows in the sitting room and saw Aunt Pauline peering out between the curtains. I waved to her, and then she was suddenly gone. Aunt Effie had probably pulled her away.

We were off.

This was my first time in an open motorcar in the streets of Richmond. The night world seemed brighter and livelier than ever. The streets were crowded and noisy, and people were moving quickly on both sides as if they all had places to go. My eyes went everywhere. I could hear pianos playing in bars and restaurants. On one corner, an elderly man was playing a fiddle and occasionally clicking his heels to attract donations tossed in a tall black hat.

"You know, the Jefferson nearly burned down completely a dozen or so years ago," Daniel told me. "Most of it is practically brand-new. The stained-glass Tiffany windows with the hotel's monogram are the original ones. In the center of the lobby, you'll see the life-size marble image of Thomas Jefferson. You know who he was, right?"

"Yes, yes," I said. Aunt Effie had been making Yvon and me read about American history.

"Did Yvon warn you about what's in the marble pools in the Palm Court?"

"No," I said. "He told me very little about the event or the hotel."

"Oh, boy," Daniel said. "Okay, I'd better tell you. There are alligators in them."

"What?"

He laughed. "You'll see. I'm not joking, but don't worry about them. No guests have disappeared. Wait until you see the grand staircase, the marble columns, and the Tiffany stained-glass skylight. I've been studying architecture, you know. It's important for our business. The façade blends Beaux-Arts and Renaissance Revival styles with something of Spanish Revival, Italianate, Palladian, and Classical Revival," he recited with obvious pride.

I think Daniel kept talking like a tour guide because either he was nervous or he was afraid I was. I wasn't as anxious as I was intrigued and excited. Even though I knew I looked very good in my new dress and shoes, I still felt like I was wearing a costume, especially tonight as we approached the Jefferson Hotel. Ahead of us, men and women in formal dress were entering the hotel. There were many fancy motorcars.

"Impressed with me yet?" he asked.

I really hadn't been listening to his continued explanation of architecture, but I remembered how my mother reacted when someone was fishing hard for a compliment or praise.

"I'm so overwhelmed that I can hardly breathe," I said, and he laughed as we pulled to the side.

He got out quickly and ran around to help me out. He held my hand, and we started toward the entrance.

"Oh," he said, pausing. "Your aunt advised that we don't mention you work at the company so you won't be bothered with questions. In these sorts of business gatherings, you have to be very careful. Everyone is looking to learn some secret, some deal in the works for other companies. Some people have been sent here to do just that."

"Do what?"

"Spy on the competition, steal a deal." He laughed. "Many a negotiation was ruined by someone talking about it too much and someone overhearing it. Even I have to be very careful about what I say and to whom."

"Does everyone walk in there with all these worries?" I asked. "It doesn't sound like it's much fun."

"It's fun, but business is business, first and foremost," he recited.

One of Aunt Effie's soldiers for sure, I thought.

When we entered, I paused to take a deep breath. I had never been in a room this large and seen so many people gathered, most of the women dressed far more elegantly than I was. A balcony surrounded the room, and there were many settees and chairs with small tables so people could sit there and look down on the crowd. We were handed a pamphlet that listed all the attending businesses and the featured speaker, the president of the Bank of Virginia.

"We had to pay to be included in that," Daniel told me, nodding at the pamphlet. He pointed out Dawson Enterprises. "Businesses that don't buy a spot aren't very impressive."

Waiters came around with trays carrying glasses of champagne. Daniel plucked two quickly and handed me one. Off to the left, there was a chamber trio with a man playing a violin, a woman playing a harp, and another woman playing a flute. I could barely hear them over the loud din of conversation that seemed to come at me in waves of laughter as well as people greeting each other.

I wanted to go look at the alligators in the fountains, but Daniel quickly spotted some people he knew and introduced me. When they heard my surname, the men especially smiled at Daniel, as if he had won the hand of the boss's daughter. I noticed that the women were silent when different business topics were raised. Their smiles seemed more like masks as they eyed each other to judge what they were wearing, how they had done their hair, and what jewelry they were displaying. My mother's pearls caught their envious eyes, but no one bothered to ask me about my obvious accent. Daniel was quickly involved in an argument about how much someone had paid for a hundred-acre lot on the southeast end of the city.

I was frustrated that we were trapped in one place in this beautiful lobby and I was unable to see more of it. Everyone in the small group looked shocked when I said, "I'm going to wander a bit and look at more of the Palm Court and the alligators."

Obviously, if a woman came here with an escort, she didn't go off on her own.

"What?" Daniel looked at the others, who were waiting for him to tell me to just wait, but the look on my face smothered any such idea. "Don't get lost. They'll be calling us into the grand ballroom, and we'll be eating soon," he said, and turned right back to the point he was making.

Other guests were gathered near the fountains and watching the alligators. I had never seen anything more than a picture of one. They looked asleep but still quite scary. I walked all the way down to the foot of the grand stairway and gazed up. Yvon and I had really done little traveling in France. I had certainly never seen a grander place. I sipped a little of my champagne. It didn't taste as good as the champagne I remembered drinking on special occasions in Villefranche. A waiter was going by with a tray of empty glasses.

"Here," I said, stopping him. He looked confused. "I really don't want it."

He took the glass, nodded, and continued into the crowd. As I watched him, my eyes drifted toward the front entrance and to the right. I felt myself explode with joy. I had begun to feel that this was going to be a stuffy, boring night and regretted agreeing to attend. I could have come to the hotel anytime to see the beautiful lobby.

But I knew the back of that head, those shoulders and neck. I was just surprised that not only was Yvon here, but he had bought himself such a formal suit and never had shown it to me. This was his plan all the time, to just appear, maybe after spying on me to see how I was conducting myself in this so-called high society. I didn't see Karen, but there were simply too many people gathered around him. Practically charging, I hurried across the lobby until I was right behind him. Then I tapped him on the shoulder firmly and said, "Very funny. *Très drôle, mon coeur.*"

When he turned around, I felt the blood drain quickly down to my feet.

It wasn't Yvon, but he had Yvon's flaxen blond hair and the same strong Roman nose and straight, thin mouth. His cheeks were fuller and his forehead a bit wider. He was probably an inch or so taller and did have broader shoulders. There was something a little more gleeful in his smile, too. His eyes could be bluer, I thought, and his jawbone just slightly more prominent, but that didn't take away from his good looks.

"I know a little French," he said. "*Mon coeur?* Have we met? Because if we have and I forgot, I think I'll stop drinking."

The men and women around him laughed. I was still speechless.

"If I can forget someone as pretty as you, I mean." His smile became a look of amused confusion. "Miss?"

"I'm so sorry," I said, looking at him and at the bewildered people around us. "I thought you were someone else."

"He must be awful good-looking," he replied, and everyone laughed again.

I was so embarrassed and looked for a quick escape. "Sorry," I said again, and had started to turn away when he reached out to stop me.

"Well, you can at least tell me your name. Maybe it's you who forgot you have met me."

"No," I said. "We haven't met. I'm sure of it."

"Let me decide," he insisted. "What's your name?"

"Marlena Dawson."

Everyone around him oohed and aahed.

"Dawson? I was just talking about the Dawsons. You are related to the people who own Dawson Enterprises, are you not?"

"My aunt," I said. "Effie Dawson."

"Marry her, Malcolm, and you won't have to worry about

being overbid," a tall, thin, redheaded man said. Everyone laughed again.

"Yes," this man Malcolm said, taking my hand and looking at my fingers. "Why don't I marry you? You are unmarried, right? I see no ring."

I pulled my hand away.

"*Excusez-moi, monsieur,*" I said. Angered, I reverted to my mother language. I wanted then just to turn and walk away, but there was something about his wry smile that kept me rapt for a few more moments.

"I'll try to please you," he said, and looked up as he thought. "*Je suis . . . désolé.* How's that?"

"A very good effort," I said, "but how do you say 'no gold ring'?"

He laughed even harder, looking at his friends. "Is she a doll or what?"

"A what," one of the young women, in a dark-blue dress, said.

"Uh, uh, oh, Barbara Ann, jealousy puts wrinkles in your face," Malcolm warned her.

Everyone laughed but her.

I was finally turning again to walk off when Daniel appeared.

"There you are. I was afraid I had lost you," he said, and looked at the man they called Malcolm.

"I'd be afraid to lose her, too," Malcolm said.

"Yeah, well . . ." He looked uncomfortable and then extended his hand. "Daniel Thomas. I work for Dawson Enterprises."

"Malcolm Foxworth," Malcolm said, shaking Daniel's hand. "I work for myself and my father. I think we bid against each other recently on something."

"Yes, we did. Sorry we won. Well, not really sorry," he said, smiling at me.

"Most likely, we will bid against each other again," Malcolm said. He winked at me. "I have more reason to now."

"We'll see," Daniel said. I thought he looked a bit intimidated. "Marlena. There are some other people I'd like you to meet."

"*Au revoir, mon coeur,*" Malcolm said to me.

I just looked at him. My face couldn't help but smile.

Daniel threaded his arm through mine and led me away. "How did you come to meet Malcolm Foxworth?" he asked.

"I thought . . . it was Yvon."

"What?"

"Did you see any resemblance to Yvon?" I asked.

He glanced back and then shrugged. "Same color hair, I guess. So?"

"I saw him from the rear and thought Yvon had fooled me and come to the convention dinner."

Daniel grimaced and shook his head. "I'm sure he'd rather be with my sister somewhere else. Ah, look, they're getting ready to ask everyone into the ballroom. We can eat. The food should be great." He leaned in to me to whisper, "If you don't want to stay for the speech afterward, we'll sneak out."

"My aunt expected we would stay," I said.

"Oh, right. I was just joking. Of course. I'll have to report to her. There, we're being called to the ballroom," he said, and hurried us ahead of others to get to the banquet tables.

Later, I wished I had agreed to sneak out. I nearly fell asleep listening to the speaker drone on about this property and that and what he saw to be the future for Richmond. In my thoughts,

I continually returned to my meeting Malcolm Foxworth. Actually, I couldn't stop thinking about him, and then, when I turned to the right, almost as if someone had tapped me on the shoulder, I saw him looking my way and smiling. I quickly turned away.

The moment the speech ended, Daniel got into a discussion with the man to his left, and I felt an actual tap on my shoulder. I turned to face Malcolm Foxworth again.

"You look terribly bored," he said. Before I could protest, he added, "So was I. Where are you from in France?"

I glanced at Daniel, who was now in a heated argument with two men.

"Villefranche-sur-Mer," I said.

"Ah. That's near . . . Nice, right?"

"Yes, it is."

"I think my father's passed through, although I couldn't swear to any of the places he's been or things he's done. He's off right now to London. Ever been there?"

"No."

"So where do you live here?"

"I live with my aunts in the Dawson House," I said.

I surprised myself at how haughty I sounded. It was his fault, I quickly concluded. There was an air of arrogance about him that made me want to overshadow him. But all I did was broaden his smile. It was as if he knew me from the day I was born and we were like similar souls.

"Dawson House? I've heard of it. Actually, I've seen it on a tour of Richmond an associate of my father's took me on last year. You weren't there then, right?"

"No, but what made you ask?" I asked. Did he know all about Yvon and me but was pretending ignorance?

"Just curiosity. I'm sorry to say that the house was boring, quite unimpressive. If you were living there, it would have more brightness."

"You're quite the tease, aren't you?"

"Tease?"

"Perhaps it's the wrong word. Flirt?"

"Ah, yes, that's the word. I probably am, but tonight I feel quite justified being so."

Despite every effort I was making not to, I felt myself blush. "And my aunt's house is far from unimpressive," I said as sharply as I could.

He didn't lose his smile. A part of me wanted to drive him away, but a surprisingly stronger part didn't.

"Without exaggeration or arrogance, Marlena, I can tell you that your aunt's house would probably fit into my ballroom at Foxworth Hall."

"Foxworth Hall? Is that what you named it? A hall?"

He laughed. "It's a lot more than that. It was named that by my grandfather, but it's twice the size since he first lived there. It's the largest private property in Charlottesville. There's even a lake on it with rowboats. I've been looking into these outboard-motor boats a friend of my father's has been building and selling, Ole Evinrude. Maybe when I get one, I'll invite you to take a ride. It's quite thrilling. Have you been on one?"

"No."

"Then you'll surely want to come."

"I don't think—"

"Oh, don't make your mind up now," he said. He sounded less arrogant and demanding. "You have to see Foxworth Hall and the lake and let that help you decide."

"But—"

Daniel was turning back to me.

Malcolm leaned in quickly to whisper, "I'll have a train ticket delivered to the Dawson House, one you can use at your discretion. You just let me know, and there'll be a car waiting for you at the station in Charlottesville. Don't let this magnificent weather pass us by," he said, then glanced at Daniel and stepped away.

Us? I thought.

"What did he want now?" Daniel demanded. "Did he ask you anything about the company? Any properties? The Foxworths have quite the reputation for stealing someone else's business."

"No, Daniel. He didn't mention business. He was just bragging about his home."

"Um," Daniel said, looking after Malcolm, who had joined his friends again.

"Is it as big as he claims?"

"Yes," Daniel said. "But he had little to do with it. He's inherited everything. Those sorts of men are spoiled and stupid. He'll lose it all eventually. Would you like some coffee or tea or . . ."

"I think I'd just rather go home, if you don't mind," I said. My boredom with most of the event had turned into emotional fatigue. But probably what most made me want to leave was the idea of being alone to think about Malcolm Foxworth. I had thought I'd never find a young man as good-looking as Yvon. Dare I think he was even better-looking? He was certainly far more outgoing and possessed what my heart told me was a dangerous charm. He seemed to have it all: good looks, wealth, intelligence, and an exciting personality.

As Daniel led me out, I couldn't help but look back, and to my delight, Malcolm was watching me go. He nodded and smiled with a very slight bow as he raised his glass. I felt my heart flutter and surprised Daniel with my quickened steps.

"Boy, you really want to get out of here," he said.

Oh, no, I thought. *I really don't.*

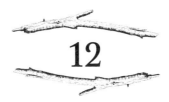

12

All the way home from the real estate banquet, I debated whether or not I should tell Yvon about Malcolm Foxworth. I doubted I could talk about him without revealing how he had touched me inside as if his fingers had grazed my heart. I had always been troubled by Yvon keeping something secret from me. Surely, it would be even more painful for me if he thought I would keep him from knowing about this. Who else did I trust for advice, after all? And he would be angry because he believed he was supposed to be my father and mother now.

But another part of me thought I wasn't a little girl anymore. I could have personal secrets and personal feelings that perhaps I could share with a girlfriend but weren't appropriate to share with a man, even if that man was my brother. Surely, he was keeping his most intimate thoughts about Karen Thomas to himself and not sharing them with me. That was rightly so.

When Mama was alive, she and I told each other things we wouldn't tell Papa and Yvon, and Yvon had done the same with Papa. Mama and I revealed intimate girl things to each other. How could I tell Yvon about the achings and longings that woke me up at night? Similar things must have happened to him and might even be happening to him now, too. I would expect he would keep that to himself. It was only natural for us all to be that way, wasn't it?

Then why did I have even an iota of guilt about it? I blamed it on my inexperience, which led to natural fear, but if I was going to be a mature woman, I would have to solve womanly problems myself. Aunt Effie was certainly no one for me to go to with personal questions, and I wasn't close enough with anyone else yet, even Karen. I also thought it might not be nice to talk to her about someone other than her brother.

Probably because I was so quiet, so deep in thought, while Daniel brought me home, he seemed quite worried that I'd had a disappointing night with him. Maybe he was afraid I would say something unkind about him to Yvon or even Aunt Effie. Or maybe he was truly disappointed that I hadn't been more excited about and more grateful for being with him.

"I'm sorry if I spent too much time talking business," he said as we arrived at the Dawson House. "But I picked up a few important bits of information that your aunt and Mr. Simon will appreciate. I really did."

"I understand, and I'm sure you did. You're right. My aunt will be pleased."

"But I was hoping to please you, too."

"Oh, it was all quite an experience for me. It was very nice, Daniel. Thank you for taking me," I said as he helped me out of the car. "And thank you for the corsage."

"Maybe I can take you to something more fun in the near future," he suggested. "I promise I won't spend a moment on anyone or anything else but you." He smiled and waited for some encouragement.

I was so reluctant to raise his expectations that even though I wanted to sound polite, I nearly choked on the words. "Of course. We'll see," I added.

"See you at work," he said.

He hesitated, hoping that I would just move my head a little toward him to encourage a good-night kiss, but I just nodded and turned toward the door.

He stood there a moment, surely disappointed, and then he got into his car and drove off.

The house was so quiet. I wondered if Yvon had come home before I had. I walked softly toward the stairway, and when I reached the doorway of the sitting room, I heard my aunt say, "Come in here."

Wearing a heavy white wool shawl, she was sitting on one of the cushion chairs reading a book. I was surprised, because it was a novel, *The Custom of the Country* by Edith Wharton. In my mind, my aunt read nothing but numbers and property descriptions. I had never seen her even read a magazine. She always turned first to the business section of the newspaper. She saw my eyes go to the cover when she had closed it and quickly put it upside down on the table beside her. As Jean-Paul would say, she looked like someone caught with her hand in the cookie jar.

"Well? Don't just stand there looking dim. Why do you think I called you in here? Tell me about the event," she said.

"The hotel is incredibly beautiful," I began. "I have never seen anything quite as big and decorative."

She grunted. "And?"

"There were quite a few people, some of the women very dressed up, so I was glad I wore my mother's pearls. Considering what some women wore, I would have looked naked without them."

"And the event?" she said, with a sharper, impatient tone.

"The food was very good. There were very good musicians playing, but there was so much noise from all the conversations going on it was difficult to hear them unless you were close. Why didn't anyone tell me there were alligators in the lobby? They were sleeping but still quite scary."

She stared at me. "Alligators. That's what impressed you the most? I do forget how young you are."

"I'm not that young."

She looked away and then at me again, as if she was being forced to talk to me. "You shouldn't be. When I was your age, I had more responsibilities than most older women, more than my mother had. That was for sure."

She pulled herself up in the chair.

"What do you think of Daniel Thomas?" she asked. "Now that you were with him outside of the office?"

"He's nice. He is very dedicated to your company."

"It's a family company," she said sharply. "But I expect no less from my employees. When you become part of something as big as Dawson Enterprises, it should become a part of you. Did you behave? Am I going to hear something awful tomorrow?"

"Of course not."

She nodded. "We'll see. What did you learn that you could bring with you to the company tomorrow? You have to prove your value every day."

"I didn't think I was there to do that. That was why you sent Daniel, wasn't it?"

She stared at me with such disappointment.

"Why didn't you go yourself?" I asked her, now feeling more annoyed.

"I was hoping by now you would be alert enough to notice that women are just not at the forefront of the business world. Men talk to men when it comes to that. Mr. Simon was on another assignment for us, but you're at least as absorbent as a sponge. Didn't you soak up anything while Daniel was discussing business? Didn't you hear anything new about our industry?"

"The bank president talked about the future of Richmond."

"And?"

"He talked about railroads and electric cars and things like that."

"Things like that? How impressive. I'm expecting you to start to develop more interest in your future, the Dawson future. It is very much tied to Richmond's future. The event should have held more interest for you besides how you looked in your mother's pearls, but I fear you've grown up believing your life could be in a novel, especially now."

I thought that would be it, the end of her reprimand. She looked down, and I was about to turn and go upstairs when she looked up again and asked, "I'm sure there were quite a few young men there. Did you flirt with anyone and embarrass Daniel?"

"What? No."

Could she have heard about my meeting Malcolm Foxworth already?

"Daniel is a fine young man. He has a future in the business."

"Probably," I said, but not with much enthusiasm.

Her eyes narrowed. "But he's not someone you could imagine yourself with?"

"As a wife?"

"Not as a secretary forever, no."

"I don't think so," I said. Was she responsible for Daniel asking me to the event? Was she trying to plan out my life, as I suspected? Did she want me married off and out of the house, maybe away from Aunt Pauline? All sorts of suspicions were racing through my mind.

"You don't think so? What? He's not a prince on a white horse or something? I am sure I am the first to warn you that romantic love is an extravagant emotion. It's rarely worth the cost. Passion lives only a short time, especially for men. The definition of a man's eyes is wandering orbs. It's in their nature to be dishonest and disloyal."

"My father wasn't like that."

She smiled and shook her head. I felt the ire stirring up again inside me. She could blow the lid off a kettle just by standing near it.

"How could a woman marry anyone if she believed that? Is that why you never married?" I asked.

"The man my father thought I should marry died very young, and it wasn't long after that my father died and my brother ran off, leaving me with so much to do that I was unable to spend that much time on my own life, developing personal relationships. Can you imagine that happening to you? Do you think I wanted my life to be like this?" she asked, her voice a bit more shrill. "My father wasn't in the ground an hour before I was troubled with one financial decision after another, and my sister . . . my sister's enough for ten of me."

She took a deep breath and looked away again. I just stared at her. Suddenly, she was sounding so different. She blamed others for her troubles, especially my father, but she never showed this much self-pity in front of me, only anger. It was as if the real Aunt Effie had stepped out from behind a wall, if only for a few moments.

"Your life flies by faster than you think," she said, now looking like she was talking to herself. "And whatever opportunities you had are gone."

"Why did you have to marry only the man your father wanted you to marry? Wasn't there anyone else?"

She looked at me again. "He was wiser."

"Always?" I asked. Should I bring up Aunt Pauline's story? I wondered. Now was a perfect time for it.

"I believed in him," she said.

"Always?"

We stared at each other. Did she sense what I knew?

"You can go to sleep now," she said, returning to the tone I was more accustomed to hearing. "I expect everyone to be at work when he or she is supposed to be there."

She picked up the book again. I stood there for a moment. I was going to say something nasty about it, but suddenly, I realized she really was suffering, and I thought I knew why. She read novels about women who sought love just the way someone without money would only stand outside the Thomases' bakery and look through the window at the cookies. What you couldn't have tormented you. Why willingly look through the window and tease yourself?

She looked up sharply as if to say, *Dismissed*.

I wanted to say something nice, something sympathetic, but then thought surely she would hate me for pitying her.

"Good night," I said, and left her.

I saw the lock was fastened on Aunt Pauline's door as usual. I listened for a moment and then went down to Yvon's room. I knocked and waited, but there was no response. I opened the door and looked in. His bed was still made.

At least one of us is enjoying the evening, I thought, and went to my room.

When I stopped to look at myself in the mirror, I saw Malcolm Foxworth smiling at me. Boys flirted with me in Villefranche, but it was never anything like this. As short as the contact between us was, it felt like there was more to it than his merely toying with me. Was I imagining it, wishing for it, or had he really looked at me with more than the usual interest he might have in a new girl? No, I was confident that something about me pleased him deeply, just as something about him touched me in a way I had never felt.

I laughed to myself, recalling Aunt Pauline's requirement for a boyfriend. He had to have sweet lips. There was little doubt in my mind that Malcolm Foxworth did.

I began to undress and then stopped, turning back to the mirror. I imagined him standing there again. He was so vivid in my mind that my face flushed with excitement. Every article of clothing I removed added to it. My heart beat faster.

In moments, I was stark naked before the mirror, which was now filled with Malcolm Foxworth gazing at me with such delight and lust that I couldn't help but touch myself just the way I thought he would. I ran my palms softly over my breasts, making my nipples erect. I brought my hands to my hips and then slowly moved them until they covered my patch of hair. I closed my eyes and imagined they were his hands and felt the surge of warmth moving up between my thighs. My heart was pounding. I moaned softly and envisioned his "sweet lips" just touching mine and then pulling back in a tease before he brought them harder to mine, the kiss lighting up my blood and sending it to every sensitive and welcoming part of me.

Gently, very slightly, I rolled my hips and pressed my body harder against my hands. My eyes closed and then fluttered open. When I saw myself in the mirror, I moved faster and faster. Malcolm was whispering in my ear. My mouth watered, my lips pursed. The excitement inside me raged and then burst, and I moaned louder and louder until it stopped, and I struggled to catch my breath. As soon as I had, I rushed to put on my nightgown and then sat on my bed, staring at the mirror like someone stunned and frightened.

What had I just done, envisioning Malcolm?

Did that make it sinful?

I don't know how long I sat there, but finally I heard a gentle knock on my door. I pressed my hands against my cheeks to see if they were as hot as they had been. There was a second knock, and then I heard Yvon whisper my name when he opened the door slightly. After a few quick breaths, I turned and said, "Yes?"

He stepped in. "Aunt Effie told me you had just gotten home. How was it?" he asked.

I looked at the mirror again, as if I thought he would, too, and see what had happened.

"Mostly boring," I said. "I nearly fell asleep listening to the speeches, but the food was good, and there were alligators! Why didn't you tell me there were alligators?"

"I was never there," he said, shrugging. "It just slipped my mind. What about Daniel? Was he nice to be with?"

"He was nice, but he spent a lot more time talking to other real estate people. I wandered about because I never saw any-place like it, and . . ."

"And what?"

I didn't want to tell him how I had rushed toward Malcolm Foxworth and why. Instinctively, I feared he would think I was too immature to have gone out on a date, especially such a for-mal one, and probably did make a fool of myself.

"And I saw the alligators, but they looked asleep. Soon after, we went in to eat."

He nodded, looking like Aunt Effie had already related all this to him.

"How about you? Did you have a good time?" I asked.

"Oh, yes. We enjoyed the show, and we had some great chicken and dumplings at this small restaurant Karen knew. Then we just walked and talked. She likes you a lot. I promised we'd go on a picnic soon."

"Not with Daniel, too?" I moaned.

He laughed. "He can be a bore, I guess. He's ambitious. Aunt Effie likes him. He's done some good work for the com-pany, and that seems to be all he cares about right now."

"I know," I said. "I'm a witness."

He thought a moment. "Well, maybe we'll take Aunt Pauline with us. I'll say you have to look after her and convince Daniel he wouldn't have any fun."

"I almost told Aunt Effie what Aunt Pauline had told me."

"I asked you not to, Marlena."

"I know, but she talks about her father as if he was some sort of perfect man and—"

"What's past is past. What good will you do knocking him? Don't do it." His face was reddening quickly. He looked like he was in actual pain.

"Okay, Yvon. Okay."

"Let's go to sleep. I'm visiting a prospective purchase early tomorrow with Daniel." He relaxed and smiled. "Everything will be great. You'll see. I believe she's thinking about drawing up papers to ensure we're part of the Dawson company's ownership. Mr. Simon sort of hinted about it today."

"Okay, Yvon."

He stood there a moment as if he was deciding whether or not to kiss me good night the way Papa often did. I think he was too embarrassed to do it and just smiled again before leaving and closing the door softly behind him.

I looked at the mirror again as if it was really a window to the future, and then I went to sleep knowing I would surely dream about Malcolm Foxworth. Even dreams seemed like a forbidden world, which made it more exciting to go there.

Once again, by the time I rose and went to breakfast, Yvon was gone. Aunt Pauline was at the table. She had remembered I had gone to the event and wanted to hear all about it.

"She's been on pins and needles waiting for ya," Mrs.

Trafalgar told me. "I swear. She's more lively than I've seen her be in years. She wouldn't eat nothin' until ya came down, Miss Marlena. Ya better eat now, Miss Pauline," she warned her.

"My aunt Effie's left?" I asked.

"Yes'm. She left with yer brotha."

I sat and smiled at Aunt Pauline. She drank her orange juice when I had mine.

"Tell me about the party. Where's your corsage?" she asked.

"It's up in my room. I'll give it to you later."

"You will?"

"*Absolument*," I said. I imagined she would put it on her wrist and parade around her room, fantasizing about herself getting dressed up to go out to a ball, too. How sad her life had been. How sad it was.

I quickly described the event, especially the alligators. Then, although Yvon didn't confirm it, I felt it was all right to tell her we were going to go on a picnic again soon, but with Yvon and his girlfriend.

"And your boyfriend?" she asked.

"I really don't have a boyfriend yet, Aunt Pauline," I said. "But I promise, I'll tell you first when I get one."

She burst into a smile, and both of us ate Mrs. Trafalgar's hearty breakfast of grits and eggs and homemade bread and jam with some fresh bacon. Before I left, the Brown twins promised to take her for a good walk and then let her do her giant jigsaw puzzle.

"And I'll wear the corsage," she made sure to tell them.

When I arrived at the Dawson offices, Doris was just as eager to hear about the event as Aunt Pauline had been.

She also, however, wanted to know what I thought of Daniel Thomas now.

"He was very nice. He tried to make it special. He bought me a corsage and had his father's car. But . . ."

"But what?"

I thought about how to say it without creating any issues in the office. When the right answer came to me, I smiled.

"What?" she asked, more interested.

"For me, he doesn't have sweet lips."

"What? He kissed you?"

"No, Doris. I mean I don't think any more will come of it."

"Oh," she said. She looked thoughtful. "He's not bad-looking, and he makes good money. My mother says I should have shopped more."

"Shopped? Is there a store selling husbands in America?"

She laughed and then grew serious when Aunt Effie walked into Mr. Simon's office, glancing first at us with those critical eyes.

"There aren't too many women like your aunt. Most need a good husband," she said. "My man is good," she continued. "We're just going to struggle a bit once I stop working, too. I hope they let me work until I can't," she added, looking fearfully at me. In her mind, I was surely breathing down her neck.

"They will. I don't intend to be ready until you leave," I said, and she smiled.

A few minutes later, Yvon and Daniel returned to the office. Daniel went quickly into his, and Yvon stood just inside the main entrance looking at me for a few moments. I had started to say something to him when he put his hand up and then pointed to his office. He marched into it.

"I wonder what that's all about," Doris said.

I rose slowly. I feared that I knew.

Yvon closed the door as soon as I entered and told me to sit. He went behind his desk.

"Daniel says you were quite friendly last night with Malcolm Foxworth."

"I spoke to him, yes. I don't know as I'd call it quite friendly. Why?"

"He said he was flirting with you. Was he? Don't tell me you aren't sure, Marlena. You know what flirting means."

"I suppose so," I said. "But I think he flirts with every girl he meets."

"You know he's our competition sometimes, especially quite recently."

"Yes, Daniel told me that."

"Well, what went on between you? Why did you meet him in the first place?"

I looked down, thinking.

"What?" he asked sharply.

"Have you ever met him?" I asked.

"No. And I'm not eager to, either."

"Have you ever seen him?"

"No. The deal he tried to get occurred before you and I arrived in Richmond. Why is that important, whether I saw him or not?"

"He had his back to me, and when I first saw him, I thought it was you."

Yvon's face quickly looked a shade or two redder. "Me? So what did you do?"

"I thought you had pulled a joke on me, and you and Karen

were there. I rushed across and tapped him on the shoulder, thinking it was you, and . . . and it was embarrassing. I mean, he has the same color hair, and I didn't look closely enough. He's bigger and taller, but he has beautiful blue eyes. Like yours, Yvon. He was surprised, of course."

"Surprised by what?"

"That I thought he was you and I said . . . something in French."

"What did you say? Exactly?"

"Why is this so important? Why are you getting so angry?"

"Just tell me, Marlena? What did you say to him?"

"It wasn't to him. I thought it was to you. His back was still toward me and—"

"Forget that. So? What?"

"*Très drôle, mon coeur.*"

He stared at me a moment and then leaned forward. "What did he say? His exact words. Think!" he ordered.

"I don't remember it word for word, Yvon. He thought it was amusing, especially when he learned my name. Daniel came over, and they met and had a little unfriendly banter, and then we walked away."

He nodded. I saw how upset he was and decided not to mention Malcolm's coming over to me after the speeches were done or his invitation and promise of a train ticket.

"Why didn't you mention this last night?"

"I didn't tell him anything about the company, Yvon, if that's what's worrying you. Otherwise, I don't know why you're so upset." I looked down and then up quickly. "Was Daniel upset I spoke to another man? Did he complain to you? Is that it?"

"Forget about Daniel. You should have told me about all this," he insisted.

"All what? It was nothing."

He looked away a moment. "It's not nothing. The man has a terrible reputation when it comes to how he treats young women. His father does, too. They're arrogant and ruthless men and not only in their business dealings."

"How do you know all this? You just said we weren't here when they were trying to get the same property in Richmond."

"I know. I listen. It's a small community when it comes to business in Virginia. You can't just walk up and speak to someone, especially someone like that. These are the sorts of men who take advantage of innocent girls."

"I'm not a child, and you shouldn't talk to me as if I were. Our aunt Effie certainly doesn't think so. She would marry me off next week to Daniel. You should have heard her."

"Don't worry about that," he said, waving his hand as if he could wave away words. Then he leaned over the desk toward me. "If you should ever see or hear from Malcolm Foxworth again, you're to tell me immediately. You understand, Marlena? Immediately. I don't care when or what time of the day."

"Why?"

"I just told you. He's not someone to play with."

"And I just told you that I don't need you to hold my hand all day and all night, Yvon. "

"Yes, you do, apparently," he said. "And you'll do as I tell you, Marlena."

I felt the tears welling in my eyes. He had never spoken to me like this. And he looked absolutely terrifying.

"I don't like arguing about it with you. I'm sorry, but I feel I have to do what I have to do. Let's stop talking about it. Aunt Effie, Mr. Simon, and I are going to dinner tonight with a gentleman who is considering investing in Dawson Enterprises. You should be happy I'm included in the meeting."

I stood up. "You are getting just like her, Yvon. Papa would hate you for it," I said, and I sucked in the cry that tried to accompany my tears and left his office.

I paused to wipe my cheeks and then walked slowly to my desk. Before I sat, I saw Daniel peering at me through his doorway. I went up to it and looked in at him.

"Hi," he said. I was glaring in at him. He raised his hands. "I didn't mean to say anything that would get Yvon angry. I don't even know why he got so angry. I didn't blame you for anything. I swear," he said.

"I want you to know that should you let Doris go before she wants to go, I will not work for you. In fact, I will never work for you," I told him in a loud voice, turned, and started back toward my desk. Doris was sitting there aghast. I nodded at her and walked out of the offices and out of the building.

I didn't head for home. I went in the opposite direction, walking fast, my arms folded under my breasts, my eyes fixed on the street ahead. I even bumped into people, but I didn't stop, and only one person bothered to say, "Where do you think you're going?"

Finally, I found a stoop and sat just so I would keep out of the way of pedestrians. Dust rose up from the street, automobiles bounced by, the drivers sounding horns that resembled dying animals. There still a number of horse-drawn carriages confronting and confronted by the automobiles. Some of the horses complained. One pair got up on their hind legs for a scary moment, but the driver had good control. After a few moments, I saw or heard none of it, because I was too submerged in my own thoughts.

After our parents' deaths, I had felt the world drop out from under my feet. No friends, not even Jean-Paul and Anne, could keep me from falling and falling, but I believed in and leaned heavily on my brother. He would somehow save us, make it possible for us to go on, and somehow find happiness for us both.

I never told him outright, but I was very disappointed that he didn't fight harder for us to remain in Villefranche. If anything, he kept more inside himself than ever, but I saw how he had shifted his thinking and his ambitions, and I thought, *Maybe he's right.* Maybe we should think of a whole new life in America and put away anything and everything that caused us to hold on to Villefranche, a world we could never restore.

But he was too different now. He had gone too far and left me feeling more alone than ever. As I looked at the crowds of people, the endless line of strangers around me, I thought I had started falling again. I was more lost than ever. What would my life be in America? As sweet as Aunt Pauline was, Aunt Effie was right about her. She was more of a burden as she grew older, perhaps more than she ever was, and I was certainly not the one to take care of her. At this moment, I didn't think I was capable of taking care of myself.

So much, if not all, of the love we had around us was gone. Perhaps I had to find my own way and not depend so much on Yvon anymore.

I stood up and headed back toward the Dawson House. Twenty minutes later, I turned into the drive. The moment I opened the door, Minnie and Emma stepped out of the dining room as if they had been standing there waiting to hear the front door open. Emma approached me first and held out an envelope.

"A Western Union messenger came by a little while ago with this," she said, her face and voice full of excitement.

I took it slowly. Was it bad news about Jean-Paul?

"He wasn't going to leave it without your signature," Minnie said. "But I assured him we'd give it to you."

"I signed your name," Emma said. "I hope that was all right."

"Yes, fine. Thank you."

I walked into the sitting room. If it was bad news, I didn't want to read it in front of them, or anyone else for that matter.

When I opened the envelope, I saw a ticket and a note beside it.

It was a train ticket, good for any round trip between Richmond and Charlottesville, Virginia.

The time for the first departure of the day tomorrow was listed first on the note and beneath it, it read:

There will be a car waiting for you at the station, a black Cadillac. The driver's name is Lucas. If you take this train, you'll be at Foxworth Hall for lunch. I look forward to showing you an estate that would make King George V jealous. There will be plenty of time for your lunch and tour and then return on the train to Richmond.

Please come, mon coeur.

Malcolm Foxworth

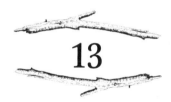

13

I wasn't the most perfect child in the world, but I never truly defied my parents or even Yvon as I was growing up in Villefranche. I might have pouted a little, but I didn't have a temper tantrum over anything my parents or Yvon had forbidden me to do. If my friends were permitted to do something that I was not and I complained or whined, Mama would tell me she suffered more over my unhappiness than I did.

But, Marlena, that is what makes it so hard to be a parent. You want your children to love and adore you, but you have to do what you think is best for them, even if they will resent you for a little while. Remember that for when you have children of your own, she would say.

In the end, I always felt sorrier for my parents and even Yvon than I did for myself.

But I wasn't feeling this way about Yvon right now, and Aunt Pauline thankfully did not give me much time to feel sorry for myself. The moment she realized I was home, she was at me to read to her again. The idea that we would be alone for dinner obviously pleased her, too.

"It will be like a party," she said, clapping. I knew that what she really meant was that Aunt Effie wouldn't be sitting at the table criticizing almost everything she did, whether it was eating too fast or using the wrong fork.

Perhaps because of how trapped I was feeling, I welcomed that same air of liberation. With only the twins and Mrs. Trafalgar in the house, Aunt Pauline and I were free to do whatever we wanted. My conspiratorial laughter encouraged her when she touched an expensive Italian vase Aunt Effie had forbidden anyone to touch, even the twin maids. We sat without worrying about our posture, took off our shoes, and put our sockless feet on the edge of the table as we slouched. I brought peanuts into the sitting room, an act that qualified as a cardinal sin in Aunt Effie's Bible of Behavior. Our laughter opened up the floodgates.

I let Aunt Pauline ramble on and on about the past, citing anecdotes about her father and Aunt Effie that she had never even suggested. Apparently, my grandfather had some dirty habits, especially when it came to his cigar smoking, grinding them into ashtrays all over the house, even flower pots. Aunt Pauline said that when her mother was alive, she was constantly cleaning up after him and complaining. She had to sleep in a separate bedroom because he even dropped ashes in their bed, and the room reeked of bourbon and cigars. She said Aunt Effie often tried to cover up for him by getting to the mess before any maid or her mother could.

"She wanted him to like her more. But he never brought her presents like he brought to me. She used to hide the jewelry he gave me. She even buried a ring he had bought me in New York in the backyard. I saw her do it. When I told her, she said she would never do such a thing. But I didn't tell on her like she would tell on me.

"When my mother died, she took all her jewelry into her room so my father couldn't give anything to me. Effie said she had to take my mother's things because she had to be the mother now. She said if she hadn't had to be a mother, she might have gotten married and had children of her own."

"I've heard that before," I said dryly.

"But that's not really why."

"What's really why?"

"She didn't want a man's smells and sweat in her bed. She once told me that," she added with firm nods. "She'll say she didn't, but she did."

On and on Aunt Pauline went with her stories. Whatever dam Aunt Effie had created to keep her memories under control crumbled as I prodded her for recollections of her childhood and especially memories of my father. From what she was telling me, I realized that early on, Papa got into spats with his father constantly, but especially after my grandmother had died. The way Aunt Pauline described Aunt Effie standing beside their father when he bawled Papa out or criticized him for being lazy or uninterested in their business made it all so vivid for me. She was surprisingly visual with her descriptions, at one point saying Aunt Effie duplicated their father's facial expressions as if "his growling lips hopped onto her face."

Maybe because I was so angry at Yvon and feeling so defiant, I asked her to tell me again about the fight my father had with his father in the bathroom while her father was giving her a bath.

"Effie told me never to tell," she said. "She said people would hate me more than they would be angry at my father."

"Why?"

"Because . . . no one would believe me, and they'd think I was a mean liar." Then she added, "But she promised me something."

"What?"

"She would always help me with my bath, and Papa wouldn't anymore."

"So she believed you," I said, more to myself than her, but she had heard it.

"Oh, yes. She was mad at him, too. I heard her yelling at him in his room. She made him stop buying me things. She even scowled at him if he kissed me. He never came in to kiss me at night anymore. Effie would stand in the hallway to be sure sometimes. Right after dinner, he would lock himself in his office anyway. Or he wouldn't come home for dinner." She leaned toward me to whisper. "Effie said he was visiting with those dirty women in some filthy place on Jackson Street. She said she once followed him and saw him go in.

"But I wasn't permitted to mention it. I almost did once at dinner, and Effie spilled a glass of water on my lap." She studied me a moment and then said, "Beau would never let her do things like that. Daddy did. He didn't care by then. He was getting old fast and sometimes drank so much bourbon that he couldn't get up the stairs and had to sleep on the floor in here. He even peed on a rug we had to throw out."

"And she calls him the perfect father. They should rename this house the House of Lies," I muttered.

Jean-Paul once had told both Yvon and me that if you refused to correct a lie or face up to it, you were a liar, too. Why didn't Yvon remember that?

Aunt Pauline was suddenly very quiet, stuck in one of her more troubling memories, I was sure.

The twins came to tell us dinner was ready.

"And Mrs. Trafalgar made Miss Pauline the chocolate cake she likes," Emma said.

"With the cherries on top," Minnie added.

Aunt Pauline was all smiles.

"Marlena likes that, too. Right, Marlena?"

"Oh, very much," I said.

For a while, at least, we should be happy, I thought. Aunt Pauline obviously wasn't as mature as a woman her age should be, but she was sensitive enough to feel when I was sad. Besides, being with her and laughing at silly things were good medicine for now.

After dinner, I read to her as I'd promised and then helped with her jigsaw puzzle until she was falling asleep in her chair. The twins were quite attentive. It was remarkable how well they knew her, knew when her energy was running low. They came to take her up to her room and help her to bed.

"Don't lock her in tonight," I said. "I'll do it when I go up."

"Oh, but—" Emma began.

"I'm the mistress of this house when my aunt is away," I said sharply, so sharply they both widened their eyes and then looked at each other. Neither said another word.

"Are you going to sleep, too, Marlena?" Aunt Pauline asked.

"Soon," I said. "In fact," I added, looking at the twins, "I'm going to come into your room to say good night to you."

"Oh. That would be very nice," she said. She thought a moment. "Effie never does."

"Well, I won't be saying good night to her. That's for sure," I said, and Aunt Pauline laughed.

"She won't be saying good night to her," she told the twins as they walked her out. She was still repeating it as they went up the stairs.

I sat for a while thinking about everything, and then I took out the ticket I had hidden inside my dress and looked at it. Why shouldn't I go? I was no longer a child in any sense of the word. If I was to be a woman, I would have to be in charge of my own life. Right?

I knew that question would roll around in my head all night, but I was also sure I would answer it before I fell asleep.

After I grew what I thought was tired enough to fall asleep, I went up and did say good night to Aunt Pauline. She told me this was the most fun night she could remember and asked me to promise we'd do it again.

"Oh, we will," I said. "We will. I promise."

When I stepped out, I considered leaving the lock undone, but then I realized Aunt Effie would only take it out on the twins. And there was that possibility that Aunt Pauline would walk out in her sleep and again fall down the stairs. Maybe one of these days, I'd come up with a way for us to sleep in the same room, I thought, and went to bed.

As I anticipated, I tossed and turned, moving from outright rage at Yvon to sadness and then to the sense of adventure and romance Malcolm Foxworth dangled in his handsome smile and dazzling eyes.

"*Mon coeur,*" I whispered. "*Mon couer.*"

I finally fell asleep with those words on my lips, and I knew what they would mean.

When I woke, I hurriedly dressed. I was eager to see if Yvon was sorry for the way he had treated me yesterday. Of course, he knew I had walked out angry. I had tried to stay up as long as possible in case he would stop at my room when he had returned with Aunt Effie from their dinner with an investor, but either he didn't, or I was already in a deep sleep and he didn't want to wake me. That was my real hope.

When I rushed downstairs, however, all that I found was a note on my plate. Emma said Yvon had left it for me. Minnie told me he and my aunt had needed to leave early to make an auction outside Richmond. The note read, *I hope you're over your tantrum. We'll talk about it later.*

Over my tantrum? This was so unlike him. Aunt Effie had her claws in him. She was turning him inside out.

"Usually, Miss Effie doesn't bid on those properties," Emma said.

"But she told us this one was worth their consideration," Minnie said.

Both looked so proud at being able to share business information. Anyone would think they believed they worked for the queen of England. A small favor, a smile, an appreciative nod made their day. How pathetic and sad, I thought. They reinforced each other's worship of my aunt.

"Where is my aunt Pauline? Why isn't she up and dressed?"

I snapped at them. Whatever patience and understanding I once had was drifting off like smoke.

"She was sleeping so soundly," Emma said.

"That we didn't have the heart to wake her," Minnie explained.

"We didn't tell," Emma said.

"Tell what?"

"That you let her have two glasses of that wine at dinner last night," Minnie replied.

I stared at them both for a moment, the rage swirling in my chest. "You can tell my aunt Effie anytime you want," I said through clenched teeth. "This isn't, as far as I know, a prison, and you are not prison guards. You're maids. Or do you think you are hired to spy on those who live here? Do you think this is a palace full of family intrigues? You're both driveling with your need to please her. I don't need your protection. *Mon Dieu.*"

Flustered, they both retreated to the kitchen, probably to cry on Mrs. Trafalgar's shoulder. I sat there steaming. Whenever Jean-Paul had seen me like this, he would shake his hand and blow on his fingers, pretending that the vapor coming out of my ears had burned him.

Suddenly, as if something had exploded inside me, I slammed my palm so hard on the table that the dishes and glasses jumped. Then I stood, paused, and hurried to the stairway. I knew the dress I wanted to put on. I had secretly bought it for myself and had yet to wear it.

There would be no better time than now, I thought. I had seen the way other customers were looking at me when I had tried it on. It was a white eyelet dress with a fitted waistband, lace detail throughout, and a button-down front. The sleeves were cuffed a few inches below my elbows, and the hem was at least six inches above my ankles. With my hair down and my mother's black-pearl bracelet, I thought I made what the saleslady said was "quite the statement." I had the white shoes to go with it.

Before I finished dressing, I heard Emma and Minnie getting Aunt Pauline up and dressed for breakfast. I also heard her ask for me. I knew she was disappointed to hear I had already had breakfast, so I rushed out to meet them as they were starting down the stairs. The twins were very surprised at what I was wearing.

Aunt Pauline clapped and said, "You're so pretty. She's my niece, you know," she told Emma and Minnie.

"Thank you, Aunt Pauline. Have your breakfast. I have to go. I'll see you tonight."

"When we'll read?"

"Yes. Choose a new book," I said.

She smiled and started down the stairs. Why she paused I couldn't say, but she did and then turned around and asked me for a hug. I did hug her and then watched her descend. I rushed back to my room to get a scarf and quickly went down the stairs.

Serendipity, I thought, when George pulled up to the front of the house. My aunt had sent him home to get a folder she had forgotten on her desk.

"Can you drop me at the train station?" I asked as he came rushing to the door.

"Oh. Sure 'nuf, Miss Marlena," he said. "It's on my way back. Give me one minute," he said, and hurried into the house.

I got into the automobile, clutching my train ticket. Less than a minute later, he was out and got into the car.

"Ya picked a beautiful day ta go somewhere," he said.

"I hope so, George. I hope so," I said, and sat back.

My heart was pounding all the way to the station.

"Ya be all right by yerself?" he asked when he helped me out.

"Oh, yes, George. I'll be fine," I said. "Thank you."

He nodded and then hurried off. I wondered if he would volunteer the information that he had brought me to the train station. I didn't want to ask him to keep it a secret. It would be unfair to put him under that sort of pressure. My aunt was capable of firing both him and his wife.

I hadn't been on a train since we had first arrived in Richmond. This one looked and was a lot more comfortable, with softer seats and more legroom. There were many more passengers than I had anticipated, most of them looking like businessmen. I sat beside one of the only women in the car. She was a grandmother going to visit her son and his family. She was so excited about her trip, her first on a train, that she hardly asked me any personal questions. And then, about twenty minutes later, she fell asleep.

I was too wound up to close my eyes for anything longer than a blink. By now, so far into my journey, I imagined both Aunt Effie and Yvon had realized I wasn't coming to the company offices. I wondered if they would think I was simply staying home. After a while, Yvon was sure to call the house and ask if I was sick or something. He'd learn I had left, and then he would ask George, unless George had already told them both.

Of course, at first he would be angry, but I was confident that after a while, he'd be more worried than mad. Perhaps he would question Doris to see if she knew anything. Poor Doris. She was so fragile now that she'd probably cry if my aunt was listening. I couldn't envision him doing anything else. Maybe he'd check with Emma and Minnie again to see if I had come home. I hoped that before the day had ended, he would feel sorry he had spoken to me the way he had.

When we pulled into the Charlottesville station, I feared there would be no car waiting, and he had not been serious about it. But Malcolm Foxworth's vehicle stood out clearly from everything else that was waiting there. It looked brand-new and quite impressive. The driver was leaning against the vehicle and watching the passengers come off the train. He was a slim man, not very tall, with graying dark-brown hair, the gray strands heavier on the sides. The moment I appeared, he stood straighter. I smiled at how quickly he had recognized me. Malcolm surely had given him a very detailed description. Of course, it was true there weren't many other unaccompanied young women coming off the train.

"Miss Dawson?" he asked, approaching.

"Yes."

"I'm Lucas, the Foxworth chauffeur," he said. He gestured toward the car and then hurried to open the rear door. After he was in, too, he turned to ask if I had a good trip.

"Much nicer than I had expected," I said. "Have you worked for the Foxworths long?"

"Oh, yes. More than twenty years," he said.

We started off. I could see that Charlottesville wasn't as big and as busy as Richmond, but the streets didn't look all that different. In no time, we were out of the city proper and on our way to Foxworth Hall.

"How far away is Foxworth Hall?" I asked.

"Oh, it's about an hour from the city," he said. "Those are the Blue Ridge Mountains ahead."

"Are they?" I said. We passed so much unattended land with few houses in between. "I wonder what brought the Foxworths so far out."

"Oh, you'll understand once you see where the house is located, miss."

Soon we were driving upward, where there were more farms and small houses, and then suddenly, as if it rose from the earth knowing I was coming, this enormous house came more and more into view. The mountains rolled along the horizon in the distance, and the forest was a sea of green on our right and left. Lucas was right. What a beautiful setting, I thought. It didn't surprise me that someone living in this mansion would feel special, even superior, being so high up and looking down on so many smaller houses, much smaller houses, some half the size of the Dawson House.

"How big is Foxworth Hall?" I asked Lucas as we drew closer and the size of it became clearer and clearer.

"Oh, it's big, miss. There are thirty-six rooms, a ballroom, and a lobby bigger than any house's lobby in the state, I'd venture. The Foxworth property is hundreds of acres, too."

"Do you live on the property?"

"I do, miss. As do all the servants."

How exciting, I thought. Malcolm Foxworth, the Foxworths, were so much richer than the Dawsons. They could probably swallow up the Dawson company. Maybe Yvon's fear of Malcolm Foxworth wasn't only because of his reputation with women. Maybe he thought he'd gobble up the company.

As we went past the fields and the forest, climbing closer and closer toward the mansion, I wondered why a man with such power and wealth would be at all interested in someone as young as me. He surely could have his pick of sophisticated older women. Then again, I thought, smiling, perhaps I was underestimating myself. Now was the time for self-confidence, not self-doubt. Only a child would fear being courted.

We pulled up to the large double entrance doors, and Lucas got out quickly to open mine and help me out. I looked up at the roof, which seemed to rise higher and higher before my eyes. Smaller windows suggested an attic. From where I stood, it looked like it ran the length of the house.

The moment I stepped down, the double doors opened as if by magic, and Malcolm stood there smiling. He was holding two glasses of champagne.

He looked even more handsome than he had at the business event, wearing a white shirt, the collar opened, and a pair of black pants. When I started forward, he stepped to hand me my glass of champagne.

"Welcome to Foxworth," he said.

"How did you know I would come?"

He shrugged with that small, wry smile.

"I didn't, but what was the risk, Lucas driving to the station and back and opening a bottle of champagne?"

"I fear you're a scoundrel," I said.

He laughed.

Lucas drove the car to the multicar garage on the left.

"I am and more," Malcolm said. "But being French, you'll love it." He tapped his glass to mine. "To a wonderful day at Foxworth Hall."

We both sipped, our eyes fixed on each other's over the edges of our glasses.

"I like your dress."

"Thank you."

"I just knew there was something special about you," he said. "I've been thinking about it ever since we accidentally met at the Jefferson. I'm sure I'm right when I say 'accidentally.'" He stepped back and gestured. "Shall we?"

I nodded, and we walked through the impressive doorway. As soon as we entered, a woman, perhaps five foot four at most, approached us. She wore a dark-blue dress and black shoes that looked heavy and uncomfortable to me.

"This is Mrs. Steiner," he said. "She cares for Foxworth Hall as she would a child."

"As I cared for you," she said to him without smiling, and he laughed.

"Mrs. Steiner, may I introduce Marlena Dawson?"

"How do you do?" she said. She studied my face when she took my hand, inspecting my features as my father would consider a subject for a portrait. "You're a very pretty young woman," she said, as if that was a fault.

"Thank you."

Oddly, she held on to my hand a little longer than I had anticipated, her eyes fixed so strongly on mine that I had to smile inquisitively at Malcolm.

"Mrs. Steiner is a little bit like a worrying mother," he whispered, loudly enough for her to hear, of course.

She let go of my hand. "I'll have your lunch on the rear patio, Mr. Malcolm. Mrs. Wilson has prepared everything as you wished."

"Delightful," he told her.

She turned and walked off.

We continued into the massive lobby. Scattered along the walls were portraits of people I assumed were Foxworth ancestors.

"Are all those people your family?"

"They are. A sad lot. A smile was a sign of weakness to them."

"Maybe they wanted to look regal."

He laughed. "That they did." He leaned in, his lips brushing my ear. "I told my father they all must have had hemorrhoids. He thought it was disrespectful, but I've heard him tell people that, especially after he's had a little too much to drink."

"Is he here?"

"No. He's still abroad."

He took my hand and led me to the end of the long foyer, where there was a pair of elegant staircases that wound upward to join a balcony on the second floor. From the balcony, there was a second single staircase rising to another flight. Three giant crystal chandeliers hung from a gilt carved ceiling some forty feet above the floor of mosaic tiles.

"It's . . . amazing," I said. "Such high ceilings."

"And you've seen less than ten percent of it, if that."

As we approached the stairway, I gazed at the marble busts, the crystal lamps, and the antique tapestries.

Before we reached the stairway, he nodded to his right. "That's our library," he said.

I gazed through the doorway at the walls lined with richly carved mahogany bookshelves crowded with leather-bound volumes. The ceiling was at least twenty feet high, the shelves of books almost meeting it. A slim movable stairway of wrought iron slid around a track curved to the second level of shelves, and there was a balcony from which someone could reach the books on the top level. It made the sitting room and library in the Dawson House look puny. No wonder he had joked about what I had thought was an enormous mansion. As I gazed about, I realized the entire Dawson House could fit in only this section of Foxworth Hall.

"Our bedrooms, my father's and mine," he quickly added, "are upstairs in the southern wing. There's warmer exposure. There are sixteen rooms in the northern wing, all various sizes. I'll show you something special later."

"It's like a hotel."

He laughed. "Few hotels have what Foxworth Hall has."

We continued on until we reached the doors of the ballroom. He gestured for me to enter, and for a few moments, all I could do was look in awe. I was sure he had staged my introduction to it. To make my first view of the ballroom dramatic, the curtains were closed so that the room was made brilliant with all five tiers of the four crystal and gold chandeliers fitted with candles that had been lit. The light that spilled from the chandeliers reflected off the grand crystal fountain, weaving threads of radiance over the walls. Mirrors captured it and carried it farther, illuminating everything silver and gold. The room was dazzling.

The ballroom was so large that our footsteps echoed, because there wasn't anything much in it at the moment except the piano. The hardwood floor looked as new as the day it had been installed. A corridor in the house ran above the far wall. It was difficult to make out too much because it was dark.

"You arranged this all in anticipation of my arrival?"

"A simple task to please a beautiful young woman. Impressed enough yet?" he teased.

"Not as impressed as you are with yourself," I said, and he laughed.

"I knew it. I knew you were witty. I'm starving. How about we get some lunch before I show you anything more? I'll want to show you the lake, maybe take a short row? How's that?"

"Sounds possible," I said, and he laughed again. He took my hand and led me out a French doorway to the patio where a table had been set up for our lunch.

There was a large bowl of mixed salad, two loaves of baguette, condiments, and a bowl of large shrimp in crushed ice.

Next to it all was a bottle of white wine, chilled in a pail of ice.

"It's a French wine," he said, "imported. My father brings back all sorts of things from his travels. I thought you might be familiar with it."

I looked at the bottle and shook my head. "Maybe it's very expensive," I said.

"Oh, I'm sure it is." He pulled out a chair for me, and a tall, light-brown-haired woman came out with a tray holding a platter of chicken and another with slices of potato.

"This is our cook, Mrs. Wilson," he said.

"Pleased to meet you, miss," she said in a clearly English accent.

"Yes, thank you, but who's to eat all this food?" I said.

"We'll find eager mouths for whatever you don't eat, miss," she said, and turned to go back into the house. She behaved as if Malcolm invited a young woman for a special lunch daily.

He opened the bottle of wine and poured us both a glass. "How do you say it in French? *Santé?*"

"*Parfait*," I said. We both sipped our wine.

"I'll be our server today," he said. "Please?" He held out the salad bowl, and I took some.

I looked out over the property toward the mountains. "You didn't exaggerate," I said. "It's quite impressive."

"Home sweet home. Now, tell me about yourself and where you lived in France."

I described our village and the seaside, the fortress, and the cobblestone streets.

"The entire village probably could fit on your property," I said.

"Probably. And your parents, they were Americans?"

"Yes."

"What brought them there? Did you have French relatives?"

"A very good friend of my father's arranged for him to teach art, and they wanted to live in France."

"Was he simply a teacher, or was your father an artist?"

"Yes, he was a very good artist."

"Anything famous?"

"In France, in Villefranche, especially. Perhaps if he had been given more time, he'd be internationally famous."

He nodded and poured more wine. "I am sorry to have learned what happened to them. Tragic. But the silver lining is it brought you to America so I could meet you."

"There's no silver lining to that."

"Yes, of course. You're right. Sorry." He smiled. "Let's think of only good things today. I want it to be special for you."

"Well, it already is. This is all delicious," I said.

"It usually is."

"You sound quite spoiled."

"Rotten to the core," he said. He looked out toward the mountains. "You're right. The problem with living here is I take it all for granted. It is quite beautiful today. You've reminded me to appreciate it. I think you'll enjoy the lake. Are you willing to risk it?"

"Risk what?"

"Why, being alone with me, of course."

"I assure you," I said. "I can swim. A lake is nothing compared to the sea and waves."

He laughed. "Well, let's hope you won't want to," he said. He drank his second glass, and I drank mine.

Both of us seemed unable to look at anything else but each other.

Yes, I thought. *Maybe I won't want to.*

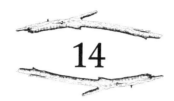

14

After lunch, after I had gone to the powder room, he waited to take me through the front door to a waiting horse and buggy he had arranged. I thought it was a very romantic and delightful thing to do. He carried a large leather bag.

"This is a piano box buggy made especially for my father. That's a black leather button-tufted cushion seat. And those are real brass decorations."

"It's beautiful."

"More important, it's more fun than walking to the dock," he said, and helped me into the buggy.

Where, I thought, would I be courted any better, and by whom?

"It truly is a magnificent place," I said as we started toward the lake. "And you have a right to brag, but with only your father and you living here besides the servants, isn't it a bit lonely? I mean, from what you say, he's away a great deal."

"Yes, well, I'm pretty busy helping him with our business, and I do have many friends, when I want many friends. Normally, I'd be at work today, but I anticipated your arrival, as you see."

"I'm still quite amazed you did. Is it simply your arrogance?"

He laughed. "You are not afraid to say what you think, are you? I thought the French were very diplomatic."

"It's the American influence, I guess."

"Stronger than the French?"

"I'm not sure yet."

"Maybe we'll find out today. It's a nice day for it," he said, with those blue eyes glittering mischievously.

"You must have been a handful growing up. You've asked me about myself, but what about your family? What happened to your mother?"

The smile practically leaped off his face. "I don't talk about her," he said. He stared ahead, the anger filling around his mouth and flooding into his eyes. After a moment, he realized the uncomfortable silence and relaxed. "She deserted my father and me when I was only five."

"Oh. I'm sorry."

"Most likely, it was the best thing that could have happened to us. I'm sure she would have brought us more pain, especially me. She was a flimsy, flighty woman, constantly thinking of herself, her own beauty, over the welfare of her one and only child. She betrayed my father, but more important, she betrayed me. My father had a difficult time for years. He even toyed with the idea of leaving Foxworth because, in his words,

278

'it reeked of her.'" Then he looked at me and shook his head. "I'm sorry. I told you we'd think of only happy things today."

I nodded. We were both silent. Ahead of us, the lake looked so still. It was as if it was anticipating being disturbed. I saw the dock and the boats.

"I can see why you want one of those new motorboats you mentioned. The lake looks large."

"A mile long." He smiled. "You remembered what I said. How nice. I take it as a compliment. Most girls I've been with couldn't recall a word I said. They weren't interested in my oratory."

He turned to wash me in his wicked smile, a smile full of sexy suggestions. A part of me wanted to be more reserved, even be a little upset, but there was that thrill of danger again. I was confident in myself, as confident as I was when I used to swim out just a little farther each time until my father came after me and bawled me out for daring the sea to capture my soul.

Was Papa's voice in the breeze that whispered past my ear? I took a deep breath and sat back as we drew close to the dock and Malcolm brought the horse to a stop. He hopped out quickly and ran around to put his hands on my waist and lift me to the ground. When my feet touched, he continued to hold me, bringing his lips closer to mine.

Don't let him kiss you so soon, I heard a voice inside me warn.

I put my hand on his chest.

He smiled and stepped back. "Not overwhelmed with me yet? Shall I impress you with my rowing talents?"

"By all means," I said, and he took my hand and walked us onto the dock.

He helped me into the rowboat, untied it, stepped in, put

down the bag he had brought, and sat across from me. Two large black birds flew low, crossing right above our heads before soaring off to the left. Their cries echoed over the water. I watched the ripples we caused travel out and disappear. The reflected images of the tall pine trees made it look like they grew in the water.

"Do you have fish in here?"

"Oh, yes. Beautiful rainbow trout. Lucas likes to fish and often provides us with a good dinner. Of course, it's Mrs. Wilson's preparation that makes it wonderful. Perhaps you'll come for a few days and enjoy the wonderful dinners. Among other things," he added, his blue eyes taking on a silvery tint, probably from the light bouncing off the water.

He began to row with long, smooth strokes, quickly sending us farther and farther away from the dock.

"Look!" I cried, pointing to my right, when a doe and two of her fawns had come out of the woods and were down on the far shore drinking.

He laughed.

"You are so lucky to have all this," I said, but not with envy, more with amazement.

"My father and I work hard to keep it," he said. "Our businesses are growing. That's why we've turned our attention to Richmond. Thankfully, or I might not have met you. Wait. Did I meet you, or did you attack me?"

"Very funny."

Now that we were out in the middle of the lake, he put the oars on the side and reached into the bag he had brought.

"Something to help us relax even more," he said, bringing out a bottle with a yellow liquid with no label and two wineglasses.

"What is it?"

"A wonderful drink my father brought to America and then began having made for us specially. He found it in Italy. It's called limoncello. Delightful. A fresh taste of spring or, as my father often says, drinking starlight, especially after a wonderful dinner."

He poured it into a glass and leaned forward to hand it to me. Then he poured himself some.

"To you," he said. "A rose in bloom."

I sipped the drink. It was good.

"You like it?"

"Yes."

The boat bobbed a little as he slipped off his seat to come closer to me.

"There's something about you that makes me think I've known you for a long time."

He reached for my hand and explored my fingers as if I was some fairy-tale girl he had just discovered and he wanted to be sure he wasn't fantasizing. When he looked at me, I felt myself slipping away from any restraint, out of the reach of any warning, and drawn to an image of love I had taken from novels and dreams. Was this really happening to me? Was I truly so beautiful that someone who had obviously traveled many avenues of romantic trysts would have such clear desire to be with me? Me?

He moved to bring his lips to mine, but the boat swayed so dramatically from side to side that I cried out. He laughed and settled on his seat again.

"I have to show you this little cove on the lake," he said, and began rowing.

I sipped my drink.

"It's good, right?"

"Very good. What's in it?"

"Secret recipe," he said. "It'll make you as light as those birds, and you'll fly."

He rowed harder. I saw the sweat break out on his forehead. He seemed quite a bit more determined. I reached over the edge of the boat to feel the cool water and let it ripple around my fingers as he rowed harder and faster. He paused and took a drink of his limoncello. I saw fish swimming close to the surface and cried out with delight. He laughed and leaned forward to pour more of the limoncello into my glass. I leaned back and looked up at the sky as he continued to row. The clouds were being stretched by the wind and broken into smaller ones. A flock of birds hurried across the water. They had rose-colored breasts.

"Grosbeaks," he said.

"It's like stepping out of the real world into a wonderland."

"Exactly." He turned the boat sharply and brought us into a cove. The lake seemed more shallow. I could see the rocks and the weeds through which schools of small fish swam. He put the oars up and slipped off his seat again to get closer to me.

I felt a little giddy and laughed at his careful and delicate moves to keep the boat from rocking. He took the glass out of my hand and put it on the boat floor and then rose slowly to bring his lips to mine.

Almost as soon as he kissed me, his fingers moved to the buttons of my dress. He was just a little too anxious and put his weight against me as he moved his body between my legs. I wasn't feeling all that steady as it was and grasped at the seat, but I couldn't get a strong enough hold on it and fell backward.

He lost his balance, too, and fell over and to the side of me, but I hit the side of the boat just enough to graze my head. I could feel the sting beneath my hair and moaned, turning over to stabilize myself. He started to laugh and reached out to bring me closer to him, when I reached behind my head and then looked at my fingers. They were awash in my blood.

"Oh, damn," he said, sobering up quickly. He sat up. "I'm sorry."

The sight of so much blood frightened me. I couldn't hold back my tears. I think it was that and the effect I was feeling from the limoncello, which now rushed through my body, bringing wave after wave of heat.

"I don't have anything with me," he said, visibly angry. He thought a moment, and then he took off his shirt and mashed it between his hands. "Here, hold this against your head."

I did, and he returned to his seat and dipped the oars into the water, turning the boat around and rowing hard and fast.

"Does it hurt?"

I nodded.

"Just keep the shirt against it hard. We'll get some antiseptic and see if you need a bandage. Mrs. Steiner is good at all that. She must have covered a hundred bruises and cuts on me as I grew up."

I wanted to laugh, but I was still feeling quite dazed and wondered if it was because of the limoncello now or because of the blow to my head. All I could think of was how Yvon would be angry when he saw my head bandaged. I guessed I was still a child after all, I thought mournfully.

"It's all right," Malcolm said. "You'll be fine. Don't cry."

I forced a smile and closed my eyes. The pain throbbed. The sight of me put more effort into his rowing, and we were back at the dock in easily half the time it had taken us to get to that little cove. He quickly tied the boat and then reached for my hand.

"Careful," he said when I stood.

I had started to step up to the dock when he simply embraced me and lifted me onto it.

"All right to walk?"

"Yes, yes," I said. The throbbing did seem to retreat. "It feels better."

"Good, but keep my shirt pressed against your head."

I looked at how soaked with blood it already was. The sight made me dizzy. When I swayed, he just lifted me in his arms and brought me quickly to the buggy. He whipped the horse, and we returned to the house. He helped me out but, afraid I would topple, scooped me up again and brought me quickly into the lobby, calling for Mrs. Steiner, who seemed to pop out of the wall as if she had been waiting for us this whole time.

"What's happened?" she cried.

I tried to smile to slow down her rush to panic.

"Little accident," he said. "She hit her head."

"Let me see."

She took his crumpled shirt off the back of my head.

"Let's get it washed. Head wounds always bleed dramatically," she added, as if I was making a big deal out of nothing. I hadn't said a word or even moaned.

Malcolm set me down, and she led me to a bathroom near the kitchen, where she reached into a cabinet to produce a clean washcloth, some disinfectant, and a box of bandages.

"Just sit here," she said, guiding me to the covered toilet. "Usually, this sort of thing happens to him and not to any guest he brings," she commented, again making me feel as if it was all my fault.

"I slipped," I offered. "In the boat."

"Ummm," she said, and worked on my wound. "Are you dizzy or nauseated?"

"A little nauseated, but I think that's from the limoncello."

"Limoncello? You were drinking in the boat."

"Malcolm had brought it along and wanted me to try it."

"Of course he did," she said.

The antiseptic burned, but I didn't make a sound. I was too afraid of what she might say. And then I felt her cutting some of my hair.

"What—"

"I have to do this so the bandage will stay. It will grow back," she said sharply.

After she was finished, she put everything away and began washing her hands. I stood up. She hadn't told me she was finished. She looked at me.

"Just rest for a while," she said. "You'll be fine."

"Thank you."

I stepped out. Malcolm was waiting just outside the door, leaning against the wall.

"How are you?" he said, standing quickly.

"I'll be fine," I said. "Really."

"How stupid."

Did he mean me or himself?

"You still have lots of time before the train back to Richmond. Come with me," he said, holding out his hand. "I have a surprise place for you to see and a place for you to rest a bit. We'll get your mind off of this quickly."

I took his hand, and he led me to the stairway.

"Where are we going?"

"You'll see. Actually, the house is famous because of it, and very few people have been permitted to see it. I should have taken you there before we went to the lake."

I could hear his regret, but I wondered what the reason for it really was: to prevent the accident or have a better place to make his advances?

We walked up the stairs, his arm around my waist. When I paused to look down, I felt dizzy again. He tightened his grip around me.

"You'll be fine," he said. Now he did sound more like he was trying to convince himself.

We reached the first landing, and then he practically lifted me up to the second floor.

"This way," he said, nodding to his right. I was breathing hard, my heart pounding from the ordeal, but I let him lead me down the hallway. We stopped at a door, and he reached into his pants pocket and took out a key. "It's always kept locked now unless someone forgets."

"Why?"

"My father wants it that way. It was her bedroom."

"Your mother's?"

"Yes," he said, and opened the door.

At the center of the room on a dais was a bed with the sleek ivory head of a swan, turned in profile, looking like swans do when they are just about to plunge their heads under the ruffled underside of a lifted wing. Visions of the picture my father had painted of the swan flashed through my mind. I stepped in farther.

Looking at it more closely, I saw that the swan had one sleepy red-ruby eye. Its wings curved gently up to its head on the almost oval bed. The wingtip feathers were like fingers holding back the delicate transparent draperies that were in all shades of pink and rose and violet and purple. It was very much like the swan in my father's painting.

"Well? What do you think?" Malcolm asked.

I was speechless. The bedroom looked pristine. There was a thick mauve carpet and a large rug of white fur near the bed. There were four lamps four feet high made of cut crystal and decorated with gold and silver. Two of them had black shades, and placed between the other two was a chaise longue upholstered in rose-colored velvet.

"The room is well looked after?"

"Oh, yes, but no one has slept in it since she left."

I looked at the walls covered with opulent silk damask in a bright strawberry-pink and then stepped up to the bed to feel the soft furry coverlet.

"It's all so . . . beautiful," I said.

"I thought it might take your mind off the accident. You can lie down on it if you want."

"Really?"

"You need a little rest. I'll get you a glass of water. Go on," he said.

There was something about the swan that was magnetic, drawing me to it. I sat on the bed.

"I'll be right back with your water," Malcolm said.

I sat there, looking around the room, and saw a picture or a painting in a frame facing the wall. For no reason I could see, as I looked about the room, I felt myself trembling. *Perhaps*

I shouldn't be in here, I thought. His father did want it kept locked. The back of my head began to throb again. I took deep breaths. I should leave. Maybe I should hire a car to take me home, I thought, just as Malcolm returned with a glass of water.

"How are you doing?"

"I don't mean to be such a burden," I said, taking the glass of water and sipping some.

"Oh, you're not. We'll make a good day of it yet. There's still some time. We have a player piano I wanted to show you in the ballroom. It's one of the newest ones. It has something called a word roll, words to the songs so you can sing along."

"I'd like to see that, yes," I said.

"Just take a little rest. You're fine. I've had worse falls, believe me."

He sat beside me on the bed. I took another sip of water.

"What is that on the wall? Another ancestor or what?"

He looked. "I told my father to either throw that out or put it in our attic. For now, he decided to leave it here. He thinks it belongs here, but I don't. That's why I turned it around. I don't want to look at it, not that I'm in here very much."

"Well, what is it?"

He smirked and looked away for a moment. "It's my mother," he said. "It's her portrait."

"Oh."

He looked at me. "I know. You'd like to look at it and see what the strumpet looked like."

"Not if it will disturb you, Malcolm. I understand."

He looked up at the ceiling. "I understand some of what my father endures. Neither of us can ever forget her, of course.

That's impossible. She was extraordinarily beautiful and very fashionable. My father spared no expense to please her."

He got up and walked to the golden dressing room in a recessed alcove. There were mirrors all around the vanity. He stood there looking down at it. "This was her altar, where she prayed to her own beauty. I'd stand there in the doorway and watch her. She was so into herself she didn't realize I was there until I made a noise or just screamed, 'Mommy!' She rarely had time for me. There was a nanny, Mrs. Steiner's niece Dora. She was more of a mother to me."

He picked up the silver-plated hairbrush, looking like he was going to slam it down on the table and smash it to smithereens. He did move his arm in that direction but stopped as if someone behind him had grabbed it. Then he slowly turned the brush and plucked out a hair.

"I guess you can say she left some of herself behind."

He held it up and smiled. Then he put the brush down.

"I'm so sorry, Malcolm."

"Ah, it doesn't matter now. I'm fine."

He looked at the portrait with its back to us.

"You can feel how special this room is, though, can't you?"

"Oh, yes. If it didn't have bad memories for you, it would simply be a beautifully unique room."

He nodded. "Well, you judge for yourself. If you saw this woman, would you think she would desert her own child and care only about her own happiness?"

He crossed the room and picked up the portrait.

Then he turned it around to show me.

It wasn't simply the resemblance. People, strangers, can look like each other. It was my papa's clear artistic style. It took

289

my breath away. I could feel my eyes going up and my whole body sinking. Malcolm would think it had to do with my head wound. When I fainted, I fell back on the bed.

I awoke with a cold washcloth on my forehead. Mrs. Steiner was standing beside the bed, holding my hand and checking my pulse. Malcolm was at the foot of the bed. He looked as drained of blood as I still felt.

"We should let Dr. Wasserman examine her," she said.

"Yes, please send Lucas right away, Mrs. Steiner," Malcolm said.

She nodded and left.

He sat beside me. "You'd better lie back," he said.

I did, and he held my hand.

"Usually, women swoon in my presence, so I'm not surprised," he said, smiling.

I looked toward the portrait on the floor, now facing forward. "Who painted that?"

"His name isn't on it," he said.

"Why not?"

He hesitated.

"Artists usually put their names on their work," I said.

"He did, but my father had it removed. He hired an artist to do just that one thing."

"Why?"

"He claims my mother ran off with the artist," Malcolm said.

Was my heart still beating?

"Did you ever know his name?"

"No. Honestly, I never cared about him. What good would that do? She's gone."

He lay down beside me and stroked my hair.

"Sometimes, when my mother was tired, I would lie beside her and stroke her hair. She would fall asleep, and I'd fall asleep beside her in this bed."

I closed my eyes. I felt Malcolm move his arm around my shoulders to turn me toward him and kiss my forehead.

"My lips have magic powers," he whispered, and had started to bring them to mine when suddenly we heard the sound of someone pounding up the staircase.

We both looked at the opened door.

My heart did flip-flops.

Yvon was standing there, catching his breath, his chest heaving, his face flushed, and his eyes blazing with what truly seemed more like panic than exhaustion.

"Get away from her!" he shouted.

Malcolm slowly slipped off the bed and stood. "Who the hell are you?"

"He's my brother," I said before Yvon could respond.

"Your brother? Dawson?"

"I'm not Dawson," he said. "I'm a Foxworth, and she . . . she's your half sister."

"What?"

Malcolm looked at me to explain. I shook my head. Yvon had confused me when he said he was a Foxworth.

He looked at the portrait of our mother. "Marlena's father did that painting of our mother," Yvon said, stepping forward. "Your father raped her for a second time before she left this house and went on to France with Marlena's father. Isn't his name on the painting?"

"His father had it taken off," I said. I was pressing my hand to my heart, fearing that it would beat a hole in my chest.

291

What was he saying? Was this real?

Yvon nodded and smiled. "So ask him who painted it," he said. "His name was Beau Dawson."

Malcolm simply stared at him for a moment and then smiled coldly. "That's a filthy lie."

"Let's go, Marlena. I have George waiting in the car. Come on," he said, and stepped forward to take my hand.

I slipped off the bed and took his hand. We started out. He noticed the bandage on the back of my head.

"What happened?"

"It was an accident," I said.

Yvon looked back at Malcolm, who was standing still, quite stunned.

"Not if he had anything to do with it, I'm sure," Yvon said.

We walked out and toward the stairway.

"THIS IS ALL A BUNCH OF LIES!" Malcolm cried. I wanted to turn, but Yvon held me tightly, forcing me to walk forward. "I KNOW WHAT YOU'RE UP TO!"

Malcolm came after us as we began to descend.

"IT WON'T WORK, DAWSON!"

Yvon paused on the stairway and looked back up at him. "What won't work?"

"You can't wiggle your way into the Foxworth fortune," he said, nodding.

"No worries for you there, Malcolm. Unless you tell people, no one besides your father and you will know the truth. If I could rip your Foxworth blood out of my body, I would. You're welcome to the whole polluted pool of it. Don't ever, ever contact my sister again. I'm sure what you know now and what your father will confirm won't be enough to stop your lechery. Marlena is not going to be the victim our mother was. That's a promise I made to my adopted father, and I would die keeping it."

"GOOD RIDDANCE TO YOU BOTH!" Malcolm shouted.

He shouted it again before we reached the doorway and a third time that the slamming of the door cut off and left echoing in the grand lobby of the mansion that surely had haunted Mama until the moment she died.

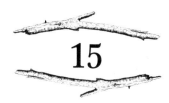

15

"When we arrive, we're going to take you directly to Dr. Lewis," Yvon said as soon as I had gotten into the car. George looked quite frightened. "What happened?"

"She had a minor accident," Yvon said.

"We could take her ta the hospital here, Mr. Dawson," he said after I sprawled out as best I could on the rear seat.

Yvon got in and lifted my head to rest on his lap. "Let's just get her away from here," he said sharply. His face was still ripe-apple-red from his confrontation with Malcolm.

We drove off. The echo of Malcolm's cries and threats still reverberated in my mind. I felt the turns and the descent as we left the Foxworth property.

It was a little over seventy miles back to Richmond. It remained light almost the entire way.

"I hope George didn't get into trouble," I whispered, looking up at Yvon.

He was quiet a moment. "She wanted to fire him and his wife," he revealed.

I held my breath. If I had somehow hurt Mrs. Trafalgar, too . . . "And?"

"I told her that if she did, I'd be out the door. There was no reason to blame him. As soon as I asked him if he knew anything about your departure, he revealed it all, and I knew the train time and where it was heading. He simply assumed we knew you were going somewhere and didn't think it was necessary to tell on you."

"I'm sorry, Yvon, but why did you make up all those things back there? Why did you tell him you're a Foxworth?"

"Because I am," he said. He put his hand on my arm but faced forward, not looking down at me. We bounced a little on the road as George sped up.

"Why would you say such a thing? How would you know that?"

"I can't tell you exactly when I sensed something, but children can, I suppose. Papa did all he could to keep the truth from me, but there were little things that gave it away, not that he was ever anything but a wonderful father to me. I loved him just as much as I could love my real father, obviously far more than this one. I doubt Malcolm and his father have anything close to resembling any sort of loving relationship."

"I still don't understand. Did someone come to you after we arrived in America and tell you all this?"

"No. That day I presented the letters to Jean-Paul, the ones I had found that told the truth about us . . ."

"Yes?"

"I kept one to myself. It was the earliest from Papa's cousin, Beverly Morris. His cousin made references to Mama being pregnant while she was recuperating at her house from some vicious attack, basically the rape Garland Foxworth had committed in a drunken rage. Papa had hidden her for a while during her recuperation at Cousin Beverly's home. It was from there that they finally made their way to France, where she gave birth to me. After I had read that letter, I put some dates together, figured things out as well," he said. He looked down at me in his lap. "Madame Sorel used to look at me with her clairvoyant eyes and nod. Somehow she knew, but we all thought she had the powers of a good witch."

I shook my head.

"I'm the same as Malcolm to you, a half brother."

"Never," I said. "You'll never be the same as him, and I could never love you any less despite learning this."

"Nor I you." He laughed. "We certainly left that arrogant, smug bastard quite shocked, no matter what sort of act he put on. He's shaken to the core. I'm sure of it. He'd have no trouble believing anything about his father. He'll be worrying that somehow it will all get out and the Foxworths will be shoved off their self-made gold thrones."

"Will he try to hurt us?"

"My guess is he'll try to pretend we don't exist. No worries. I have some ideas about ways to help him with that, but more important for now, I think the time has come to have a shed-light-on-the-truth talk with our aunt Effie."

"Yes," I said.

"But let's take care of you first."

297

We were both quiet as George drove onto wider, better roads and sped up.

"When I saw that portrait, I knew instantly," I said after a while. "Papa didn't have to sign it to tell me he had made it."

"*Oui.*"

"I saw her in the picture, but I still can't believe she once lived here, that she gave birth to Malcolm."

"This is why they kept their past so hidden from us, why they avoided talking about family. There was more pain to remember than there were smiles and laughter. Her life was so difficult, and she was so young, really not much older than you are now."

I could see in his face that he knew more, had more to say. "What, Yvon? There's no sense keeping any of it secret now."

"Before the accident, I told Papa about my reading that one letter I didn't produce. Papa told me most of it and I kept it from you," he revealed.

"What exactly did he tell you?"

"Malcolm's father seduced Mama, and her father agreed to the marriage in exchange for Garland Foxworth's votes on the bank board to make him president of the bank. There's a history of betrayal that is sickening. It was no wonder Mama and Papa fled to France and started a wholly different life for themselves and us. They were both ashamed of their families."

"That's why you want to have a truth talk with Aunt Effie now, tell her everything?"

"I don't want to live in a house—"

"Of lies?"

"Exactly," he said.

I closed my eyes again.

"Rest," he said, stroking my hair. "Facing the truth takes more strength."

I nodded. Everything that had happened back there flashed across the inside of my eyelids, including the lake, which until I fell was like something out of a fantasy, a place where birds could talk and deer could smile. Fish followed us with trust, enjoying our very presence. I wondered now if Mama had even a few seconds of what I had started to feel.

"Foxworth is truly a beautiful place, though," I whispered, with my eyes still closed.

"The devil knows the value of property," Yvon said.

I almost laughed, but it hurt too much to do so. I just smiled and fell asleep for the remainder of the journey.

When we arrived in Richmond, we went directly to Dr. Lewis's home and office. He examined me and said I'd be fine, that whoever had treated my wound and bandaged it had done a professional job. He gave me a new medicine for headaches and prescribed more rest for a few days. I did feel better soon after my first dose and sat up for our ride through the city.

Aunt Effie came rushing out of her office to greet us as soon as we had entered the Dawson House. Her face looked swollen with the invectives and reprimands she was about to unload at me, but Yvon put his hand up and stopped her before she could utter a word.

"She was in a minor accident and needs rest," he said. "We'll talk after she has a chance to recuperate, the three of us. It's time for the truth. Take it out of the closet," he added, which was one of Jean-Paul's favorite expressions.

Impressed with Yvon's firmness, she turned and stepped aside as he escorted me to the stairway and then up to my

V. C. Andrews

room. Aunt Pauline was already in hers, apparently. The lock told us that.

"I'll have some tea and biscuits with jam brought up to you. You don't want anything heavy right now."

"Yes, Dr. Yvon," I said, and he laughed.

Then he did something he hadn't done for a while. He leaned over to kiss my cheek. "I'll always be a full brother, Marlena."

"I know."

I fell asleep before Minnie and Emma came up with my tea and biscuits but woke as soon as I heard them enter. The two looked very concerned, their looks of apprehension were so identical I couldn't help but smile and thank them. Yvon had obviously told them and Aunt Effie I had already been to the doctor.

"Are you in pain?" Emma asked.

"Does it hurt?" Minnie said, her face grimacing in anticipation.

"No, no. I'm fine. My brother babies me. How's Aunt Pauline?" I asked.

"She was very upset when you didn't come home for dinner," Emma said.

"And worried about you. We had a hard time getting her to bed."

"I'll see her first thing in the morning," I said.

They nodded and watched me sip the tea and eat my biscuits.

"Where is my brother?"

"He's in the office with Miss Effie," Minnie said.

"Oh, is he? Thank you."

They left. I finished eating and lay back, wondering what sort of things Yvon was telling her. I kept falling asleep on and off, and after a while, I wasn't sure how long, I heard Yvon come into my room.

300

"How are you doing?" he asked.

"Just tired."

He sat on my bed. Before I could ask anything, he took my hand and looked down.

"We don't have to talk about what made you go there, but I think it might have something to do with me," he said. "I should have been honest with you instead of just forbidding you to do things."

"Why weren't you, Yvon?"

He started tracing circles in my blanket. I knew my brother well enough to know how hard it was for him to admit to his deeper, inner feelings, especially if any of them even grazed the concept of fear.

"I always felt that if you knew the truth, you'd not think of me as your brother so much anymore and we would grow far apart."

"That's—"

He put his hand up. He had more to confess. "I was very angry, Marlena, angry for most of my life, and until I read those letters, that one letter, I didn't understand all the conflicts raging in me. Sometimes, when you weren't with me, I'd beat a branch on a rock until the branch was all splinters. It doesn't make sense to you, I'm sure, but that's how I was."

"And after you knew it all?"

"That's what truly gave me the real rage. Right after Papa told me Mama's story, I wanted to come to America to confront Garland Foxworth one day, to look him in the face and tell him who I was and what I knew he had done. I wanted to hate him and hate him, and then I learned about Malcolm and thought perhaps I could do something hateful to him."

"You did," I said. "When you told him the truth."

"Yes, but he almost hurt you and therefore hurt me."

"I'm sorry, Yvon. I was just being a spoiled brat."

"No," he said, smiling. "You were just being an independent young woman."

He took a deep breath and smiled.

"All right. Get some sleep," he said, standing. "None of us is going to work tomorrow, at least in the morning."

"What did you tell her just now?"

"Nothing, as it turns out, that she didn't know about me. Cousin Beverly was her cousin, too."

"Really? But if she knew the truth, why would she still want you, want us?"

"Maybe after we all have that talk, you'll tell me," he said. He kissed me good night and left.

Oh, Mama, I thought, *I need your angel wings hovering above me tonight.*

I went to sleep thinking they were.

Yvon was back in my room to see how I was almost as soon as the sun rose in the morning. The back of my head was sensitive, but I didn't have any headaches and was actually quite hungry since I'd had little for dinner. He insisted my breakfast would be brought up to me. He had already told Minnie and Emma.

"But I'm fine."

"It's all right. You need to be pampered a little. Take your time afterward getting up and dressed. I am leaving the house for a little while to make a proposal to Malcolm this morning via Western Union. We'll see if he responds as quickly as I expect."

"What is the proposal?"

"We'll discuss it all when we meet in Aunt Effie's office later this morning. Perhaps by then, I'll have the answer," he said.

Minutes after he left, Minnie brought me my breakfast. To my surprise, she said that Emma was bringing Aunt Effie hers to eat in bed as well.

"It's not usual," she told me, "but Miss Effie's feeling poorly this morning."

I wondered how much my visit to Foxworth Hall and all that came after had to do with it. I didn't look forward to having our meeting with Aunt Effie, even though I was overwhelmed with curiosity. I was also quite nervous. When I went downstairs, Aunt Pauline was already in the sitting room doing her jigsaw puzzle and listening to Billy Murray singing "Pretty Baby," her new favorite song. She was singing along with it and didn't see me standing in the doorway.

"To my office," I heard behind me, and I turned as my aunt Effie came down the stairs.

I followed her, and when I entered, I saw Yvon was already there looking at some papers. He had been to Western Union and back. She went around to her desk chair, and I sat beside Yvon. Aunt Effie looked pale and tired, her hair not as neatly brushed and pinned. She leaned forward, her arms on the desk.

"Your brother has insisted we have this family meeting. He threatened to return to France today if we don't make an effort to—"

"Tell each other the truth from now forward," Yvon finished for her.

She took a deep breath. I was holding mine.

"My father started this company, and as brilliant as he claimed to be and as I've credited him with being from time to time, the truth was, he nearly bankrupted us two years before he died. Your father," she said, looking only at me, "was long gone by then. I was the one who brought Mr. Simon into the company. As Yvon will explain, he has a percentage of ownership, and he's well worth it. He made some economic decisions that kept us afloat. By then, I was quite involved but, as you might say, in the shadows."

I looked at Yvon. "I think we know most of this," I said.

She stared at me, looked away, swallowing hard, and then turned back, her eyes more glassy.

"Together, he and I turned the company around and built it to what it is today. It's growing well, but . . . what for?"

"Pardon?" I said.

"What do I have? Money, this house, a sister who needs constant care? In short, there is no future for me. I have no children, and any distant relatives are more like parasites to me. The only time I hear from any of them is when they cry for money.

"Therefore, I have asked Yvon to think of himself as truly my nephew, my father's grandson. Perhaps someday you will marry a man who will work for us. I know you're not blown over by Daniel Thomas, but someday there'll be somebody, and you'll feel more attached to the family business and future if he happens to be able to work for us. I am a realistic woman, and I know there is not much more I personally can do to make all this worthwhile, give it any meaning.

"Yes, I wanted you both to pay for what I considered your father's betrayal, practically turn you both into indentured servants, but seeing who you both are and what you can do, I want you to want to be here yourselves. This has to be your home and your company because you want it to be. I promise to let you become who you are and not force you to walk in my footsteps.

"There," she said to Yvon. "Is that good enough?"

"Almost," he said. She looked as surprised as me.

"Well, what—"

"I'd like you to tell us why our father—he will always be my father—ran from this house and this family. It was not only because his father had no respect for his talent and dreams and his disinterest in being a businessman, was it?"

She was so still and dark-looking that I thought she wouldn't say another word except maybe tell us to get out. Then her face seemed to crumple before our eyes. Her lips quivered, and her eyes watered. Her habitually stern posture softened. She looked up as if she was trying to pull her tears back into her eyes and then took a deep breath and said in a voice barely above a whisper, "No."

"Just say it," Yvon said. "Tell us."

"My father's affections for my sister were not normal for a father and a daughter. He was a sick man, and he took advantage of her. Your father discovered that and disowned any relationship with him. That's what drove him away the most. It was partly my fault. I didn't want my father's unnatural affections, but I wanted his affection. He gave it all to Pauline right from the beginning. I know you won't believe it now, but I was jealous of her."

"I believe it," I said quickly. "She's sweet and loving and beautiful."

I thought she was going to say something nasty, but she only nodded.

"She was the victim, not me," she said. "I didn't protect her soon enough or fast enough. Thanks to you and what I see you've done for her, that will change. I promise that."

Yvon looked at me. It was my turn, I guessed.

"I'm glad," I said. "I'm glad the lies will stop."

"They will. Now," she said quickly, returning to her Aunt Effie self, "what about the Foxworths?"

"I proposed a deal to Malcolm."

"A deal? What deal?"

"Neither he nor his father nor the Foxworth company will bid on any property in Richmond or the immediate environs. In return, I will never, ever claim to be a Foxworth."

She smiled. "That's very clever. You are a little of a Foxworth, but I think my brother made you a bigger part of him."

"I think so, too," I said.

He held up the paper that was in his hand. "He's agreed. I believe he will keep the truth about us, our being here, from his father, too."

Aunt Effie sat back and smiled more warmly than I had ever seen her smile at us.

"I think we'll take the whole day off," she said. "I'm going to have a picnic lunch put together, and we'll take Pauline to the park. Perhaps," she added, looking at Yvon, "you might ask Daniel's sister to join us."

He looked at me. "Feel up to it?"

"Oh, yes," I said.

"Then go tell my sister," Aunt Effie said.

"No, Aunt Effie," I replied.

"No?"

"I think she'd really like it better if it came from you."

"You are going to be a handful, you two," she said, still smiling.

EPILOGUE

There was truly a difference in our lives, in the very air we breathed in what was once the dark Dawson House. We all worked with a new energy, too. In the evening, our dinners were more enjoyable. There was laughter and music. Aunt Pauline, at first looking confused by her sister's kindness, began to participate more. Many of the things that she said made us laugh, and sometimes they made us think. I know my thoughts always led to the question, was she smarter than we all assumed?

Yvon asked Karen to dinner often. He went out with her more, at times taking me along. Daniel realized he wasn't going to win me over and started to date someone from the Richmond National Bank. I met young men who were good-looking and even interesting and fun, but no one set my heart on fire the way Karen had set Yvon's. I was jealous and told him so.

He was successful not only in the romantic world but in the business world as well. He obviously impressed Mr. Simon more and more. I could see the respect building. Aunt Effie was happy about it and depended upon him more and more.

Despite all this and all the new things I had learned and discovered in Richmond, I still felt a strong longing for Villefranche and the life we'd had. Sometimes, on warm nights, I would sit out on the rear patio and just remember the sea, all of us on the beach, and the music. There was always music. Here there was music drifting out of bars and clubs, but it seemed more like noise to me. None of it compared to the sound of a French accordion coming from a street in the village or outside a café by the dock. But I was admittedly biased about it. It was the music I grew up with, the music inside me. Why shouldn't I long to hear it?

Despite that, I tried harder and harder to become an American through and through. I did enjoy my days with Karen and some of her friends. Finding new things in the department stores and clothing stores was fun, but everything seemed to have a short life to it. We seemed to flit from one thing to another, nothing truly lasting. There were simply too many changes occurring; everything was coming and going so fast because it was improved or changed, and when I complained, there was that simple explanation: "It's America."

Maybe it was, but I couldn't shake off my longing for things that seemed to live forever and ever.

And then, one day when Yvon and I came home together, we found an envelope waiting for us on the table just inside the main entrance. When we saw from whom it had come, we both felt our hearts dip. Neither of us wanted to open the envelope.

Yvon did and unfolded the letter. He held it so we could both read it together.

There was probably not a night or even a moment during the day when either of us didn't pause to think about Jean-Paul. We knew this day was coming; the news was traveling across the ocean and into our eyes eventually. Whenever we spoke about him and Papa and Mama and Anne, we looked at each other and, without speaking, confessed our dread, our fears, and our sadness.

We didn't speak now. We hugged. Yvon tried to hide his tears, and I went off to be alone. We told Aunt Effie later in the day, and I surprised them both.

"Although it's past his funeral, I want to go back. I want to go to his grave and Mama and Papa's."

Yvon nodded. "We should."

"I'll have Mr. Simon make your arrangements," Aunt Effie said.

Later I told Yvon he didn't have to go if he didn't want to. I knew how painful it would be, but he insisted.

"I would never let my little sister go alone," he declared, but then confessed he truly wanted to go and had dreamed of doing it himself.

The trip back seemed to go faster, but perhaps that was because our memories of the trip that had brought us here were so full of sadness and fear. We had sadness now, but it was expected sadness, and there really is a difference between the sadness you know is coming and the sadness that hits you like a horrible gust of cold wind coming from nowhere. That's always unreal and something you fight to admit, you refuse to acknowledge until the dark day when you must.

For me and, I suspect, Yvon, the sight of Villefranche-sur-Mer was like waking from a long sleep. In a moment, I thought we'd discover that all that had happened had been nothing but a dream, a string of nightmares. But there were things that did look different. First off, we didn't arrive with a horse and carriage. We had hired a car and a driver to take us from Nice.

When we pulled up to what had been Jean-Paul and Anne's house, she came out immediately, and immediately I thought she had aged so fast. Her hair was grayer, the lines in her face deeper, and her body less firm and confident. The anxiety age brings with it had settled comfortably in her.

But her smile was truly warm and wonderful. We all embraced, and then the talking began, all of us rushing out what had gone on since we were away. She told us how proud of us Jean-Paul had been, how strong he thought we were the day we had to go. He had tried to go back to work, do a painting, but never seemed to get beyond a few dozen strokes of his brush before sitting down and staring at the canvas. Nothing he could think of was good enough.

"He'd go to the gallery every day to look at your father's work to see what was sold but also, I think, to see your father. That was the way he could, *n'est-ce pas*? It's the way we all can, really.

"He so looked forward to your letters," Anne said to me, and then turned to Yvon and said, "and yours."

I looked at him. He had never revealed writing one. He blanched a little but nodded.

"And our house?" I asked.

"No one has bought it yet. It's almost as if everyone wants it to be a historic site or something. But I'm sure it will sell. The location, the view . . . it will sell."

"Maybe we shouldn't sell it," Yvon said, surprising me. "We'll brag that we have a vacation home in France," he said.

"That's fine with me," I said. I looked at Anne. "The painting, the swan?"

"I know. I was supposed to send it to you, but every time I went to do it, I couldn't get myself to take it off that wall. It was like—"

"Admitting they were gone," Yvon said.

"*Exactement*," she said.

"Then leave it there. I like knowing it's there," I said.

She nodded.

After we had something to eat, we all went to the cemetery. Yvon held my hand. Neither of us said anything, nor did Anne, until we were ready to leave.

"When we look at the stones, at what they say, I don't believe it," I admitted. "To me, all cemeteries are gardens of lies. Our parents and Jean-Paul are not there. They are here," I said, pressing my hand to my heart.

Anne nodded. "Maybe we go there just to let them know," she said.

That night, we went to dinner in the village at La Maison de Pierre, a new restaurant Anne liked. So many of the villagers heard we were there. We could barely take a bite of the delicious food. Before the evening ended, Monsieur Appert appeared. He was walking with a cane and complaining about his arthritis. He said the pleasure of seeing us took away his pain. He held on to my hand so long that I thought he would never let go.

"So what have you learned in America?" he asked.

I smiled and glanced at Yvon and Anne. "What else?" I said. "It's all Eve's fault."

311

The laughter washed away the sadness the way the outgoing tide could clear the sand. Thinking about it, I could feel the cool grains between my toes.

Later, before we went to sleep, Yvon and I went to the hill where Mama and Papa often stood to look out at the sea. I felt they were there with us, all of us holding hands. The four of us, for just a few moments, stopped time, stopped all sorrow, and watched a star grow brighter and brighter until the darkness surrendered and let the light travel into our hearts to keep us forever safe.